THE **CHILDREN OF THE ORB**
SERIES

A JOURNEY OF MAGIC AND MYSTERY
THROUGH THE REALMS OF THE CRYSTAL ORB

BOOK FIVE

DANIEL LIGHT AND THE
EXILE OF ARADON

BY
C. MICHAEL PERRY

Leicester Bay
B O O K S

Newport, Maine

Paperbound Edition(CS) 2017 by Leicester Bay Books—
ISBN-13: 978-0692930915
ISBN-10: 0692930914

Kindle Edition available.

BISAC: Fiction / Fantasy / Epic --
Adventure—Coming of Age

Leicester Bay Books
P.O. Box 536 Newport, Maine 04953-0536
www.leicesterbaybooks.com

Cover Layout by Brook Bowen

Visit us at: **www.childrenoftheorb.com**

To my wife and children,
they are in every book, parts of them or all of them;
they live and breathe in the Realms of the Crystal Orb

Other books in **THE CHILDREN OF THE ORB** SERIES:

www.childrenoftheorb.com

Books in *Wembley Tewkes On The Edges of Time* SERIES

www.wembleytewkes.com

DANIEL LIGHT
AND THE EXILE OF ARADON

CHAPTER LIST

Year in Colabos Time: 2726

NOTE: The initials ⓂL at the end of every chapter stand

for Ⓜiraden Light, the historian of the Realms.

CHAPTER ONE—
THE PRINCES

•• 5th day of 4th Month ••

Daniel was accustomed to the whiteness all around him now, no longer having to squint to see what he was supposed to see through it. He was seeing quite clearly—with his eyes. His ears and heart and mind were another matter.

"I miss you, Boncaster."

"I miss you, too, Uncle Daniel."

"Do you really need to call me Uncle?"

"No. But I like to. I still yearn for the old familiar—the mortal. Even after eight of your years."

"And I'm stuck here yearning for the Immortal—for what I have been shown—for the things I cannot have—yet."

"The Creators have chosen us to walk the same path in different spheres, Uncle."

A chuckle of surprise—then: "You always were too smart."

"Not half as smart as you. But I am still the Child of Promise. It was not just a mortal title. I still have a promise to give you."

Daniel sighed. "What am I in for now?"

"Not you—Aradon."

"What more? Uncle Emeron—ill. Aunt Rose—missing. Raileon and Galderon—lost."

"All is not as it seems to be. But, Evermon is now in danger."

"From who? How?"

"All I am allowed to tell you is that Kwuktw and Nathan and others are destined to help—somehow. The Second Generation will now begin its official service to the Orb. There will be many changes in Mirador...and all the Realms of the Crystal Orb."

"What do I do?"

"I can say no more. Just remember—'all is not as it seems to be.' But your promise? A good end. Goodbye, Uncle."

"Goodbye... Nephew."

The brightness of the room vanished with the disappearance of the being who was once the hope of all the Realms. Daniel was alone—again.

It had been eight years since Kerrayu had killed Boncaster in the tower of Castle Panador. The Creators have a plan. (They always have a plan.) Within a few months after the young Prince's death the visions between Boncaster and Daniel had begun.

Aside from Boncaster's parents–Valor (now also dead) and Snow (now solitary Queen of Panador)–no one had been closer to the Prince, The Child Of Promise, when he was alive than his 'Uncle' Daniel–The Prophecy–The Miracle of Mirador. All was as it should be; good things, bad things; success followed by disaster; small defeats followed by smaller victories. Life—as it was designed to be by the Creators of Colabos.

•• 5th day of 4th Month ••

"You can't afford friends, Baladar. You are a Prince—and you will soon have a Kingdom..."

"How, Mother?"

"When it is time, you will know."

"All I want is a big brother—and I want him now!"

"Now—later—that is an impossibility!"

"Then why can't I at least be friends with Evermon? He's a Prince!"

"That is exactly why he cannot be your friend. Nor you, his. Princes, like you... and Evermon... must be alone in the world. You will always be alone."

"I still want a big brother," was pouted out through pursed lips.

Baladar, almost ten years old, tall and strong, as handsome a boy as his mother is a beautiful woman, drooped—moped— deflated himself so that he looked very small when he sank into the chair. Alindra looked on. Her heart (what little was left of it) went out to her son. She had outlined a hard road for him. Although she loved him, she loved power more. He was the key, now. If all continued to work in her favor, she would have that power, and not only her magic; her son would be a Prince! He could never have friends—other than her.

Baladar shot out of the chair and across the room. He stood in front of his table with its racks and racks of potions and ingredients. His anger had motivated him into a solution! He grabbed his wand and started flailing it about. Beakers, ampules, vials, packages of herbs and other things began to fly through the air, then empty themselves and intermingle in a small cauldron on the table. When the air was clear of the flying objects, and the mixture was bubbling in its own heat, Baladar, the boy, leaned over the pulsing pot and spit into the percolating brew. It spat back. He spit again! The brew was silent. He scraped the potion into many small jars and stoppered them. He labeled them 'poof' and placed all but one on the shelf. Had he done it! Had he really done it at last? Would this solution, arrived at in anger, work? He took that still warm jar with him to the door of their cabin. His mother followed him.

He stepped outside into the bright morning of an early spring day, jar in hand, and walked up to the edge of the waters of the Purple Lake—in Aradon. He picked up a small stick and immersed one end of the stick in the gooey substance in the jar. He then threw the stick at the water's surface. There was a small 'crack' and a flash of smoke at the impact of stick and water. There was also a smile growing on the young Sorceror's face.

He walked over to a nearby copse of trees. He picked up a stone this time, dipped it in the mixture and blew on the congealed mass to dry it onto the rock. His mother, at the cabin door, watched with great, almost amused interest. He set the jar carefully on the ground. He placed the rock, nestled it in his fingers so that he could grip it properly, drew his arm back and released the rock towards the trees with a mighty and very accurate heave.

The rock hit the tree. There was more than a crackle this time as the rock exploded. Then there was much less than a tree standing where it had stood a few seconds before. The rock had hit the tree dead center and the tree had disintegrated from its center both upwards and downwards. It was like a flash-fire without the flame. All that remained was the ash and cinder around the base of an almost-stump. No wonder it hadn't done anything when he threw the stick at the lake except disintegrate the stick.

Alindra approached her son and wrapped her arms around his shoulders, no longer just amused.

"That was very good!"

It was more than very good. It was amazing! Her son had invented a substance that disintegrated solid matter.

"Thank you, mother. Now, can I have a brother?"

She kissed the top of his head, ignoring his impertinence and rewarding his industry.

"How are your spells coming?"

"All right, I guess," he said with an indifferent shrug of his shoulders.

"Just all right?" She really wanted him to be a powerful Sorceror—not just dabble in alchemy. He was content so he didn't care what she really wanted.

"Yes. What do I need all that black magic of yours for, anyway?"

"To make you the greatest Prince in all the Realms."

"Greater than Daniel?"

She was silent. He knew that the mention of the King of Mirador's name always shut her up. It was his one and only trump. What he didn't know was just how much she hated 'the Prophecy!' What else he didn't know was that Alindra had gained, through her son, another weapon in her arsenal for the war against the King of Mirador and the Realms.

"Mother—why can't we just live at the palace? I like it there. I have other children I can play with."

"Because you can't practice your magic there. What would your step-father or even your precious Evermon do if they knew about you—or me?"

He was silent now. He didn't like what he knew.

"So all we do is hide? We cover up what we do? We lie? I have no friends and you have no Kingdom, Mother."

She stared at him open-mouthed. He always stopped her with his wisdom. His nine-year-old wisdom.

"It's lonely here."

"It's private, son. Our plans require privacy."

"<u>Our</u> plans?"

"Soon they will be ours! Mine—and yours."

The Purple Lake of Aradon was indeed a lonely place. Eight years ago, when Alindra and her small son had arrived, there had been some neighbors around the lake. But when the formerly deserted cabin on the western shore seemed to awaken in the darkness, most of the people fled and never returned. Alindra set up her stores of alchemy and magic. Soon, sounds and strange lights frequented the night-time former-stillness. Even the animals of the surrounding forest avoided them. When Alindra actually turned the waters of the Purple Lake to purple (on a whim) well, that was the last straw and the remaining neighbors disappeared. Alindra and Baladar were finally alone. Comfortable for her. Unimagined torment for him.

He was a social creature, not a solitary one. He was not like his mother; or his father—whom he had never known, but he knew he wasn't like him. His mother had been his companion all of his life but around the age of four he had started, as most children do, to yearn for others. That is when his mother, completely unintentionally, started going to the Purple Palace of Aradon, which exposed him to the others he sought. She became advisor (with some quickly invented credentials) to King Emeron. When Queen Rose disappeared, without a trace, Alindra became his second wife.

Now she had two boys to raise. The oldest two of the three Princes of Aradon had gone off on some foolish quest a year ago. So her own son, the talented Baladar and Prince Evermon, handsome, young, courageous, but still a boy—all of the qualities that drew her to him—became her charges. The Prince was irresistible—as his father must have been in his own youth.

"Shall we go visit your brother?"

"But you... ? Really?"

Baladar was all smiles as they 'popped' to their private

chambers in the Purple Palace of Aradon.

•• 6th day of 4th Month ••

"The only thing I want for my birthday is to have my real mother back! If I can't have that, it's no use celebrating my birthday at all!" Evermon, the soon to be fifteen year old Prince, stomped out of Alindra's room with tears streaking his handsome face. Then he stopped, turned and said: "And while you're at it, you might try bringing my brothers back; it's their birthday, too—remember? Then... you can cure my father. I want my family back. A family you are not, and never will be, a part of!" He was just a little angry, don't you think? "So, keep yourself and your own brat away from me!"

He spoke these words in anger and unthinking haste to his step-mother but Baladar heard it all and ran from the room. Alindra, with a nasty glance at Evermon, followed her own son out the door. He ignored her glare. What was she to him? This woman who had tried to take his mother's place; this woman whom he suspected was responsible for his Mother's absence and his Father's illness; he didn't know how but she would soon be exposed—as soon as he could manage it!

His mother had disappeared over five years ago. He was only ten, then, and his Mother had been his entire world for each of those ten years. His father had been ill for most of those last five years, as well, and now he was completely bedridden and uncommunicative; and getting worse.

Evermon would sit for hours, just talking to his father who could not answer him, but the youth was convinced that his father could hear him—somehow. His brothers—his idols—had now been gone for over a year in the search for his Mother and for a cure for his Father. They had finally reached the age where they could no longer be told what to do by their step-mother (or their Father) so, they had decided to go in search of their dear and long-lost Mother.

The Kingdom is no longer a happy one. The Purple Palace of Aradon seems quite empty at times. Queen Rose is grieved over. Her kindness and wisdom are missed. Her loss in keenly felt. So much so that many believe that magic or sorcery was involved in the disappearance and also in the illness of the King. Many even pointed to the new Queen.

"Father, you never should have married that woman. Nothing good has happened to us or to our Kingdom since she arrived! She had the nerve to tell me what was going to happen tomorrow for my own birthday! I told her what she could do with her plans. I wasn't very polite." Evermon chuckled. "But it sure made me feel better." He stopped for a moment. A regret. "But I was rude to Baladar. He didn't deserve what I said about him." He stared into his father's eyes, searching for a response. He usually found one, but it didn't come from his father.

"I know! I know! I should apologize. You're always right, Father. But there are times when he is like the little brother I never wanted. Sometimes I hate him because I hate her. But then there are times that he's like the little brother I can't do without. I should tell him, huh? But he'll never replace my real brothers!" Those eyes again. "I know! He's not meant to."

Evermon sat there in a pregnant silence looking at the placid, seemingly disinterested face of his father. After all, this was the man who had carried him on his back; wrestled with him; taught him. This was the man who had saved Panador and Aradon (as Boncaster, the gardener) by restoring the Talismans to both Kingdoms over twenty years ago. Now he just laid there—inert, unresponsive—but alive, at least. Thank the Creators—he was alive! He was here and he was still breathing. Evermon had no such fortunate knowledge of his brothers or his moth...

His body shook lightly as a new wave of sadness overtook him. He sat, head bowed, hands dangling uselessly at his sides, in the great armchair at the side of the canopy bed his parents used to share—where his father now laid alone. The plush velvet curtains, the satin sheets, the thick downy comforters, the majestic hardwood frame, the portraits of the grandparents on the walls—the unused dressing table and mirror of his mother—everything that surrounded Evermon tortured him.

His memories of long ago; the laughter-filled hours spent with parents and brothers—those things that he had left of them—only memories—he couldn't even hold in his hands, his arms couldn't wrap around them. So, he wept. Every day he would sit like this by his father, talk to him and lose control. Tomorrow was his birthday and things seemed closer to the surface than ever, now. After all, he was only fourteen—well, fifteen, but sometimes that extra number in the year of your age doesn't help to make the difference it is supposed to make in how you behave. For tomorrow was the end of his childhood—where he must put away childish things. His father had prepared him for it for years. Something, somehow, stood there; solidly in the way of that preparation. He didn't want to grow up without his mother, father, brothers and friends. Especially not with a stranger who made him uncomfortable. He was suffocating here!

There were those looks from Alindra. Those looks that made him feel—naked—even when he wasn't!

"Mother is not dead! I know it!" he shouted to his deaf father. "I would feel it if she was."

He left the room and moved out onto the balcony. Fresh air. He breathed deeply. He tried to calm down. He focused on the beautiful golds, greys and purples of the sunset happening in front of him. There was beauty in his world—just none in his life; not at this particular moment, anyway.

The bell of the city tower began to ring. It seemed like a hollow, mournful sound. He remembered when the call to evening prayer was a joyous occasion and his family and even some of the servants would gather in the castle Chapel—and he would feel loved.

Oh, no! He sure felt something—right now!

"Evermon?"

So much for feeling loved! "Yes, Alindra—what do you want?"

He was trying to be civil but it was oh-so-difficult. She had interrupted him just as he was kneeling to say a prayer. He wished she would just go away—permanently. He knew that it wasn't a nice thing to wish for but he wished for it anyway. He got to his knees and stayed there; facing away from her.

"Can we at least go through with the party for lunch tomorrow? I've invited many of your friends..."

"I don't have any friends, Step-mother. I am a Prince! I can't afford friends."

At least that is what she had taught him for the last four years. 'If you would be King you must stand alone!' So, he had thrown her words back in her face. A real fifteen (well, fourteen) year old thing to do.

"Please?" was her only reply. A new tactic maybe?

"Will Baladar be there?" He regretted his question immediately. Baladar was not his mother.

"Now, Evermon—he worships you..."

"Yes. All right! I... I'll be there. But no presents!"

"Just good company!"

Evermon held his tongue. He could only roll his eyes.

"You'll be glad... it will be good ..." she stared at his back as he had not yet condescended to turn his face to her in his petulance. She thought, *'He is magnificent when he is angry! Too bad Baladar is not more like him—but he is only ten.'* She slipped silently away.

He knew she had been staring at him! He felt unclean. He knew he was alone again—he recognized silence; it was one of his most constant companions. The silence always welcomed him. It didn't pressure him. It left him alone; mostly, unknown to him, it turned others away.

In the present silence, the dark corners of the room were becoming brighter. He could feel the warmth on his back. It certainly wasn't the proximity of Alindra. He was not alone! He turned slowly to see a glow emanating from the northwest corner of his father's room. It was warm and inviting and he walked inside, off the balcony, and toward the radiance. As he reached the edges of its welcoming influence the light began to take the shape of a human body. The more that Evermon stared into the light the more enchanted he became and the more he began to recognize the figure within the light. The Figure was fully formed now and Evermon could not believe it.

"Boncaster?"

"Cousin!"

Evermon grasped forward into the vision and his arms wrapped around solid flesh.

"But you're...

"Yes. I am with the Creators, now."

"I miss you, Cousin."

"And I you."

"Why are you here?"

"To tell you that you must follow your heart."

Evermon looked perplexed. So the dream-figure continued.

"Do what your heart tells you. Don't listen to your mind. Your heart knows. It understands. I will try to speak to your heart. Listen!"

The vision began to fade. The body in Evermon's hands began to lose its solidity.

"Stay—please!"

"Follow your heart!" and the brightness faded from the room, taking its warmth with it. Evermon collapsed to his knees. He felt empty—but he also felt good. Tired, yet alive in hope. His best friend ever, the person be shared a birthday with, had brought him a promise as a present. He had told Alindra 'no presents' but it was a good thing that Boncaster hadn't heard him; or if he had that he had known better than to stay away. Boncaster had always seemed to know better.

The vision of his cousin in his father's room would not leave Evermon. The memories associated with Boncaster—the last memory that Evermon had of the brave Prince of Panador—was of his bloody death. The torn body of his cousin in the lap of his Aunt Bianca was forever seared into Evermon's brain. He had been only nine when Boncaster had been ripped from this life by the minion of the evil Dajinn. The magnificent Boncaster, after being mortally wounded, had slain Kerrayu, the monster. There had been no monsters since that day. But Evermon suspected that monsters lay in his future, as well as the future of the Realms.

ᴍᴌ

CHAPTER TWO—
HAVE WE MET BEFORE?

•• 6th day of 4th Month ••

The feeling of the water's currents as they brush past your naked body; the pleasure and warmth of the water near the surface; the stab of the cold—right through you—as the deep ocean occasionally seeks the surface; the cries of the whale and dolphin as you interrupt their pods while they feed; interfere with them by asking questions they can't answer about where you are in relation to the land. This is how it felt to be one of the Skwatwaela. He was Kwuktw—Prince of the Merfolk. Kwuktw knew that they could not explain it to him. The creatures of the sea had not seen the other half of the world in which Kwuktw was privileged to live. His world was both above the water, on the land; and under the water. These creatures only knew the world beneath the waves, while he was comfortable in either sphere.

He was on a journey. His friend's birthday party was tomorrow. These silly humans! What use was it to keep track of how many years you had been alive? Even though the parties themselves were fun, a birthday was nothing to a Skwatwael. Yet it was something to his friend, Prince Evermon. He was determined to be there and also determined to do it on his own. No magic of the Circle. It always made him feel odd, uneasy, to transport. He loved the water and swimming was easy for him. He preferred it—using his own muscles, creating his own power. Evermon's brother Raileon had been Kwuktw's closest friend. Although the MerPrince was twenty, he had also grown attached to Raileon's youngest brother, Evermon. He was not going to miss this birthday!

Kwuktw surfaced. The cliffs of Aradon were in front of him and the City of Aradon was not too far inland. He submerged again and used his powerful fluke to propel him towards the delta of the River of Hope—that same river that passed the City of Aradon and the Purple Palace and led to the center of the continent and the Crystal Lake of Mirador.

The change from salt water to fresh water was gradual but noticeable. The MerPrince swam on, upriver to the Palace. He would arrive sometime before dark. But Alindra had told him to come silently. She would hide him to surprise her step-son.

Alindra was a confusing mixture of power and poise, love and lust, kindness and killer instinct. She would use whomever and whatever to accomplish her goals; even if it benefitted someone else, even temporarily. Boncaster had been right to warn Daniel and Evermon.

•• 6th day of 4th Month ••

The feeling of a brush through your long, yellow hair is relaxing. Even if the hundred strokes of the brush have to come from your own hand and have done so for over twenty-five hundred years.

It is restful, concentrative, restorative, as the years fell away in the mirror in front of her as well as off her actual appearance. It helped her think. Thinking was something that Alindra did all of the time, but she never let anyone catch her doing it; thinking, that is. It was thinking that had gotten rid of the old Queen; *'What a lovely and innocent patsy she was.'* It was thinking that created the marriage for her with the King; *'What a fool to be so easily advised!'* It was thinking that, after exhausting every old and musty book in all of her collections, she had found an illness so rare that it laid the King low—without a cure. It was thinking that sent Raileon and Galderon, Evermon's brothers, on their futile quest. At least Alindra liked to call it thinking—maybe you or I would call it plotting, lying, cheating.

Queen Rose, Evermon's real mother, was safe. Sort of. Even though she was far outside the borders of the Realms of the Crystal Orb. They would never be able to find her. There was no cure possible for their father. She had thought it, planned it all out. She had planned well. All she needed now was to get rid of the last remaining Prince. Then, exalt her own son. Oh, and find the Gentle Jewels; that Talisman that gives power to the throne of Aradon and helps to stabilize the Crystal Orb and its Sceptre.

She must have those jewels! Why else should she endure the jibes, hatred, suspicions and distrust of the Court and the Kingdom? When she could probably just wipe them all away? Because simply wiping them away had never worked! Why else would she have gone to all this trouble? How else could she hope to bring Daniel down? Why else would she force herself to drink that nasty potion every morning? A potion what would maintain her appearance, in a changed form, and force her to seem... nice... interested... fair... decent... trusting... even loving—with her own son and others—when exactly the opposite was her fondest wish. Why? She had learned patience. She had had to...Tophet, Wyara, Dajinn—all of those who, in their incompetence, sought to destroy the Light and had failed due to their impatience.

Her duality was carefully planned—engineered, thought out. You can always catch more flies with honey than with vinegar. (She hated honey!)

Why else had her father, Orthon, (Tophet's son), taken a concubine and sired her? It was for one purpose only and that purpose had nothing to do with love or children, it would have been only to fulfill the measure of his evil transformation. She now wanted power as he had wanted power—through his children! That was the only reason for them! She had a right to power! She was born to be powerful—the daughter of a Prince! There was nothing that fool called Miraden could do about it; because the Magician didn't even know she existed—at least not as Alindra. Tophet, her own grandfather, had not recognized her as Accosta when she had helped Dajinn. They were all fools. They were never patient...but she was. She had been for over two millennia. One hundred strokes through her hair each night was a small price to pay for eternal youth and beauty—and power. No body knew of her origins. Her father had given her the enchantment before he was destroyed by the Forces of Light—the forces led by Miraden in the Great War.

She would make them pay! Once she had the Jewels. Where were they? The guards of the Talisman performed their duties in an empty room. Where was the Talisman? Who had hidden it? It was not Queen Rose—she had known nothing when Alindra had questioned her. It wasn't King Emeron.

She would find it! All it would take is time. She had plenty of that—with her brush and per potion and no King, Queen, and soon, no Princes in the way.

But there was that boy! Ooooh, how she loathed the way she had to coddle and cajole the little birthday-snot. Plus, he was so blasted attractive. He reminded her of a boy she had once, not so long ago, almost gained the affections of. The opportunity had not yet arisen to get rid of the Prince. (And it would be so difficult to do it to him.) One day the opportunity would present itself.

All she had to be was ready! When her path to power would be absolutely unencumbered by anything called opposition. Then, she thought, then Miraden—you will also die!

•• 6th day of 4th Month ••

The feeling that the Spring in Mirador was a near perfect time was not a vain one. The warmth of the sun, while refreshing outside his cave, never dared penetrate its cool walls. It was enervating to come from the tepid open air into the slightly chilled temperatures of the cave. Besides, if it ever got too hot in the cave it would probably blow up, what with all of the chemicals, and potions that he kept in the laboratory.

There were others appreciating the cool of Miraden's cave today. He had been entertaining two soothsayers. Men of wisdom who were going to take the messages of prophecy to the court of Aradon. There was too much happening there! This woman—this Alindra—where had she come from? What did she want? How could he find out?

The soothsayers had brought some word for they had already traveled through Aradon.

"It is a doleful place," said one.

"There is no joy. On every level of the Kingdom, despair shows through," said the other.

"It has been contaminated by the presence of this woman."

"She is evil and must be dealt with."

Dealing with her—they were. Miraden had the cure for the King. There was only one small, little, teensy-tiny problem—he must find the location of the source of the once well-known cure. He had better hit the books again. His memory is not what it once was nearly three thousand years ago. But he would find it. By the time that the Quest was ready—he would have the location! He had a little surprise for Alindra, whoever she was. Something that would stir things up a bit and maybe cause her to make a mistake or two to show her hand in some other way. Something to maybe even reveal who she really was? He must know. This new prophecy, real and not imagined, would stun the people of Aradon, not to mention the other Kingdoms of the Realms of the Crystal Orb.

They checked and double-checked their plans. Then the soothsayers were on their way to Aradon to deliver the prophecies and Miraden was alone again.

A thousand years of being alone can begin to have an effect on a person. His beloved Enchantress wife, Aradella, had been killed in the Great War by their niece, Reugella, along with many other Magicians of Light. Reugella, it seems, would also have to be dealt with, but that is another story for maybe the next book of Orb tales. Miraden married again, this time to a mortal. She had given birth to Liliana—former Queen of Mirador—now retired. Miraden was the last of the Great Magicians—the originals of the race—left alive. All the other nieces, nephews, brothers and sisters, aunts, uncles—dead; except that Anna, Estrador's daughter (Miraden's niece) had recently turned up at Lake Estrella. All else were dead—gone.

There were people who stopped by his cave at times. He invited others there for fun and games like Dragon Wars—a game somewhat like our chess. These visitors, for the most part, were not people to share a life with. Daniel had now even moved out of the cave to live with Tilly at the Crystal Castle. He was King after all. Even that company, when visiting, was never the same as being with the one to whom you have given your heart and who has left you, however unwillingly, taking a piece of your heart with them;

no matter how much of their heart has remained with you—it is a lonely existence.

How? How had he managed all these years? He had lived since the Creation—The Time Before—through The Age of Magic. He had been there at the birth of the Age of Men and Dwarves. He had even helped create them. He had lived through the Age of Kings and the Great War; The War of the Realms; the Taradal Treachery; The War of the Arikkans. He had lost everyone who had ever meant anything to him—except Daniel and the Circle, and Lily, of course.

He had kept busy. So many people to take care of in the Kingdoms of the Realms. So much evil in the world to defeat and destroy. His cave in the mountains of Mirador was chocked full of spell books, histories, prophecies, potions, ingredients. It was a thirteen room, Dragon hewn cave—huge! Alas, with no Dragons either.

Now there was trouble in Aradon. Troubles continued to hang like a cloud over Balador. Just a few years ago he had solved the mysteries involving the Kingdoms of Mirador, Panador, Zanadon. His evil brother and nieces had been destroyed. He even missed them, which in a way, was a good thing. They had turned to the Darkness in order to seek out their life's path. They killed, maimed, stole, tortured, purloined, lied and cursed their way across a continent in two and a half thousand years.

Even with all of that, it had all ended for them in the forests of Zanadon and Panador; on the plains of Balador, Aradon and Caladon. Now, he was facing another battle. Some new evil had arisen inside the Realms. This would not be a battle of armies—he was sure of that. Aradon was in serious trouble and he could not get his mind around the entire happening. He could cure the King. He knew the cure existed. He just had to find its resting place, either in his books or out of his Orb of Sight; they had always come through in the past. Even his Orb had been lost—probably during the War of the Arikkans. So, that left him only his books!

Where was Queen Rose? Who was this Alindra? He must have missed something—for he, if anyone, should know of all of the Magicians and Enchantresses since the Creation, whether good or evil. They were all related to him someway. Someone... somehow... somewhere would know.

What if it was someone not related to him? Someone from outside the Realms? The Dajinn, Kerrayu and Blad were all gone. But that woman! He would talk to Arik. He had a mission for him anyway. Besides, he probably had known her best. (At least better than the boy had wanted to know her.) Or maybe Kalaal! What was that woman's name? He would find it. It would come. It had to— for Aradon's sake.

ML

CHAPTER THREE—
TRANSFORMATIONS

•• 6th day of 4th Month ••

As Evermon was berating his step-mother on the day before his party, the Court of Mirador—the Crystal Castle (home of the Frosted Flask and the ruling family of Mirador: King Daniel, Queen Mathilda, Princesses Caelith and Raelle, the throne that leads the rest)—was having a ripple of its own across its golden threshold. Mirador is first in all things, including troubles. All Kingdoms of the Realms looked to its leaders; to Miraden, to 'The Prophecy' and the Circle of Light for guidance. Unfortunately, even the highest of all did not have the answers for all things. For who, indeed, can have answers for teenagers?

"Why can't Raelle do it?" Caelith complained for the fifteenth time.

And for the fifteenth time a patient Daniel replied to her. "Raelle is already promised—you know that—to Capostral of Caladon. You are the only one who can take up the throne here. You must be patient and accept the responsibility that comes your way, whether you like it or not." He paused to see if any changes appeared in her troubled expression. Seeing none, he continued, "Do you think it was easy or fun for me to change from an eleven-year-old boy to a teenager almost overnight, to turn white all over?"

Silence.

Her father had been fair to her, was being fair to her, but she still didn't want to admit what her responsibilities were. After all, Princess Caelith was a young and pretty eighteen year old who had no thought whatsoever of tying herself down to a husband and

Kingdom and all that went with it. (At least no thought at the present.) But she also still suffered an ache in her heart for the loss of her good friend and cousin, Boncaster. She wanted to do something with her life before death overtook her also. Boncaster's early death had haunted each of the Princes and Princesses of the Realms.

"But Father, I am—I

"There is nothing to be done, Little One."

She gave him a look that could have exploded honey. "That's just one of the problems. I am still your 'Little One.'"

"And you always will be."

"Which proves my point, Father. How can I rule or wed when I am still your 'Little One?'"

He held out his arms to his frightened and frustrated daughter. She ran into them, like the child she had always been, searching for the security she had always found. Although it was only temporary, on her part, not her father's part, she managed to feel better. The Queen also gave her a heartfelt hug and a squeeze. Caelith then begged her leave and went off to her room with Daniel and Tilly casting looks after her that were filled with great concern. They hoped that all of their advice, counsel and instruction would accomplish the job of helping their troubled daughter to make the correct choices. For there is nothing a parent wants more than for their children to be happy in making good choices.

"I hope we have done the right thing,"

"Tilly, is there such a thing as 'the' right thing? I only hope that we have done a good thing."

"Of course, you are right—this time. So much is riding on her decision."

"No more than the fate of this and other Kingdoms, and the future happiness of our strong-minded daughter, and her entire family!"

"Yes, well—nothing to worry about then, eh?"

They smiled tentatively at each other and exited the room arm in arm. The courtyard was full of afternoon sun and, as usual, their walk in the warmth managed to bake a few of their worries away. It was a glorious day despite the disposition with their daughter.

•• 6th day of 4th Month ••

Caelith kicked an urn full of flowers as she rounded the corner of the hallway near her rooms. The urn was made of a delicate porcelain and shattered spreading water and stems and blooms all across the corridor. She stopped. She stamped her feet. She looked around for any signs that she had been seen. There were none. She picked up the biggest shard of porcelain and catapulted it down the hall and at the same time uttered a little petulant cry of frustration. It shattered. She then took off to her chambers where she opened the door, flung her cape on the floor and hurled herself onto her downy soft bed, letting her leg kick down at the mattress every few minutes in a release of extra pent-up frustration. It is hard when you are young, and yet not young, and are forever, or so it seems, being kept from the very things you yearn to do. She laid there for hours. Even her parent's hugs had worn off. She was still thoughtful—resentful—and anything but calm inside! Her outside appeared restive (except for that occasional kick of her leg against the bed), but her heart and mind were a roiling, racing menagerie of entangling and conflicting feelings and thoughts.

She knew her father and mother were right. That's what hurt her the most. She knew what her duties were and she knew that her parents knew she knew. However, the difference between knowing and doing are often difficult—the connection that leads from one to the other is a tenuous thing. Especially in the young. It is always there when we don't want it to be and rarely there when we really need it. When it is there we want to forget about it and pretend that it does not exist. When it is not there we cannot stop thinking about it. Such are the paradoxes of life at any age, but for the young who have not always learned, yet, how to summon the powers that help them make their most valuable and telling decisions, it often becomes a guessing game with all choices appearing equally, deceptively appealing.

"I will do it!" she thought as she stood up.

There. She had made her decision. Then why did she feel so terrible?

Sometimes, not only is the decision difficult to make but even more difficult to carry out. This is where Caelith was about to fail. She knew that the right thing to do was to stay and support her parents and... well... be an adult. That's the decision she had stood up for.

Now, she had to carry it out—but she could not—she sat down.

She stood again and picked her rucksack out of her armoire, stuffed it with her clothes, a bulging coin purse, and sat back on her bed again. Waiting. For what? She did not know, so she just waited. Maybe for a voice to talk her into or out of the choice she had made—remade—but no voice came.

Instead, dark came. She pitched herself over the balcony of her room and landed, feet first on the stones of the courtyard about ten arms below her railing. She rushed through the shadows as she made her way to the kitchen. Once there, she had to avoid the cook and her assistants.

She sneaked into the larder and nicked several small wheels of cheese, a couple of loaves of bread and some dried fruit. She filled her water skin from the pump near the sink. Her pack full, and her water skin slung over her shoulder, now all she had left to do was to get out of the castle without being noticed.

She started out and heard the voices of Cook and the gardener. She flattened herself against the wall. She tried to disappear by pressing herself through it. It did no good, for she was not a Magician and could not disappear through it; she was still there. Eyes shut, she sensed that he voices had not passed by her. She heard them fade away, taking another hallway, not the one she was sweating in. She waited and then quietly made her way to the trap door in the floor. She had done this so many times as a child when she and her sister wanted to sneak out of the castle. No one had ever caught her! She and Raelle would go for long walks in the moonlight, searching for faeries. They never found any but the hunt was certainly enjoyable. (They never found any because all the Faerie Folk lived in the mountains of Caladon, now—ask Daniel!) She and her sister would sneak back in just before the kitchen staff arose for their early morning food preparation.

It is funny that she should think of Raelle now. Her sister was to marry Capostral in two months. She had to be back for that! Maybe her absence would show her parents that she was really serious about what she wanted. She descended the ladder through the trap and hit the dirt of the lower storeroom floor. She made her way in the mustiness past the baskets of potatoes, bushels of corn and beans, jars of fruit and barrels of flour, oats and barley. She passed the drying rack of herbs and spices. The door was right there. Almost... but then she heard voices again. They seemed to be just outside the door. It sounded like the Captain of the Guards, Montcalm, with...Lilith, his intended. It surely sounded like they were doing more than talking.

"Montcalm, stop!"

A giggle escaped Lilith's lips.

"The moon is just right for a stroll in the orchards."

"Drat!" Caelith thought. *"The orchards are the fastest way away from the castle. I'll have to go out over by the stables."* Then an idea hit her. She waited again. Montcalm and his lady strolled away and all was silent outside. The Princess eased the door open and saw no one. She made a beeline for the stables, just a few spans away, across the moonlit courtyard. She stumbled in through the open door and sank against the far wall. All was still quiet. She saw several men's shirts and pants banging on a line across one of the stalls. She went over and took a smaller pair of pants and a shirt, entered a stall and changed into them. They were not even very big on her. They must belong to Henry, the stable boy. The shirt was just big enough but it was a tight squeeze. She didn't have a large chest (one of the many things that she was disappointed over), but then the shirt of a fourteen year old boy would be tight on most eighteen year old girls. Except for Caelith who was short and petite.

She then had an 'ah-ha' moment. She salvaged her sash from the pile of her clothes and wrapped and bound her chest, just to make sure. The shirt then slipped on much more easily. The transformation from Princess to peasant boy was progressing. She thought she had come up with a very novel idea.

She reached into her pack and left a silver coin on the stall post under where the clothes were hanging. If she was going to be a thief, it was an honest thief she would be. She re-slung her backpack and her water skin over her shoulder. She passed out the front of the stable. She had decided 'no horses.' Yes, it would be faster—but too traceable. Especially if she wasn't going out as Caelith. She made her way along to the Queen's Gate, across the drill yard in the moonlight with the noises of the sleeping soldiers in their barracks a few spans away impinging on her ears. As she rounded the corner some guards passed the other way and she snuck out the murderer's gate and into the awakening streets of the Crystal City. It had taken her all night to get out of the castle.

The first shop she stopped at was a barber's. She thought and thought and then—broke in. She found a pair of scissors and brought them to her hair. She could not force herself to do it. Her hair had been growing since she was eight. It was down to the small of her back—long and golden—but then she closed her fingers and a large piece of hair fell away from her head. Well, that was it. Another decision made. She had to finish it. She bit down on her lip and soon she looked most unlike any Princess you have ever seen. In fact, she looked very much like Henry, the stable boy. Caelith looked almost fourteen—she hoped; much younger as a boy than a girl, she thought as she stared into a mirror. It must be her baby face, her slight build, her fair complexion, her long, slender fingers. Was she crazy?! No. She could be Henry. She had a nice alto voice—clear, pure. She could do this!

She gathered up her hair and put the scissors back. She went out of the shop and threw her long, beautiful hair in one of the nearby refuse barrels. She walked, without concern, down the street. She tried not to flounce; she strode—much more masculine. She looked in window after window of the shops as she passed them. She found the shop of the Harper and Master Instrument Maker. She went in. The Harper was just opening up as the sun began to rise over the roofs of the buildings across the little street. She asked the Harper if he had any good harps for sale.

"Why, yes, son. All my harps are good!"

'Son,' she thought. *'He called me son!'*

"I have this harp here that might fit you perfectly. You are right handed, I hope?"

"Yes, sir."

"Have you been playing long?"

"For several years."

"With whom have you studied?"

'Uhh—with you,' she thought, but said "Oh, Harper Ford from Caladon. I am here to buy the finest harp possible for my money. He said that you made the best."

"I am grateful for the endorsement. How long have you been gone, young sir?"

"I arrived here last night and must choose and be on my way. My father gave me leave only to buy the harp and get home. The cows need milking and he cannot do it alone. I'm afraid that he is not very happy with my desire to be a Harper."

"Neither was my father, but, when you have the gift..."

The remainder was unspoken but understood. Caelith was relieved that she had not been recognized by one of her former teachers. She was also grateful to find someone who understood her longing to be a Harper. She was quite good at it. She took the harp and strummed her fingers across the strings, lightly. It made a fine, rich sound for such a small harp and she reached in her rucksack and extended five gold pieces for the instrument,

The Master reached out his fingers hesitantly.

"This is too much."

"It is worth every mark."

The Master plucked two gold pieces out of the Princess's hand. "This will do nicely. I thank you, young sir. Have a pleasant journey home."

"Same to you, Master Harper."

"By the way, boy, what was your name?"

"My name?... is... Hen... Holder."

"Hen-Holder, eh?"

"No, sir, just Holder."

"Well, Holder, play well and love often."

"Thank you again, sir," was said in a rather red-faced blush at the innuendo of the last remark.

And Caelith (Holder) was off. Now, this was going to be an adventure! But what had she gotten herself into? Sneaking, stealing, disguising, masquerading, lying—and what more was to come? As of yet, she hadn't even left the Crystal City!

Out of the city across the narrow plains to the shores of the lake, across the Straits of Light to Hope Peninsula, then down the Well-Traveled Road and through the Forest of Hope, it was a most pleasant day to be out on your own. Even if 'your own' was completely alone. Cheese never tasted so good as it did that day to Caelith. She was free. She was the master (or mistress) of her own fate.

She had been walking west for several hours since arriving on Hope Peninsula. She had passed the High Forest of Hope, many farms, a few small hamlets, the Grove of Grace, and was just into Aradon. But it was now getting late and she must find a place to rest for the night. She passed another farm, a large one. The house was of mud and wattle with a tightly thatched roof in good repair, sturdy fences, with a wooden barn. The chimney to the house was issuing the smoky smell of food cooking—that wonderful smell of fire-braised meats and boiling vegetables.

She saw at least a dozen children running around the yard, playing, chasing their dog and laughing and yelling. One little boy held a baby lamb close to his chest. Every once in a while he would bury his face in the soft fleece of the young kid. She entered the gate.

"Hello, children. Are your parents home?"

The children stopped dead. They stared. The little boy clutched the lamb to his chest even more tightly and the poor little thing let out the most pitiful of bleats. The boy let up on his pressure and the lamb licked his face as the boy petted the soft, wooly head. One of the other children had run into the house and soon returned with his father.

"Good day to you, good Sir," Holder called out.

"It is a good day. Will it stay that way?"

"I am only looking for a place to lay my head. I am Holder, a Harper and as I travel the Kingdoms of the Realms looking for a position, I ask the favor of the good people of the land to give me shelter and a little rest in exchange for a coin and a few songs."

"Aye. A little young to be a Harper, though, but I've never turned anyone away from my door who was hungry nor refused a night's sleep to a single soul. Not many have looked as pitiful as you do."

Holder heard the children snicker, the little boy with the lamb was grinning from ear to ear. Their father was so clever.

"Come in and sit at table. Children, wash and join us. William, the lamb must stay outside. Your mother will not have the beast in the house."

The children scattered as the man led Holder into his humble home, where they washed at a pitcher and basin. There was a long table in the center of the large kitchen. The man directed Holder to the place at his right, at the head of the table.

"May I have your name, kind Sir?"

"William, Master Holder."

"Well, William—are all those children yours?"

"Every last one of them..."

"And he ought to know. And if he doesn't know I don't know who would!" came a voice from the other room. That voice soon became a person as the wife of William, the Farmer, swept into the room. She was not an overly large woman; not a 'typical' farmer's wife. She was pleasant looking and her face was made even more appealing by the giant smile she had placed on it.

"And you know it's why I married you, Tildy. You were always one to know how to help folk."

"And you were always the one to help me help them."

They kissed each other very demonstratively, like a just before mealtime ritual, and there was the loud sound of giggling and even a few groans from the now assembling children.

"Take your places, young ones!"

The children rushed to their places at the table in a very orderly manner. They knew the drill. Each child shifted one place from their usual, allowing for the guest to sit at the head of the table, next to their father. Holder noticed this. Tildy took her place at the end opposite to that of her husband. Holder counted: one, two, three, four, five, six, seven, eight, nine, ten, eleven... "Where's number twelve?"

"Nought but 'leven, Master Holder. Nought but 'leven."

Holder noticed also that the room had gotten a little quieter.

"We lost our oldest when he fell from the hayloft."

"I am sorry to hear that. What a great family! Such fine children."

Each child strained to sit up a little straighter and be a little more proper.

"Thank you, Master Holder."

"Holder, just Holder." She wasn't handling this 'Master' business very well as she had been a 'Mistress' all her life.

"Fine. Join us in a word of thanks?"

"I'd be honored."

Holder had not looked at the table yet but when he turned it was loaded with fresh farm goods: baked bread, sliced ham and some cheeses, vegetables steaming out of a pot. Little William was the last one to close his eyes and he caught Holder's attention and smiled. Holder smiled back.

"Oh—Creators of the Realms—we thank you for this bounty on our table—we ask for a blessing on it to build us strong in body, mind and spirit—so that we may build the Kingdoms you created, help others and give freely."

"You are a most Humble man, Farmer William."

"Aye, that he is," agreed Tildy.

The bread was broken by the Master of the house, the cheese sliced and passed. The family and Holder ate their fill.

Little William then grabbed a utensil and started banging in on the table. The other children soon picked up the rhythm and joined the chant that came out of their little brother's mouth: "Sing-a-song, sing-a-song, sing-a-song!"

William, the Farmer, went to quiet his brood with a look but Holder laid his hand on the farmer's arm.

"I would be honored to sing for this family," was spoken over the continuing chant of the children and when they heard it they clapped happily and silenced themselves in preparation for their entertainment.

They watched in eagerness as Holder went to his rucksack and took out his harp. The children 'oohed' and 'aahed', for it was a beautiful looking instrument. He plucked a few strings, Little William patted the bench next to him and Holder sat down. With the first and third fingers of his right hand he plucked two strings on the harp while he held it with the other hand against his leg.

"Since the great dawn of time
With a vast span of rhyme
Songs have been sung,
Bells have been rung of happy times.
Realms among the Crystal Orb
Shared in wealth of hill and vale.
Miraden of old has said
Listen well to every tale.
Men of valor, women bold,
Dwarves who gather as of old;
All good creatures must agree
Mirador will leaders be!"

Now, the family lived outside of Mirador, in Aradon, but all peoples of the Realms understood that the leadership of Mirador was first and foremost in all the Realms, so they clapped along.

"Fall to! Fall to! Join in the celebration.
Behold! Behold! Each man fulfills his station.
Within the Realms of Light there be
Not one who's better off than me,
For I can sing, and I am free
To tell you each that you can be -- like me!"

The songs that followed carried the family away into the evening. Holder sang and sang and the children loved him for it. At each new song they clamored to sit next to him and Little William, being the totally gracious child he was, moved over so each of his brothers and sisters could have a turn next to Holder. The parents just sat there and beamed at the family.

As Holder sang, he thought, *'How can I bless this wonderful family?'* He would not make any hasty decisions. He would take his time and make sure that this family was taken care of—not that Farmer William couldn't do it on his own; even if she was from Mirador and they were of Aradon. It became a vow, and Caelith would see to it being kept.

As much as the children enjoyed the singing; as much clapping and foot stomping as they did to the varied rhythms that Holder sang out; they, being normal children, grew tired, their eyes and heads drooped and their parents took them away one by one to their beds; their limp little bodies attesting to the fact that a hard day was spent at work and at play on this most wonderful of farms. Little William, as hard has he tried not to, was the last one to fall asleep. As his father picked him up the boy murmured:

"Thank you, Holder. It was wonder..."

Farmer William, with a soft chuckle, continued out of the room. Tildy cleared the table. Holder got up to help her.

Tildy looked amazed and shocked at the Harper. "You sit down! I'll not have a guest helping with the chores like a common laborer!"

She had only done what she was used to doing for herself at the castle. Oops! She was NOT at the castle and she was NOT a she! "It is my privilege to assist you. How else can I repay you for your kindness and hospitality?"

"Your songs and the joy of my children is payment enough."

Caelith was—well, stunned. She had thought that the people of the Realms were just as self-serving as some of those at court—the pretenders. She was refreshed of her opinion, now, having stopped at the Farmer Family's home. She thought that maybe, just maybe, she could rule over people of this caliber—someday! She chased that thought away!

Farmer William re-emerged from the back rooms and faced the Harper.

"Never have we had a night like this one! Come, I'll show you to your room."

He led Holder outside and to the back of the house. He opened the creaky door and inside was a bed, a chair, a washbasin on a stand. Holder's expression was as one astounded.

"We keep it just for the occasional visitor. Never has there been one to rival your songs."

She was very grateful for the hours she and her parents had spent at music-making. A melancholy came over her. "Thank you."

"Little William will be out here to fetch you for breakfast."

"There is no need... It..."

"There is every need. There is no stopping Little William.

Besides, we will not see anyone go away unfed. Goodnight to you, Master Holder."

"Goodnight to you, Farmer William."

Holder sank onto the bed after William had closed and latched the door. Even to Caelith it was very comfortable. She laid back and fell asleep almost instantaneously. She dreamed of children— lots of them—running, playing, singing and calling 'Caelith!' She awoke with a start and had just a little bit of trouble falling back to sleep. When she awakened in the morning it was to the persuasion of the very gentle shaking of the bed by Little William.

"Please, Master Holder. It is breakfast time and the family awaits you," was his little way of saying 'I'm starving! Hurry up!'

Holder turned over and clutched the bedclothes to his/her chest. "Well, good morning, William." He sat up off his pillow. "How are you this morning?"

"I am well but my lamb is sick."

"The one you were holding yesterday?"

"Aye. He is not well. Father says he could die."

"I am sorry, William. I hope he will be all right."

"Father also says that if he dies it is meant to be. What do you think?"

Holder was amazed at the attitude of this tiny boy over death.

"I think your father is a very wise—and lucky man."

William's brows knit as he pondered on Holder's words for a few moments. But then he smiled and ran out of the room.

Holder finished dressing and came up to the kitchen in the front of the house. Bread, cheese and fresh milk were on the table. Holder sat in 'his' place, they had a blessing on the food and all partook of it in the same spirit that had prevailed last evening. When the repast was done, Holder stood and announced he must be off. The children whined for him to stay.

"I must go. I am needed elsewhere."

"But we need you here!"

"I would love to stay here, but you could not afford to support me and I am afraid that I could not afford to pay for too long. And my work is not the kind of toil done by the hands that you require here. But, I will stop by again and visit."

The children were sad but somewhat pacified. All said their goodbyes and Holder set out of the house and down the lane and through the gate. The children ran to the fence to see him off, waving and shouting:

"Don't forget to come back!" "Thank you, Holder!"

As hard as it was to leave that little family, it was more difficult to head away realizing that she had been spoiled in her first night away from home. She could hope that her Kingdom and others could be filled with families like the Farmers; but she realized that hope was not entirely realistic.

She turned her face westward, toward the city of Aradon. She again passed through fields, glens, hamlets and villages. She stopped for rest at mid-day by a cool and refreshing stream where she slaked her thirst with fresh, cool water—and filled her waterbag again. She then headed onward. She was hoping to be able to find shelter in the village of Pemberton, really nothing more than an expanded farming hamlet with a way station. Then it hit her! Aradon—and Evermon. Today was his birthday! In her rush to do her own will she had forgotten all about her 'cousin.' And to appear there now would put an end to all of her plans. She was saddened at facing the first major consequence of her decision to leave.

Meanwhile, back at the Farmer's house, a morose group of children had taken a terribly long time to do their chores that day. They had sat around the yard instead of running and playing. Then Little William paced around to the back of the house where Holder had slept. He pushed the door open and his eyes lit up. On the well-made bed, right there on top of the pillows, five golden coins were set out along with a note. He grabbed the coins and the note and took them into his mother. She read the note and then held it to her breast. The children gathered around her.

"It is Holder, saying how much he enjoyed... our family. 'This gold,' he says, 'is to see to the education of the children. And there will be more.' He is a fine man, children. A fine man."

The children were no longer really sad, but they missed their new friend—almost like an older brother. They would see him again. Oh, would they see him again!"

ML

CHAPTER FOUR—
A YEAR OLDER, A YEAR WISER

•• 7ᵗʰ day of 4ᵗʰ Month ••

He wasn't a little child anymore so why was there this Dwarf Magician at his birthday party? He was fifteen for goodness sakes! He had reached his majority, in Aradon. He could take a bride! *'Well, maybe not,'* he thought *'at least I wouldn't, not yet.'* Besides his mother and father had been 'gone' so long that there had been no arrangements made for him as there had been for his older brothers. Watching the tricks being performed, even the birthday boy had to admit that the Dwarf was really good. Most Dwarves had a marginal acquaintance with magic; they did card tricks and made small animals appear and disappear. This Dwarf, on the other hand (or is that sleight-of-hand) was different. He had a gift for making anything disappear. Including himself. Evermon would crack up every time he would reappear, because he would be sitting on Alindra's lap. She would get so mad, but then laughingly join in with the others of the party praising the Dwarf and his abilities and cleverness. Her moods shifted so rapidly. Evermon noticed it but did not know what to make of it since it had been happening ever since she had come into his life.

Now, there were other special guests at the party—Lindara, the Princess of Panador, sister to the slain Boncaster. She was three years older than the Prince and she was so pretty, so smart, so able to hold anyone's interest, that even Evermon was smitten. Hopelessly and totally. He fawned on her every word. He laughed at her funny jokes. He worshipped her own smiling laughter over the prestidigitation of the Dwarf. He drooled all over his best pantaloons just looking at her. It was very embarrassing. But he was being stupid. (He was being a fifteen year old boy!) His mother and Lindara's father were siblings. That made Lindara his cousin. Eeeewwww! (Well, not to everyone in the Realms, to whom it was a part of tradition—but to Evermon—eeeewww!) He straightened his thoughts out immediately and his eyes fell on the lovely face of Raelle—not a cousin! Still a Princess! Oh, yeah—but Raelle is the promised Princess of Mirador. Capostral is certainly a lucky guy. Too bad Evermon wasn't a lucky guy. Mother gone, father sick—he was promised to no one. As he looked around at all the beautiful girls in his life he realized that they were all unreachable—untouchable—in one way or another—either already promised or somehow... related to him.

"Where's Caelith?" Evermon asked suddenly and eagerly—maybe too eagerly. (She was not a cousin!)

The party patter was subdued as Raelle, Caelith's younger sister got up and ran from the room. Everyone looked at Evermon.

"What did I say?"

"I am sorry, Prince," Alindra broke in, "but in all the excitement I didn't have a chance to tell you."

"Tell me what? It seems that the others know!"

"The others have not been secluded in their rooms for days!"

There was silence.

Lindara spoke up, "It seems our cousin, Cousin, has disappeared. No word—no trace—no nothing."

"When, Lindara?" Thoughts of Boncaster, his mother, his father, his brothers, flashed through his mind.

"Last night."

"I... has... has she run away?"

"That is what the note said."

Evermon thought that this was not a particularly keen birthday present—he had definitely asked for no presents. He thought a minute in the silence that follows unwelcome news. "I'm sorry. I'll be right back."

He got up and went to search for Raelle. She was sitting in a speck of sunlight in the corner of the stairway leading up from the Great Hall. As she heard him approach she wiped her eyes but her breathing was still ragged and her body trembled occasionally with a silent sob. Evermon sat next to her. He said nothing. She leaned her head on his capable shoulder. He took her hand in his. After all they had grown up together.

"I'm sorry."

"It was nothing you did, Evermon."

"I'm glad about that."

Raelle, charmed by his sincerity, choked back a laugh.

"But I am sad for you."

"Thank you, Evermon."

They sat in silence again. Sometimes it's just the best thing to do. Evermon liked the feeling of her trust and warmth. It had never been a part of him to be serious around a girl before. He was enjoying this contact of close friendship and a problem shared. He didn't enjoy the situation that had brought it all about, but he didn't mind being close to Raelle. He stood up with her hand still in his. She looked up into his strong, caring eyes, standing also. He led her slowly back to the party.

Also at the party were others he considered his 'friends' whether he was related to them or not—no matter what Alindra said. Evermon found his thoughts straying to those nearest him.

Evandra, a distant cousin who was kind and gentle, but only thirteen; Jayden, at fifteen, was probably the one he was closest to besides his own brothers. Jayden is the son of the local Townesman—kind of like a mayor. They were good friends and frequent companions both in and out of trouble. (As long as Alindra didn't know—all was well!)

Then there were the daughters of Duke Alfrond, his father's brother—so they were direct cousins. If anything were ever to happen to himself or to his brothers the girls would then be in line for the throne. Can you imagine—Queen Testra or Queen Palanca? They were good girls but would you ever listen to them? Just what were their parents thinking when they chose those names?! Of course, their parents had been stuck with questionable monikers also—Alfrond and Elayda!

Elias and Nancy's children were there. Second Generation Circle of Light for sure. Evermon had grown up with them: Sean,

16; Molly, 15; Michael, 14; and Matthew, just 13. Now that Daniel was King of Mirador the mantle of the leadership of the Circle of Light had fallen on Elias' capable shoulders.

Aradon's leader for the Circle of Light, Nathan, and his wife, Malika, had sent their children also: Mara, 18; Sala, 17; Alan, 16; Will, 15; and Cort, 14. Whenever the Circle met at the Palace the Jameson children had come to associate with Evermon and his brothers.

His brothers! He knew how Raelle was feeling. He was still holding her hand and he squeezed it. As Evermon and Raelle reached the end of the greeting line, there were four children he didn't know. He was introduced to them by Alindra who got all their names right: Stephen, Silar, Aylara and Kenton; four orphans all round ten or eleven years old or so. Every year four orphaned children were invited to the Prince's birthday. Evermon didn't mind at all. This year there seemed to be something causing a little more distance from the 'royals', even though he and the others tried to make them feel welcome. Then, last and certainly least, was his Step-mother Alindra, and young Baladar.

There were a few guards and serving maids, but in most Royal circles they don't count for much. (Unless you live in Panador.) Although he had heard some pretty good stories from two of the Guards (the Princes and their companions); stories that Queen Rose would have cautioned them NOT to listen to. Evermon guiltily enjoyed them whenever he heard them in the halls. The funny thing about it is that everyone got along with Evermon. He was really an amazing individual, despite his sorrows; his melancholy. His parents had raised him and his brothers with the greatest of love and care. Evermon was just in a blue funk lately. He realized that it was because of all the people who were NOT at his party!

There was a loud "AHHH!" as Gladenwreath, the Dwarf Magician, magicked Evermon's stunning bay stallion into the Great Hall in front of the party goers. Evermon caught it just in time and clapped along with his friends. For friends they were (except for and in spite of Alindra). He had grown up with all of them and had always enjoyed their company before. He knew it was just him—this mood. He liked and even loved these people! (Lindara!) Even when he had been rude over the last year or so; everyone of them understood (except Alindra) why he was acting so 'out of himself.' During the party each of them had carefully stolen a glance in Evermon's direction, and gradually they began to see the old Evermon re-emerging from the clouds that had hovered over him.

More applause as a Knight in full armor was summoned magically to sit astride the stallion and ride him out the main doors of the hall—but he didn't stop there. The youths followed the horse to the door in time to see both horse and rider gallop magically up and over the castle's battlements. They turned and Evermon started an ovation for the Dwarf. They then shook his hands and congratulated him as they crowded around him.

The Dwarf held up his hands. "And now, My Prince, I have a special trick just for you."

"More?!"

The Dwarf nodded and smiled, then motioned to the stairway. A blue mist began to appear and out of the mist the shape of a human form began to coalesce. As it solidified there was awe at the beauty of the illusion; the shimmer, the sparkle, the gleam, the phosphorescence. Around the room, there was confusion as to exactly who was standing there in the brilliant blue, floor length robe as he or it was facing away from the group of the youths. Slowly, as the form turned around, a smiling, slightly blue-tinged face revealed itself under long, bright yellow hair.

"Kwuktw!" was screamed by Evermon as he ran forward. The two princes shook hands, and the others, who knew the MerPrince well, crowded around. The four orphans held back. Evermon stopped the reunion of friends and motioned his special guests forward. The four children came forward meekly. Kwuktw loosed his robe and stood there in a small, white shift, kind of like a Greek chiton; a pleated skirt topped by a garment that draped over one shoulder leaving half of his upper body exposed.

The children stopped and gasped. He was so blue! Evermon stooped to whisper the visitor's identity into their collective ear. They just stood there staring.

"A real MerPerson?"

Kwuktw smiled and stooped low to meet the young ones eye to eye. He extended his hand carefully and shook the hand of each child. With the children still clustered around the Princes, they all turned to the Magician.

"Noble Gladenwreath, you have truly amazed us. I am heartily glad for your presence here at my party." (At which Alindra smiled.) Evermon was trying to sound grownup and it didn't always work well. He was only fifteen and still a 'child' at heart. "Thank you for your feats of magic," sounded much more like Evermon speaking.

"I has been an honor to serve the court of my King. I thank you for your hospitality. Now, where's the cake?!"

The laughter and applause that greeted the Dwarf's last words were warm and genuinely felt by all, because the Dwarven fondness for cake was legendary. Even Alindra broke her mask of stone and cracked a smile. It's a wonder that crack didn't cause her face to disintegrate. But we can hope!

The tables, laden with hams, fowls, sides of beef, corn, peas, hominy, dishes of pears and peaches, apples and flagons of lemonade were brought in along with the chairs for each of the guests. Evermon sat at one end, Alindra at the other and the rest arranged themselves in between, with Gladenwreath seated in the place of honor at Evermon's right and the orphans seated close to him on the left. They chatted and chewed though a wonderful meal. Then the cake was brought out.

"Here, at last, Gladenwreath—the cake you were promised!"

"About time, Young Prince. About time!"

Another round of laughter. Evermon looked across his cake and his eyes fell on Baladar, at the other end of the table, seated next to his mother, Alindra, looking ignored. Evermon was hit with the pain of conscience. He whistled. Short and sharp. All eyes looked towards him but he continued to stare at Baladar who was busy studying the dust on the toe of his boot. Another whistle. Now, everyone, seeing where the Prince was gazing, looked at Baladar but he still did not notice. Will was sitting next to the boy. He tapped Baladar on the shoulder and once the child's eyes were focused on Will, Will pointed to Evermon who was motioning for Baladar to come and join him. Baladar looked shocked. Some of the others suppressed giggles. Some held their peace. All knew of the sometimes-tension between the Prince and his step-brother. Baladar proceeded around the table. Evermon pointed to a spot at the floor next to his chair and Baladar stood there. Nervous, anxious, about to wet his breeches if Evermon embarrassed him in front of all the others. Slowly, Evermon leaned close to Baladar's ear.

"Baladar—I'm sorry."

Baladar looked at his step-brother (his idol) silently with stoicism on the outside and a growing elation on the inside.

"Your mother makes me mad sometimes!" he whispered again.

Baladar giggled. He understood. "Me too!' he admitted in a returned whisper..

Then Evermon spoke up. "Baladar is going to help me blow out the candles. He and I will then serve the first four pieces of cake to our four honored guests!" The orphan's eyes lit up. So did Baladar's. Evermon made his wish and he and Baladar blew out the candles. (Do we all know what the Prince wished for? Maybe. Baladar also made a wish—although, technically, it was not his cake.) Then with great ceremony Evermon passed the knife to Baladar in order to cut the cake. Evermon took the slices and placed them on plates. Together they served the orphans first, followed by Gladenwreath and Alindra and then the rest of their friends and relatives. (Did I mention that Evermon was Baladar's idol?) After the cake had been mostly consumed, meaning that only some of the delicious morsels remained on the faces and clothes of the party-goers, Evermon rose to propose a toast.

"To my Father, King Emeron—a great man and a good Father. To my Mother, Queen Rose." He paused for a few seconds and got his control back. "To my brothers Raileon and Galderon—may their quest have great success—wherever they are. To Caelith, my dear friend." Raelle beamed. "And to my step-mother for talking me into a wonderful party. To you, my friends—I am grateful to you all for coming here. I must apologize for my sometimes lack of courtesy and attention. I have been preoccupied as of late. Again.

Thank you." Now, that didn't sound too childish or too adult. They all drained their cups dry as the Prince of Aradon led them.

"Did you enjoy your cake, Noble Gladenwreath?"

The Dwarf laughed in loud, castle-shattering guffaws as he nodded and poured another goblet of wine with which to chase his cake. They all refilled and drank again.

•• 7th day of 4th Month ••

During a moment of calm as the partygoers talked and waited for what was to come—for among the cousins of the Realms there was always something coming—Lindara was pulled aside by her cousin, Raelle. They had not spoken or even seen each other in months.

"I'm so glad you came," said Raelle.

"I had hoped to see Raileon. But all the boys get to go off on their quests and all we get to do is sit home and knit."

Raelle laughed. "That's why I'm glad you're here. I love Evermon and all, don't misunderstand—all the cousins—but you have always kept me sane. You and Cael..." She couldn't finish her thought.

"I miss Boncaster terribly even after eight years so I know how you feel about Caelith. I still hear his voice in the castle or see him streaking across the yard. I miss everything about him."

"I feel the same way about Caelith. Although...

"What?"

"Caelith could come back."

"I hope so," said Lindara. "The loss of one of our generation is already too many."

"Remember Boncaster's parties with Raileon and Kwuktw?"

"It was fun spying on them when we were young. It felt like something naughty, watching them swim naked, but we were all children then."

"All the fun went out of it as we grew older. We giggled because they looked so silly—those little boys. But after their change they didn't look silly anymore."

"They sure didn't!" and Lindara blushed.

They giggled.

"Were we wrong? Was it wrong?"

"No. We grew out of it because we began to respect each other."

"Did you and Raileon ever... ?"

"Raelle! I should say not!"

"Swim together? is what I was going to say."

"No.

"Kiss?"

"Well, yes, that—once or twice. How about you and Capostral?"

"He's a good kisser!"

"Raelle!

"What?! We only kissed once or twice. He was too shy to do it more often!"

"You are shameless, Daughter of Daniel!"

"No. There was never a desire to go further than his kiss. It told me everything I needed to know about him—about us. And it left something to be discovered later. That something that I know, after it happens, I'll cherish. And it will make me cherish him."

"I like that."

"I do too. Do you think Raileon and Galderon will return?"

"They have to!" She paused, overcome a little. "So does Caelith."

"Then they will."

"How can you be so sure."

"I'm Daniel's daughter, his shameless daughter," she laughed, "and he would be 'told' if there was something wrong. He has said nothing to me."

"I don't understand the Creators and their plans."

"I don't either. But Father does. We'll have to be content with that."

"Lindara! Raelle!—Come on!" shouted Evermon, the birthday boy.

The party was officially over—at least the part he had agreed to let Alindra plan. But now it was time for his idea. All of the nobility, and the Circle members could ride. He proposed that the Royal Stables be opened and that they all go riding. He, Lindara,

Jayden, Evandra and Raelle would each take one of the orphans or Baladar on their horses and go double. A great cheer was raised and they headed off for an afternoon of horsemanship with one of the best horsemen in the Kingdom. Baladar was aglow as he sat behind his half-brother on the great bay stallion.

•• 7th day of 4th Month ••

They rode for hours. Across the fields in front of the castle, around through the hills and up and over the rolling farmland of this prosperous yet unlucky Kingdom. They stopped at the river before turning around to return to the castle. All were still with them. No one had lagged behind. Even Alindra had been persuaded to accompany them—and she was still smiling. (Maybe with all that potion in her she could do nothing else but smile!) Gladenwreath had ridden his sturdy little Dwarven pony. After they watered their mounts and set them to graze by picketing them in the lush green grass of the field, they decided to get together a grand game of Castle and Standards. (Better known to us as Capture the Flag.)

Alindra and Gladenwreath decided to sit this one out but were gradually persuaded with the suggestion that they serve as the officials for the game—a relatively easy task. It gave Gladenwreath a little time to study the enigma that was this strange lady—the Queen of Aradon.

Lindara and Raelle were chosen as the Generals of each army. Lindara chose Evermon, Testra, Sean, Sala, Will, Kenton, Silar, Baladar, Michael and Mara. Raelle chose Jayden, Molly, Matthew, Cort, Palanca, Kwuktw (who had never played before—but was fascinated to learn more about his human friends), Stephen, Aylara, Evandra, and Alan.

As the sides lined up and chose positions Jayden thought to play one of his jokes after conferring secretly with Evermon.

"What do we use for flags?"

Evermon took his cue and said, "We could use Baladar's and Cort's breeches!"

Both the boys grabbed their breeches tightly to them and screamed "No!"

All the youths laughed.

Evermon said, "I was only joking. You're safe."

However, the two boys only relaxed a little. Their hands were near their breeches until Alan and Will, who were dressed in their favorite and most romantic of costumes for the party—Taradal Rider black—offered their bright red and yellow sashes. They would be perfect flags!

Dungeons for the prisoners and Keeps for their flags or standards, were set up on each side of the river about a quarter of a league back from the shore. Gladenwreath helped to make the transparent structures look more realistic but Sean and Alan, being the oldest sons of Circle members, used a magic of their own, which made things look wonderful. Everyone suggested that they had to swear an oath not to use their magic during the game—they did. (Swear the oath, that is!)

The objects of the game were carefully placed in plain sight inside the walls of the temporary Keeps. With both flags and dungeons now guarded, the generals deployed their teams and the mock war began.

In this game you captured members of the opposing team, trying to get to the others' flag and take it back to your Keep. Boys were required to lift their captives into the air and count to three. Girls just had to hang on to their opponent and then count to three. But quite often the girls would lift their smaller opponents into the air and tickle them for the count of three as they squealed with glee even though they had been caught by the bigger youths.

Gladenwreath and Alindra patrolled the borders and the river side. It was a shallow, narrow river through this stretch and the youths could easily ford it. With sopping breeches and riding clothes, it made it difficult at times to run. So, all leggings were pulled up to the knees and thereby avoided getting soaked.

As Baladar was sneaking across the river leading Silar by the hand she slipped on a mossy rock and tumbled both of them into the wet. He laughed. She cried. He helped her out and they ran, tripping and stumbling over the tall grasses and tussocks of the field. Gladenwreath saw them and took out his wand. With careful aim he sent a spell, a gust of wind, that knocked them off their feet, but it did dry them off! They looked at each other, wide-eyed and both started laughing. But Kwuktw was bearing down on them. They rose and ran, much faster now that they were dry, but tall, long-legged Kwuktw caught up and tumbled Baladar in the air and counted to three while Silar ran off. Kwuktw took Baladar to the dungeon. He didn't ever think that being captured would be fun—but it had been. It must have been the MerPrince's way of doing it.

Once the prisoner was installed, Kwuktw ran off in search of other prisoners. As jailer he forgot that he had to stay there. As soon as the MerPrince was gone Evermon streaked in and stole his step-brother away. Silently, and with a big smile on Baladar's face, they made their way along the back of the playing field, through the tallest grass, toward the Keep of their enemy. As they hunkered down, making a plan, a cloud began to rapidly cover the open sky. Action on the field stopped, as all crouched down to remain hidden in the grass, and to watch the sky's unnatural change.

Gladenwreath thought it was most unusual and unsettling. He looked around for Alindra. She was nowhere to be seen, at least not out in the open. Then he spotted her in a shaw of trees at the back corner on the opposite side of the river. She was gesticulating wildly, focused on the sky. Her fists closed and lightning shot from the clouds and hit the ground near the river. The gamers recoiled and ran to the Keeps on each side where Alan and Sean were creating a protective purple warding. As the players reached the wardings they were allowed inside as the lightning continued to crash around them.

Then Alindra saw him—Evermon—running crouched. She sent a bolt at each protective bubble to distract the others and then one at the Prince. He went down as a loud crash sounded by his ear. A few more lightning flashes hit the field and a few trees were set aflame and then the storm abated as quickly as it had arisen.

As the clouds rolled away to the west—almost as quickly as they had rolled in, Gladenwreath noticed—the bubbles were collapsed and the participants gathered near the river as Alindra and Gladenwreath came to check on them. Evermon was missing. So was Baladar. Raelle shouted:

"There's Evermon!"

He emerged from a tall wave of grass that had concealed him and Baladar as they fell. But he was running toward them—bent over—it looked like he was carrying something in his arms.

Jayden shouted, "It's Baladar!"

Sean and Alan were suddenly in the lead as the group sprang toward the Prince. Alindra's heart sank. She raced to the approaching Prince. She was nearly senseless as Gladenwreath arrived on his short legs. Baladar was unconscious and unresponsive but Sean and Alan had their hands on his legs where there were charred patches of flesh that were being re-enlivened by the talents passed down to the brothers through the magic of the Circle.

"Water! We need water!"

Jayden cried, "I'll get it!" as he raced to the river, dipped his hat in and raced back to his fallen friend. Alindra wrung her hands and Evermon did something he thought he could never do—he comforted her. He tried to ease her concern.

"What are they doing?"

"Healing him, step-mother. He will be all right. It was just his legs."

"How?"

"They have been taught by Daniel and Elias—two of the greatest healers in the Realms."

Jayden stood there with the water. Sean and Alan sat back on their haunches, exhausted, and asked for the water. They dropped tiny drops onto Baladar's lips, onto his face and poured more over his charred legs. The crowd of youths and adults was in awe that there was now not a trace of injury as the water washed the remaining ash from the skin of Baladar's legs.

Baladar's eyes opened. He saw Evermon leaning over him. He reached up and pulled Evermon to him and began to cry.

"It hurt so bad! How did you stop it?"

"I didn't. Sean and Alan did."

Baladar pulled back from his step-brother and looked over to the two youths near his feet.

"Thank you." Baladar smiled and reached out his hand and shook the hands of his two doctors. Alindra stooped and lifted her son in her arms.

"I'm sorry," she whispered as she enfolded him.

Neither the boy nor the others that heard the comment understood what she meant other than that she was sorry this had happened at all. But Gladenwreath knew; he understood and his eyes narrowed.

Baladar stood down from his mother on legs whole and well—although a bit shaky from the experience. Even those who had experienced a healing before were thunderstruck at the miracle.

Baladar spoke up. "My breeches are ruined now. Maybe they would have been more use as a flag!" There was laughter and friendly jostling.

Then it was suggested that the game should be ended and all would return to the Palace but Baladar protested.

"I'm not going to be the cause that spoils everyone's fun! We play! I'm not going back until someone wins!" Then he winked at Evermon.

So they began again.

Evermon and Baladar tried to implement their strategy, the one they devised in the previous game but didn't have the favorable circumstances to obtain their goal. It was Stephen and Evandra who won the day for Raelle's army.

Then they reluctantly saddled up and rode back to the Palace. They marched in a single file line. They pretended to travel in military formations, as in a parade, with Evermon calling out the formations, which were not always perfectly and immediately arranged, but they all got the hang of it eventually. Then they held up at the edge of the field across from the castle. The storm was far away from their memories.

"First one to the drawbridge is a winner!"

They were off. The race was between Evermon on his bay stallion (without the Knight, but with Baladar), and Lindara (with Silar), and Alindra. The others tried valiantly but their steeds were not the horseflesh of the three purebreds. But, shock of shocks, Alindra won.

"What is my prize?"

"A kiss from the birthday boy!"

Evermon looked at Jayden and Jayden wished he had been quiet, but the Prince was a good sport.

Alindra, flushing a bright red (for once), was unaccustomed to this type of a show of affection, especially from Evermon. She turned her cheek and accepted the proffered kiss. It was all she and her potion could do not to ravish him right there!

"Thank you, Step-mother, again, for the party. I'm glad I came."

Jayden piped up again—totally incorrigible—"He just wishes that Lindara had won the race!"

There was laughter as all, including Evermon and Alindra, joined in. Then Evermon rushed over to surprise Jayden, picked him up and counted to three and tossed him into the lake-like moat! Well, the Dwarf and Alindra didn't need their magic powders or Orbs of Sight to know they needed to sit this one out. All the young people ended up jumping into the lake surrounding the Palace, laughing and splashing for a few minutes. The grooms came out and took the horses back into the stables. The soggy party people dragged themselves out of the lake and shook violently to get the water off their own clothes and to get Gladenwreath and Alindra as wet as possible. Alindra ran across the outwork, passed the bridge, and approached the gate, screaming. Gladenwreath pulled his wand out and pointed it at each guest, in turn, and magically dried all their clothes. He then flipped his wand toward the gate and all heard Alindra yelp. She then reappeared, her clothes still dry, but her hair standing straight up. Baladar burst into a fit of giggles. The rest of the crowd sputtered, then suppressed. The Dwarf quickly fixed the problem and the Queen lost her maddened look.

Evermon began to wonder if he had misjudged Alindra. She had really seemed to loosen up today. (Little did he know!) She was nothing like what she normally was. (Really?) Not nasty, just reserved, detached—not a killjoy. (Well, a kill something.) He could almost like her. (What a thought!)

The party broke up and all went their separate ways, except of course, for Raelle, Alindra and Evermon, who returned to within the castle walls. Raelle would stay the night in the far wing of the

Palace, near Alindra's quarters. Her father would send a coach for her in the morning. Or just come over and magic her away. The Prince may be honest and upright, but it is always better to be safe than sorry.

Alindra led the way and Raelle and the Prince followed behind her. As they crossed the courtyard they slyly took each other's hand and held it softly and in great friendship.

"Game well played." whispered Evermon.

A squeeze and a smile came back at him from the Princess. Alindra pretended not to notice. Maybe there was something she could do here to get in the way? Maybe there was a rumor she could spread?

At last they entered the hallway, they passed Evermon's room and he begged the ladies 'goodnight'. They proceeded on to their chambers. The Prince walked across the hall. He opened the door to his father's room and sat down in the comfy chair by the head of the bed.

"I'm glad I went. It was good for me to see my friends again. Now I know that a Prince can have friends. I just wish you could have been there. You should have seen step-mother. She was not herself today. (Or was she?) You would have been pleased. I don't know what she is up to, but if it is genuine—I hope it lasts—at least until Mother gets back and you wake up."

"Caelith's missing too. What's happening, Father? Baladar almost died today. A freak storm came up out of nowhere. I'm sure glad he didn't die. I got to know him today and I like him." Then there was silence. "Goodnight, Father. I love you."

Evermon stood slowly and walked around the huge bed as he had done every night for over five years now. He crossed the hall to his room. The room he had slept in since he was a tiny child. The room right across from his mother and father. They had always been there in his night terrors, his bad dreams, his accidents in the bed; yes, even Princes are human.

Evermon's end of the castle was quiet and still. He disrobed for bed and reached for his nightshirt. He caught his naked torso in the mirror and like most adolescent boys, innocently flexed his arms to his 'otherself' there in the reflection. Just wondering if there had been any more bulking up of his biceps in the last few hours since he had flexed before. No conclusion being reached, he pulled his nightshirt over his head and climbed into his oversized bed. He snuggled down in the warm sheets and thick duvet and lapsed into sleepy dreamland.

He was awakened by the pattering of feet across his stone floor and the jouncing of the bed as a small terror landed at his feet and then crawled up the covers to lie flat next to him. Evermon looked over and stared into the eyes of Baladar. Baladar smiled.

"Thanks, Evermon!" was whispered.

Then the boy padded quickly away and out the door.

"You're welcome, Baladar," was shouted after the departing form of the boy and Evermon laughed a little as he settled back into the covers.

•• 7th day of 4th Month ••

> *Cold. Wind. Snow. Ice. (Ice? There was no ice in Aradon!)*
> *The hollow ring of laughter, as if echoing through a cave.*
> *Sunless days. Moonless nights. More cold.*
> *Flashes of light. Screaming.*
> *"Get her!'... Bind her!"*
> *Rose's face—frightened. Worried.*
> *Chains. A carriage—enclosed, drawn by four coal-black horses. Alindra pointing a stick at the sky. Light.*
> *Disturbing.*
> *"Where Am I?"*
> *A long, uncomfortable ride. Hands tied. Mouth gagged. Enwarded. Terrible thirst. It's getting colder!*
> *There's a snap, a crack. The horses are being whipped. The smile on Alindra's face. Terrible.*
> *Foreboding. Fear!*
> *Look out the window. Mountains—tall and icy where there had just been forest! This cannot be Aradon!*
> *Openness. Driving snow. Torches.*
> *A motion—as if traveling on water. Rocking, listing.*

A narrow canyon of rock. Dizziness. Sickness in the stomach. Walls of ice! All around.

More yelling. Rough handling. Being thrown down. Landing hard on the floor, face scraping the hard, cold surface of the floor—the ice!

Being jerked to your feet. Alindra's evil laugh and horrible grin, that stick again, as the vision blurs and you cannot see anymore except through and/or around some substance that bends the images that you see.

"So cold! So cold! I can't breathe! I'm dying!"

"Mother!"

Evermon screamed as he sat up in bed. He was sweating. Amid all the encumbrance of cold his nightshirt was stuck to his skin—all over. His bedclothes were scattered on to the floor. His body was racked by great, heaving sobs.

"Where are you, Mother?"

He got out of bed and crossed to the balcony and opened up the double doors and went out into the cool night.

A dream!

It had been—a nightmare. Was it real? Had Alindra indeed kidnapped his mother? He felt with every fiber of his being that this was more than just a dream. It was a premonition—no, a revelation. But... why? How? Where? What could he do?

Should he confront his step-mother? Who could he tell? He was alone.

Was he next? The storm!!! His birthday. Was he safe? Father, Mother, brothers, Caelith and soon him?

'Listen to your heart,' echoed in his mind from the memory of another dream.

He sat on the cold stone bench. He had to think clearly.

That's the last thing he remembered—sitting on the cold bench.

The next thing he knew he was on the cold stone floor of the balcony, asleep, well, just waking from a sleep. He didn't remember anything since sitting down. All he remembered was that on his fifteenth birthday—he had missed his mother so deeply—that in

his yearning a link to her had come alive in a dream.
    'Ice. Cold. Somewhere north!'
    Now, he must ask.

CHAPTER FIVE—
WHAT USE, WISDOM?

•• 8th day of 4th Month ••

As Raelle arrived at the Crystal Castle after leaving Aradon and Evermon's party, she stepped out of the coach and Tilly, her mother, enveloped her in a panicked embrace. Raelle endured it. She knew her mother was just worried about Caelith and was making certain that Raelle was all right, too—but still, why the fuss over her? She could take care of herself. Her father hugged her tightly but without the panic, and she was grateful for that.

After lunch, after the news of the party had been shared, the topic of conversation turned back to Caelith and her disappearance. Tilly became frantic again and both Raelle and Daniel tried to calm her. Daniel then divulged that Boncaster had visited him again last night.

"He's alive?"

"No, Caelith. It was a vision."

"You said, 'again'!"

"He has been appearing to me since shortly after his death. He is the Creator's messenger now. A Child of Promises."

"What did he say?"

There was no question of Daniel's statement by his daughter; no doubt in her mind; her father had visions. It was as simple as that. No one knew that better than Tilly. After all, the visions came at the most inconvenient times.

"He said that Caelith is on a quest. She will be protected. She will come home to us."

So, it really wasn't her own volition that drove her to leave home? She was following the promptings of the Creators? That was one explanation—the most convenient one.

The ladies heaved a sigh of deep relief. It could not stop their worrying but it would certainly assuage it.

"Does Miraden... ?"

"Yes... he knows."

"Where she is?"

"No—only that she is safe."

That was all that anyone could know at this point. Miraden's Orb Of Sight had been lost since the Arikkans attacked. Besides, it was no longer a necessary object to Miraden, as contact had been made with the Creators directly. So, it turned into a waiting game for the Royal Family as they prayed for another miracle in Mirador.

•• 8th day of 4th Month ••

Two dark robes, with someone or something inside of each of them, appeared at the portcullis gate to the city of Aradon. They requested entrance. The guard was feeling both somewhat above himself and a little suspicious.

"Upon what business?"

"We have prophecies for the Queen's ears and for the ears of the Prince."

"Soothsayers?" was snidely thrown at the two figures as they leaned upon their staves.

"Yes—with messages from Colabos for Aradon."

Colabos. That shut up the guards.

"You may pass."

As the two hooded figures entered the city and merged with the throngs they made their way towards the castle for an audience with the Queen and her son.

•• 8th day of 4th Month ••

The throne room was full. Another busy day in Aradon. Petitions, requests, complaints—maybe, if they were lucky, a prophecy or two! Alindra sat bored with it all. Baladar was resting on a cushion at her side. Evermon sat on the second throne and handled each matter presented to him with intelligence, passion and wisdom. He was currently considering a request from a farmer of the Yellow Plains to divert water for his fields from the River of Hope. The problem was that it would cross three neighboring farms between the river and the property of the petitioner. No one else wanted to pay for the canal, as was the law. Yet, the three intervening farmers would love to use the water; if they could get it for free. Evermon did not trust the looks of the other farmers. Something was wrong. Something was not as it used to be. Was it the Kingdom—its people—or something else? Or was it a lack of something?

Evermon turned to Nathan Jameson. "Can the Circle build and ward such a canal?"

"I think so. We can skirt the three intervening farms completely. I'm sure of it."

There were scowls from the three farmers.

"Done! Farmer Severn, does that meet with your approval?"

"Indeed it do, Your Highness."

"Nathan—have the Circle Council arrange it."

Evermon banged his silver sceptre on the pad at the end of the throne's armrest. He looked to the door. The Chamberlain's staff hit the floor twice and the room quieted.

"Two soothsayers with a message from Colabos, Your Majesty."

"Let them approach."

Alindra leaned over to Baladar; "More prophecies. More, weary words. It's all too boring." She slouched back in her throne as Baladar giggled and covered his mouth and leaned forward. Evermon smiled at him and winked.

Baladar removed his mouth-covering hand and smiled back.

"Welcome, noble Seers. Who is the subject of your prophecy today?"

"You, for one, Noble Sire."

Evermon was taken aback as he leaned against his throne carefully observing the two hooded figures.

"Reveal yourselves to us before you reveal your prophecies."

"We cannot, oh, Prince. Our Order forbids us to be seen. We can only be heard to be believed."

Evermon smiled. *'Secret or sacred?'* he thought. "Who is the subject of the other prophecy?"

"Your father, Sire."

Evermon and Alindra both leaned forward; he anxiously, she cautiously.

"Speak of my father."

The Seers faced Evermon, spread their arms and alternately pronounced the prophecy.

"As the King lies ill he can be cured;"
"The Waters Of Life must be secured."
"To sip one drop restores mind and health;"
"To partake of more brings questioned wealth."

That caught Alindra's wandering attention, as the Seers knew it would. "What wealth?"

"We say the sooth, we do not interpret, My Lady. Ask Daniel or Miraden for they are the interpreters of dreams."

Alindra pouted. Evermon came alive.

"Where can we find the Waters Of Life?"

"It is your task, my Prince, to find and bring. But know this: the King can be cured."

"Mother, do you hear?"

"Yes," was her measured rejoinder.

"It is good news."

"Yes." But she considered it carefully.

Baladar regarded his mother, then his 'brother'. She didn't seem as happy about this whole matter as Evermon did. But, yet, she smiled at him and Evermon. But there was something—different—behind the smile.

Alindra spoke out. "Gladenwreath—what do you know of the Waters of Life?"

"Nought but that they are an ancient myth and they are believed to have restorative and curative powers as well as the ability to extend life."

There was a gasp in the room. Not the least of which was issued by Alindra. *'Permanent, eternal youth? No aging?'* she thought. *'It could be mine! It beats a nasty potion and a hundred brush strokes into the mirror every night!'*

"And what is the prediction that concerns the Prince?"

"We would speak with the Prince in private. It is for his ears only."

"What can be said to him can be said to us."

"Are you counseling the Creator's in their wisdom?"

There was a murmur (and a shock of glee) at the audacity of these Seers to question the Queen. As Alindra merely smiled, a half-smile, it lacked heart and conviction, yet still appeared to be a smile.

"Very well—clear the court!"

The many people made their way through the giant entrance doors to wait in the hall. Alindra, Baladar, Gladenwreath and Nathan exited the door behind the throne but not before Alindra had left one of her earrings on the seat of her throne. The soothsayers stood silent, unperturbed, as the room emptied. Evermon watched for the sign of 'all clear.' He was at last alone with the two Seers.

"Speak. I alone can her you."

"My--Prince, you will triumph."

"You alone will rule over all."

"Mother, Father, brothers..."

"Kingdom--"

"Step-mother and step-brother:"

"All will bow to you."

"All will learn to serve you."

"It is your destiny."

Evermon was astonished. It went against the entire order of things. Everything he had been taught.

"What of my own brothers? They are older. Their birthright comes before mine."

There was a silence.

"You are not destined to rule in Aradon."

Evermon sat down quickly. "Are they alive?"

"Yes."

Evermon sighed. "And my Mother?"

"That we do not know."

"But it is said that even she will bow to you"

"Yes. I think I understand." He thought about Caelith. He liked the thought. She must be alive, also.

The long-sleeved arms of the Seers raised in a salute to the Prince of Aradon. He returned the salute out of habit and sat again on his throne. The Seers departed. They knocked, the door was opened and they left. The court slowly reassembled. The rear door was opened for Alindra and the others. They took their places and still the Prince sat silent. Not just at the news—but at the salute he had shared with the two Seers. There were only a few people who knew that salute!

Alindra picked up her earring and put it back on her ear. Her face went slack as she heard the voices of the Seers and the Prince repeated for her. Her eyes widened. Her forehead creased.

"What is it, Mother?" asked Baladar.

"Shhh!" and she waved him off.

Baladar looked over at Evermon who stood and walked out the rear door without a word. Alindra's face changed. She then came back to herself and to the room.

"All petitions will be continued tomorrow. The Prince needs his rest."

The low babble of the interested and questioning voices became the undercurrent of the room as it emptied. The doors were shut leaving the Chamberlain, a few guards, Alindra, Baladar, Gladenwreath and Nathan staring at each other.

"You are all dismissed!"

They quickly and silently left the Queen absolutely alone in her thoughts—except for Baladar who lingered, concerned, and he was motioned back to her side. There was a moment of consideration as Alindra tried to take in what she was hearing. Baladar stood patiently.

"You may not rule after all, son."

"It is all right, Mother. I don't really want to. Evermon was born to it."

"I was born to it!" she corrected him.

Baladar cowered a bit at her angry outburst. This was a side of her that didn't surface very often—but when it did...! She then extended her hand and lifted him to the other throne, as if to say 'see what you are missing?' He sat there and stated at her.

"You may think that you were not born to it. But you will grow accustomed to it after Evermon... is out of the way."

Baladar objected but she silenced him. He sat there, worried. Would his 'brother' be safe from his own mother?

•• 8th day of 4th Month ••

Pemberton had been rather sparse in its accommodations but the room had been clean and the food palatable. Now a brisk morning's walk would bring her to the City of Aradon. In the distance, Holder could see the bright blue and gold banners on the city walls, flapping in the stiff breeze that sometimes brought the smell of the salt air with it towards the city and the Yellow Plains as it wafted landward from the sea. She felt a little nervous. This was a city of thousands. One of the largest in all the Realms. Could she maintain her facade as a young Harper here? Or would she be unmasked as the runaway Princes of Mirador?

Maybe she wouldn't stay long enough to find out.

As she entered the city from the Well-Traveled Road she received no challenges from the guards at the gates. She passed quite anonymously into the colorful and churning humanity that was typical of the cities of the Realms. She would be just passing through. Ahead, there was a commotion as she entered the southern square and beheld the Purple Palace surrounded by its glistening, lake-like moat. Distracted by the beauty in front of her, she paused. The rectangular battlements surrounded the bailey and the Keep. Four huge towers, one at each corner, marked the battlements. Two lesser towers flanked the gate house and then there was a small drawbridge from the island of the castle to another island. A four towered Barbican, on its own island linked to another shorter bridge, then to the outwork of earth that led to the plaza of the square of the city. It was a massive jewel of beautiful construction, with a slight tinge of lavender in all of the masonry. Something the Blue Dragons of Aradon, Kallowmere and Ekladar, could be very proud of.

As it was nearly noon the sun was almost directly behind the lake and its castle, and it all just sparkled. Caelith was captivated, as she always had been with this particular palace, but Holder had to keep moving. As she was still focused on the castle the commotion broke in and brought her attention back to the present time and place.

A long stream of people had been flooding out of the Barbican gates, chattering, arguing, shouting. At their center were two dark-robed figures who seemed to be trying to rush away from the crowd. The guards on the square formed a line between the two. The crowd and the dark robes fled the environs of the square as Holder continued his crossing to exit out the north gates of the city. She headed north on the Zanadon Road instead of taking the road that crossed the River of Hope and led to the port city of Aramar. Right now Caelith wanted distance—breathing room—and she hoped Holder, her Harper self, could get it for her.

•• 8th day of 4th Month ••

Knock! Knock! Knock!

Silence.

Knock! Knock!

"Evermon, are you there?" Baladar asked.

All afternoon the Prince had been silent, pondering, staring off into the air beyond his balcony window.

Knock! Knock!

He heard it this time. "Come in."

Baladar rushed in but came to a quick halt as he saw his step-brother's dejected and troubled face.

"What did they say to you, Evermon?"

Evermon looked up and considered his reply; should he even make a reply? "That I will rule over all."

"I could have told you that."

Evermon harumphed.

"That's not bad—is it?"

"No, but..."

"But what?"

"How would you feel about ruling over me?"

"Strange. I don't think I would like it."

"I don't like it, either."

"Does it have to happen?"

"I don't see how it can't. It's been prophesied."

Evermon was now standing at the railing of his balcony. Baladar joined him there. He stood by him. He looked up into the eyes of the brother he looked up to. Where yesterday he had seen joy—today he saw something darker. The face of the person who had saved Baladar's life made the boy tense. Baladar reached out and took Evermon's hand in his. He just held it. Evermon looked at him and smiled. There was almost something behind that smile. Baladar smiled back.

The boy always felt better being around the Prince than he had felt in anyone else's presence, including his mother's. He thought that was strange, too, but it was the truth.

The sun was directly in front of them as they stared at it in the act of setting. The entire sky was golden, then red, then bright orange and the edge of the orb sank out of sight behind the horizon while blue—whole, quiet, full—descended and took over.

The tower bell chimed. Evermon sank to his knees as Baladar watched in silence. Evermon's lips were moving but the boy could not hear anything. The bell rang again and Evermon concluded his prayer and stood.

"Do you do that every night?"

"Every night."

"Will you teach me?"

"Starting tomorrow night."

Baladar smiled broadly.

"I've got to go to bed, Baladar!"

"Oh, no!

"What?"

"I forgot. Mother is going to be so mad at me."

"Why?"

"She sent me to fetch you before bedtime."

"What does she want now?"

"She didn't say. But she has to see you."

"All right."

Evermon headed to the door. Baladar ran and jumped in the large, overstuffed chair and nestled into it.

"I'll wait here for you."

Evermon laughed as he left the room. He walked down the corridor to Alindra's chambers (at the other end of the castle—in the southwest tower.)

Alindra liked sunrise. Evermon liked sunset—and to be near to his father's room. He paused by his father's door. Then he decided he would say goodnight after he found out what Alindra wanted. Alindra certainly lived in a secluded part of the castle. Her door was suddenly in front of the brooding Prince. He knocked.

"Come in," was spoken from behind the door.

He entered. Alindra was not to be seen.

"Step-Mother?"

"Yes, Evermon."

His eyes found her in her big bed. As she rose out of the bed she crossed to him. Through her filmy nightdress he saw more of his step-mother than he had ever wanted to—or even imagined was there. She seemed totally unconcerned about it and met him halfway across the room, nightclothes still open. Evermon tried not to stare. She was beautiful, after all, and young enough to be still shapely. She looked no more than twenty-five. She smiled at Evermon's stare. There was a slight motion of her hands.

"Never seen a woman before?"

He shook his head as his body rattled like a leaf in the wind—all over trembling. He stared, his feet frozen to the floor.

He tried to move them. His feet would not do as he ordered them to. She ran her fingers along his smooth jawline. He started to panic inside. He felt confused—agitated. She walked around him. He did not turn to look—he could not. Her fingers continued to play across his shoulders and the back of his neck. When she came around his other side she was naked. The nightdress was gone. Evermon swallowed so hard that it hurt his throat.

He panicked but he could not move. Then he noticed the nightdress in her hand. She stood in front of him and ripped it in half and dropped it to the floor. She grasped his hand, moving it and using his fingernails to scrape trace-marks across her stomach and down her arms. She winced as the pressure drew a little blood. She walked back to her bed and grabbed a comforter. She undid her hair and let it fall to her shoulders. She whisked her hands through it causing it to become tangled. Comforter in hand she walked back to Evermon. He was terrified! He was rooted to the floor as if by magic!

She slapped his face. She enjoyed it too much, that was evident. His head jolted back, her finger marks across his young cheek. She dropped the comforter to the floor. She knocked over several chairs and tables and began to scream. Then she 'popped' Evermon's clothes off his body, strew them around the room and across the floor, creating a trail, leaving him naked and still rooted to the floor, barely able to cover himself with his hands; which she reluctantly allowed. She broke a pitcher, over-turned another table and screamed again, never taking her eyes from the body of the young Prince. Footsteps were heard in the hall. Pounding on the door. More screaming from Alindra and just as people burst into the room she released her magic hold on Evermon's feet and he staggered back, as she knew he would. He stood there, naked, embarrassed, ashamed—frightened.

"Get him out of here—take him away!"

Alindra ran for the comforter and wrapped up in it, expertly timed to reveal the scratches on her body. Evermon was led, naked, passed the imcoming Baladar whose face was shocked.

Evermon whispered fiercely: "I didn't do anything! You know me!"

"Get him out!" She screamed.

The guards pushed and shoved the Prince. Baladar turned his back on his mother, in a quiet rage, and left the room.

Evermon was tossed in his own room. The door was locked and two guards stood outside the door. He ran to his armoire and put on some breeches. He sat. He stood. He paced. He sobbed. Why would Alindra do this to him? He ran to the balcony. There were guards on the lawn below. That was quick! Like he was a prisoner.

What was happening?!

Baladar ran down the hall. He ran to Evermon's room and the guards restrained him. He tried again and they knocked him to the floor.

"No one allowed in!"

"Or out!"

Baladar picked himself up, glaring at the accomplices of his mother and walked down the hall and around the corner. He stopped just out of sight. He had formulated a plan. He had to do it. He had wanted to do it for a long time but there hadn't been an opportunity. He concentrated. He focused. He saw Evermon's room. He knew it well. He commanded his body and disappeared from his place in the hall. He almost calculated correctly!

Evermon turned. There was a peculiar noise in his armoire. He approached it and threw open the doors to find his clothes tangled and moving around by themselves. He leaped back. Gradually the clothes fell away and revealed Baladar—smiling.

"How?... What... ?"

Baladar hopped out of the armoire and hugged his brother tightly. Evermon returned the hug.

"You know I didn't do..."

"I know. But mother would do anything! I'm sorry I didn't forget about her summons."

"How could you know?"

Baladar shrugged.

"How did you get in my armoire?"

"I...now don't get mad..."

"I won't."

"I 'popped' there."

A blank look from Evermon.

"I'm an... Enchanter—I can—do—things."

Just at that moment Alindra entered with three more guards. She grabbed Baladar and dashed out of the room. The guards glared at Evermon, almost in mock disgust. They pointed to the bed and he climbed into it. They placed themselves at each side and at its foot and stared as Evermon tried not to go to sleep—and he failed.

•• 9th day of 4th Month ••

The throne room was packed again. The sun was streaming through the windows leaving colored patterns on the walls. Alindra was seated on her throne trying to hide the glee she felt inside. She had finally been able to do it! She was rid of them all.

Baladar reluctantly occupied the other chair. He wasn't standing; as it was impossible because Alindra had frozen him to his seat. The murmuring of those present rustled around the hall; tense, a foreboding urgency filled the air like a heavy dew. Rumors had spread!

Alindra nodded to the guards at the door. They opened it and four other guards marched in with Evermon at their center. Barefoot, shirtless, disheveled, with only his breeches to attempt to hide his shame and anger; his hands being bound behind him. He was led to the 'dais' where his 'mother' sat. He was pushed to his knees at the foot of the steps. The Chamberlain then walked forward, his face a mask of confusion, to confront his former Prince.

He could not believe what he had heard. The appearance of the unkempt youth almost convinced him of the youth's guilt. He certainly didn't want to believe the charges, but after the guards and the Queen gave their witness there was nothing else to believe.

"Evermon—Prince of Aradon—you have been accused and now, stand guilty of the assault and rape of the Queen. I wish it were not so."

"I'm innocent," Evermon whispered.

"But the evidence is against you—overwhelmingly. You are hereby stripped of your Royal holdings. You are no longer Commander of the Armies."

"I'm innocent," was louder this time.

"You are no longer... Prince of Aradon." That was the hardest one for, the Chamberlain. This was the boy, the youngest—the one he had helped to raise! He felt the pain knotting up inside of him.

"I'm innocent!" was shouted.

"You will be exiled to the River of Sadness in Zanadon where you wilt live out the rest of your days. If you return to Aradon it can mean your death."

"Mother!" cried Baladar. "No, Mother. This is wrong!"

"Be still!"

"I hate you mother. I hate you!!!" was said through clenched teeth.

Alindra blinked and moved her hand. Baladar could no longer talk. All he could do was sit mute and motionless as his brother was defamed.

If there was any heart in Alindra, though, it had finally broken as her son told her just how much he hated her, since she knew that he was not playing any part, like the Queen and the guards. His performance wasn't scripted. He had meant what he said. She steeled herself against the loss of her son's love. She had been alone before he was born and she would be alone again. She would survive. She pounded the silver sceptre on the pad at the end of the armrest of the throne.

The guards yanked the former Prince to his feet and marched him out. The people were shocked, torn, angry—betrayed—they felt a condemnation toward whom? The Prince? The Queen? They wanted to believe the Prince but even so their eyes were cast down, their faces long and full of pain as Evermon was led by them.

As the youth exited the room Alindra motioned for the room to be cleared and the people filed out. All left her alone with her son.

She leaned in to Baladar, after the room was entirely empty, except for them. She stared at him for a long while, and even though they were alone, she whispered, "I did this for you. You will rule after all! Starting tomorrow!"

She 'popped' out of the room, leaving her son a prisoner of the throne; unable to speak, unable to move.

•• 9th day of 4th Month ••

The guards tormented Evermon. It was almost a jovial atmosphere as they beat him black and blue with the shafts of their spears. They mocked him. They made fun of him as they tore his breeches from him. They lightly pierced the skin all over his body with the points of sword and spear, leaving tiny spots of blood in a hundred places. Then they threw him in a cell in the dungeon—naked and cold and bloody. They locked the door and their laughter continued to ring back to him as they ascended the stairs to freedom. Who were these men? They were not his soldiers!

They must be loyal to Alindra! Why hadn't he seen it?

One the cold stone, without clothes, without a bed or blanket, without even some straw to sleep on, the young Prince shivered and his skin began to sting from the cold of the stones—and he cried. Not for himself, but for dozens, even hundreds of others. Baladar! He would face his mother alone, now. The boy would end up just like he had. What of Aradon—under Alindra? The Kingdom was doomed!

He heard a noise and sat up. Nothing. He laid back down.

There it was again. He looked around.

"Follow..."

      "... Your..."

           "... Heart."

That was it! *"I will speak to your heart!"*

"Boncaster?"

"Follow... your... heart."

The cell was silent again. Even Evermon's sobs had stopped. Ne sat up princely—but frightened for, after all, he was a boy—yet he had the responsibilities of a man. The morning would bring something—be wasn't sure what.

  •• 10th day of 4th Month ••

The morning brought cold—numbness—fear. Baladar had spent the entire night on the throne of Aradon. As his eyes opened he found that he hadn't moved. He ached terribly. Alindra 'popped' in. She waved her arm. Her son was then able to stand, defiantly, but then collapsed to the floor due to his rubbery legs. She had released him. He massaged his legs and his bottom and soon the blood started flowing through them again. He tried to speak to her. He couldn't. He stood up again. She handed him a long, narrow cloth. He looked at her quizzically.

"For Evermon."

They 'popped' to the cell. Alindra stared and smiled as Baladar carefully wrapped Evermon, avoiding contact as much as possible with his bruises and cuts. The boy's tears flowed and he cried a little at the damage done to his brother. He would never forgive his mother. Evermon ran his hand through Baladar's hair in thanks, and to comfort the boy. Baladar stood, finished, but he remained standing, closer to his brother than to his mother. Alindra walked over and took Baladar's hand and dragged him away, crying and digging his feet in against the stones of the floor. His mouth opened in wordless phrases.

"I love you, too, Baladar!" mumbled Evermon.

The boy had never heard those words before. They were like a balm. He stopped struggling and stood proudly in front of his brother as his mother tried to control him, but no longer needed to. His allegiance was sealed to his brother. Alindra stopped, stared, seethed in hatred at the words of the former Prince. With nothing else she could think to do she and Baladar 'popped.'

The guards came and took Evermon up the stairs and out to the yard. They placed him, seated, in a small boat, a coracle, really. He sat still, bound and wearing only the loinwrap. The yard emptied. Then Alindra appeared.

"It's a shame that we never did what you were convicted of. I know I wanted to—many times!"

The Prince recoiled, repulsed at the degeneracy that emanated from the Queen. He went white on the outside—while he burned with anger inside. It was one thing for him to have a crush on a beautiful woman, and quite another thing for a beautiful woman to desire a youth. *I was right, she shouldn't have been trusted, Father!'* was screamed internally.

Alindra dribbled a black, oily potion over Evermon's body. She then moved her hands as if casting a spell. "You will never be able to set foot in Aradon again unless you bring the Waters of Life with you and only give them to me. Once you do that your exile will be over. Then, I will live forever and rule your Kingdom while you live. I will rule forever and when you die, my immortal son will take my place."

"Who are you really, Alindra?"

"It is not important, now. You have lost. I have won."

"The prophecy said that..."

She slapped him. "Your prophecy is now only to serve."

She clapped her hands and Evermon in his coracle vanished from the yard.

ᒪ

CHAPTER SIX—
ANSWERS? OR MORE QUESTIONS?

•• 10th day of 4th Month ••

Evermon sat, still bound, in the bobbing coracle. He had been floating for—well, it seemed like a long time but it had only been hours. The River of Sadness was low. The coracle almost scraped the riverbed with its hull. As it was made of animal skins stretched over wicker, that could be dangerous. As Evermon sat there he wondered why he had been so stupid. Hindsight, in every instance, sees far better than the most lucid vision of the moment.

He was tired of immobility. He began to struggle with his bonds. He was young, strong—they were only rope! He twisted and stressed the bands. As his hands were behind him, he scrunched himself up tightly in a ball, on his side, then rolled to his back and tried to pull his hands around the ends of his feet. The cords slipped over his heels and stopped mid-sole. He tugged. He strained and the ropes on his wrists sprang passed his toes and sent him sprawling. The coracle tipped and deposited him into the rocky, shallow bed of the river, then completed its own somersault by landing on top of him. He pushed the coracle off and kicked it over to the nearby shore as he stood in the ankle deep water at a bend in the river.

As he faced downstream the Black Mountains were to his right—north, be figured. The Broken Borderlands were to the south and every bit as dark and depressing as the stories made them out to be. No wonder no one in Aradon wanted to farm near them! He kept nibbling at the cords that bound him, trying to loosen them with his teeth. It was frustrating. Not only were the ropes tight but now they were wet and if they dried again before he could get them off he might even lose the use of his hands. He stood, muscles clenched and teeth engaged. He spit out bits of nasty tasting rope as he felt something slither across his ankles. He jumped with a yelp. He looked down. Just an eel. He figured he could work on the rope as safely on the riverbank as he could in the middle of the river. So, be slogged through the shallow water, barefoot across the rocks, to the security of the nearest shore—the edge of the Borderlands.

He sat down next to the overturned coracle and attacked the ropes again. He leaned against the tree and bit more fibers out of the bindings. The rough bark on the tree irritated his back and he sat up. He turned around to his knees and stared at the bark, thinking. He spread his hands apart, as far as be was able, and started rubbing the ropes against the roughness of the tree's bark, occasionally taking off a layer or two of skin with the imprecise practice. The bark began to separate the damp, drawn fibers of the rope and soon, between teeth and bark, he was free!

He then knelt at the riverbank and soaked his sore wrists in the cool water; watching for eels and other denizens he had heard of in the stories about the River of Sadness.

It was now an empty place, and had been for twenty years -- since even before his Uncle Daniel's victory against Tophet. *'Maybe that's why its so sad"* be thought. He looked around him, from that south bank, barren and lifeless, across the river to the north; into Zanadon, where there were forests and mountains. He picked up the coracle and held it over his head as he waded into the river again. It was an easy crossing but a long one as the river was particularly wide along this stretch. He tossed his coracle up onto the opposite shore as he climbed up the small embankment.

Pine trees. A nice smell. It doesn't smell like the Zanadon he had read of and heard about. He looked around. He gathered piles of twigs, sticks, branches and needles. He found a sharp rock and gave a point to a straight stick. He found a piece of thick bark and hollowed out a drill hole and a shallow trough. He piled on some dried needles, bark and twigs around the trough. He took the straight stick and spun it between his palms. Something the Master

Huntsman of Aradon had taught him. Being a Prince had its advantages—and its disadvantages, if you considered his present situation. The tinder was all very dry and the smoke came rapidly and he blew the embers to flame and piled larger material around the growing flames. Soon, a nice fire was warming his cold, goose-pimply body, for the sun had not quite reached this part of the forest. He stoked the fire and stood drying his loin-wrap, front and back. He heard a chittering in the woods. He reached for some rocks and held a half-a-dozen in his hands, peering into the blackness of the forest. He saw movement and hurled a rock in its direction. He heard a voice—an animal squealing. He ran towards it and found it twitching. He used a larger rock to still the life from it, took it back to his fire and used the sharp rock to skin and gut it. He built a spit over the fire and skewered and roasted the squirrel. His mouth watered as the animal's juices dripped into the fire. He hadn't eaten for a long time. Almost two days. (Six hours is a long time for most teenagers to go without food.)

After he finished his meal, he drank carefully from the river. He made a bed of pine boughs, stoked up the fire and in the sudden darkness of the edges of the Black Mountains, pulled his coracle over him as he settled into the boughs next to the fire.

•• 11ᵗʰ day of 4ᵗʰ Month ••

Baladar was pacing his room like a caged—well... mouse. Because at age almost-ten what kind of power do you have? He may have been as mad as a lion—he knew he felt that angry—but it was all an impotent exercise. What could he do; other than release his energy into the empty room? Which made him feel better but didn't hurt those who had caused the anger. He wanted to hurt someone!

He did know what he could not do: he could not 'pop.' Where could he go? Besides, he could not let his mother know just exactly what kind of magic he possessed. In order to 'pop' somewhere, you had to have been to that somewhere. He hadn't been anywhere that his mother hadn't been and she would find him soon if he did 'pop.' He couldn't transform yet, but he did have a funny image of himself as a chair trying to walk down the hallway without being seen. So, what could he do?

He could summon things!

He sat at the table gnawing on a roasted chicken leg with a pile of creamy potatoes and steaming vegetables on his plate with a flagon of lemonade awaiting his lips. Why lemonade? He liked it!

There was a jangle of keys and a knock at the door. Baladar quickly 'popped' all the evidence of the food away, but not too far. He had managed to get it out of the room and to the bottom of the wall under his balcony just before Alindra entered.

"Are you ready?"

He opened his mouth to speak and the only thing that came out was a deep belch. Alindra looked at him suspiciously. He blushed.

"I'm sorry, mother."

"It smells like chicken in here. Do you usually have chicken for breakfast?"

"I was hungry and cook brought it up."

Ooooh! He lied! Since it was to Alindra, it was all right. He was not liking her very much at this moment in time.

"I asked you if you were ready?"

"Yes, Mother, I'm ready," he begrudged to her.

She motioned him out the door where a guard joined them and they made their way in a tight little uncomfortable knot to the throne room. Upon entrance, Gladenwreath, Nathan and the Chamberlain greeted them. A large table covered in sheets of parchment was set before the throne. A quill was waiting in its holder and a pot of ink was set next to the quill. Alindra motioned for Baladar to sit on the throne. She sat next to him on 'her' throne. Gladenwreath and Nathan, at Baladar's side, and the Chamberlain at the side of the table nearest the parchments, watched the interaction, or lack of it, between mother and son with great interest.

The Chamberlain would hand Baladar a parchment and the boy would earnestly read the entire document. If he approved of it he signed it and passed it to the Chamberlain who poured wax on it. Baladar pressed his seal into the wax and the Chamberlain powdered it all off to help the wax and the ink dry. However, if he had a question he asked it—and it was answered by someone in the room—usually Alindra. If be didn't like the answer, which was the usual thing if Alindra answered, or if he didn't like the document in general, he set it aside on an ever growing pile of 'questionable' decrees. Alindra's mouth tightened—perceptibly—with each placement of parchment on that pile. After the twentieth document Alindra had lost her patience.

"Why do you have to read each page? Just sign them!"

"Mother, you told me never to sign anything I haven't read."

Nathan and Gladenwreath suppressed their laughter; the Chamberlain only smiled—slightly.

"At this rate you'll take all day!"

"A job worth doing is worth doing well."

Another maternal platitude thrown back in her face. It had the desired effect. She stood, rebuffed and left the room. After the door closed the laughter came loud and long. As they quieted down, through the shushes and splutterings of the Chamberlain, he spoke: "I saved these for last. I feel that there are some major details that the Queen—missed—as she had the documents prepared. Maybe you could edit them?"

Baladar smiled. He read each word, seeking out the evidences of his mother's pride and selfishness. He scratched out words, phrases, sentences, whole paragraphs and in a very neat and professional hand he rewrote his mother's carefully deceptive laws. After an hour Alindra came back in to the room and the Chamberlain whisked the stack of parchments away. Two servants removed the table and another brought Baladar some lemonade.

The Chamberlain smote his staff on the floor and court was in session again. Baladar put his not yet empty cup underneath his throne, and seated himself on the chair of power.

With every decision handed down his mother grew more weary. Baladar had been watching Evermon for many years now and his style, not hers, had fortunately rubbed off on the boy. A good model to have unless you think like Alindra. He naturally gravitated to be a problem-solver rather than an instigator and irritant—like his mother. Nature over nurture? Love over cruel indoctrination? Baladar over Alindra!

At one particular decision, though, she stood and glared at him. He smiled and silently indicated the room full of people. She looked around, smiled weakly and sat down again.

Bested by a nine year-old! She seethed, then realized she had taught him. She, too, could play those subtle games. She motioned the Chamberlain to call a recess. Once again the room emptied leaving only her and her defiant son.

"What do you think you're doing?"

"What you told me to do—I'm ruling!"

"You're not doing it right!"

"I am doing it right!"

"Well, stop!"

"Make up your mind, Mother. Either I rule or I don't. Either I'm right or I'm not. And it looks better for you if I rule. You always mess it up! But I don't care either way. It's Evermon who should be making these decisions—or his mother or father!"

"You will do it my way or you will not rule!"

"If I rule—I will do as I see fit!"

"You will obey!"

"I will tell the truth about Evermon to all!" (It was worth a try!)

She waved her hands and Baladar couldn't speak. He stood and ran but she hit him with a spell that immobilized him. She walked towards him shaking with fury. Everything she had done she had done for him! (Lie!) He was an ungrateful wretch! (Lie!) Just like his father! (Well, truth.) This was it; he would not defy her again! She flipped her hands in the air and he was in his loin-wrap and surrounded by a purple warding.

"To the Mountain Hold!" and she clapped her hands again.

The boy disappeared.

•• 11th day of 4th Month ••

Alindra 'popped' herself immediately to her cabin on the shores of Purple Lake. She procured several vials of Baladar's explosive concoction. She returned to the Purple Palace of Aradon; to the Room of the Talisman. The Dwarven Guard were no longer maintaining their vigil as the Talisman had disappeared—again.

They marched in daily and marched right back out again with nothing to protect.

She began smearing the glop from the vials over the pedestal, the window sills and jambs, the doors.

She 'popped' out and returned with several article of Baladar's clothing which she draped over the window sill. She picked up a couple of the empty vials of potion and coated them and 'winded,' them dry. She then threw them at the pre-glopped targets. The room exploded as she 'popped' to the safety of her chambers where she was able to remove all traces of the glop from her person and her clothes.

•• 11th day of 4th Month ••

Soon there was a knock at her door. Her tearful maidservant motioned her to follow. She was led back to the Room of the Talisman. The room was a shambles; windows and doors blown right out of their casings in the walls; the pedestal was only a pile of dust. She was 'shocked' at what she saw. Then her maidservant held up a swatch of what looked like Baladar's breeches. She clutched them to her chest and 'ran' from the room. As she neared her private chambers, the halls were empty and she 'popped' the rest of the way to her room. Once inside, with a silencing charm engaged, she laughed, a long, loud, evil, exultant cackle.

•• 11th day of 4th Month ••

Evermon strapped the coracle to his back and began hiking upstream to the trail that would lead him to the top of Broken Spirit Pass. The sun was just up. The forest was cool. The dew fresh. He would travel up and over the Black Mountains, through the Forest of Fear, the swamps, the mire. He expected Darkness and desolation, but the Pass was exhilarating. The air was fresh— clear. Not as his grandfather had described it to him in the stories he told about the War of The Realms. Zanadon was still changing—thanks to Daniel—changing everywhere but in the Broken Borderlands.

The trek over the Pass took most of the morning and as it neared noon he came to a precipice; a place where the trail started to descend. He recognized it from his grandfather's stories. It was unmistakable. So, the remainder of his stories must be accurate. He wondered, *'Why the change?'* Daniel and Miraden were the answers. This spot is where the forces of the Realms defeated the Ballarks and the Demons of Dark Tophet.

It wasn't dark now and he could see the ruins of the Fortress of Fear in the distance. As he descended into the forest he found some bushes with red berries on them. He tasted one. Wild Raspberries! He picked and ate as many as he could until his lips, chin and chest were stained with the juice of the luscious fruit. He wished he could take some with him but he had nothing in which to put them. Except his loinwrap—and he didn't quite feel like giving that up, again.

The forest was cool and shaded—not dark and cold. Then he heard a snapping of branches and a low rumble. He shimmied up the bole of a tree until he and his coracle were safely hidden in its branches. A bear lumbered by beneath him heading in the direction he had just come from. It sneezed. It limped along on three feathered and taloned legs. Where its cute little black nose should be was a beak. There was something on its back—it looked like a wing, or part of a wing—but there was only one. A good look revealed the foreleg, shoulder and the wing on its left side were ripped away. Was this one of Tophet's monsters? At least what was left of one? How had it survived for over twenty years?

Evermon felt sorry for it as he watched it struggle up the trail. It paused. It riffled through the raspberry bushes. It found some and chewed contentedly. Then it caught an unfamiliar scent. It pulled back—out of the bushes. It sniffed the air (through a beak?—yes!) but that's what it appeared to be doing. It rose up on its hind legs trying to catch and place the unfamiliar scent. It hobbled to the tree where Evermon crouched, safely above its reach. It rose up and pawed at the bark with its one good leg, sniffing. It let out a strange and pitiful moan. Evermon held tight to the bole of the tree as it shook a little. The tree shook a little more and the Prince's feet slipped off the branch to leave him straddling it and trying to catch his breath from the pain; daring not to let go of the bole of the tree.

Not a sound escaped his lips. The Prince maintained as the creature found nothing more and strode off and away—up the trail. As it disappeared Evermon groaned and sat there, limply. He waited until be felt he had legs again and climbed down the tree and winced off in the direction of the Fortress.

He came to another river—*must be the River of Fear*, he thought. Its waters ran clear—not black as in the legend. He set his coracle on the river and paddled across the slow stream with his hands. He made it across with all fingers and hands still attached to his body. Well, where there was one creature there may have been more! As he stepped out and strapped the coracle to his back again, he had expected swamp and found none. The swamp was no longer swampy. Tophet's magic must have been powerful in its day, but no trace remained. He walked over the solid 'swamp.' No sinking—no squish. Where were the Mists of Mire? He could see the castle ruins clearly. The barriers Tophet had so effectively created had dried up!

He trotted up the trail to the former Fortress of Fear where he picked through the ruins for hours. He found a bent tankard, lots of rotted cloth, broken furniture, the bones of various creatures, including humans. He discovered a door standing in a cube-shaped wall—undamaged—the only structure still above ground amid the rubble of the fortress. He pushed on it. It opened and somehow remained on its hinges. He entered. It was little more than a closet; completely enclosed. He found a dagger in its green sheath. He tucked it into his loinwrap. He found a leather belt big enough to go around him twice. He strapped it over his shoulder as a bandolier and then re-clipped the dagger to it.

There were faded parchments—maps, most likely—but the writing and images were so faded that he couldn't make them out and left them. He found, under the rotting shelf, another blade—short, but longer than the dagger, double-edged, rusty but not eaten away. He slid it through the bandolier also. Nothing more. Just decay. He closed the door.

He made his way back to the river, launched his coracle and it took him down the River of Fear. He passed through the river-cut gorge in the Black Mountains and found himself at the confluence with the River of Sadness. He paddled to the right and it took him West. He thought back on the many stories of power and glory. Then he recalled the emptiness of the ruins he had just visited. What was all the strife, the hatred, the struggle for? Why is power the object of so many? Why—when it all ends as if it never was to begin with? Why does it happen time after time after time? All good questions for a future ruler to be asking—even if he didn't have any answers.

He was on familiar river now. He drifted with the current until he pulled his coracle out near his camp of the previous night. He had made the entire circuit around the Fortress in a single day! He rebuilt his fire and settled on his bed of pine boughs as he pulled his coracle over his exhausted body in the oncoming and welcoming dark.

•• 11th day of 4th Month ••

As he settled in, he heard a rustling in the undergrowth of the surrounding forest. He located his bandolier, holding the dagger and sword, draped it across his chest and crept out to the shadows at the far edge of the trees dragging his coracle along. Soon a human shape emerged from the other side of the forest, nearer his bedding. He watched. He waited. He noticed that the man had his sword drawn. He was a big man—much taller than Evermon was. The man used his sword as a club and the bed was thrashed through and scattered, the fire and its spit were hacked to pieces and then he noticed who it was. He wore the emblems of Aradon. It was one of the guards that had beaten him! Alindra had sent him to finish off the Prince. Or maybe he had come on his own. Evermon remembered the injustices that had been inflicted on his body by this man.

His own hand tightened on the rusty sword he had found at the ruined fortress. He slowly drew it out of the bandolier. He let it fall to his side, ready at a moment's recall, hand tensing on the hilt, squeezing it, forearm and biceps flexing in nervous anticipation. He didn't have a prayer against this mountain of a man, but he stepped boldly out of the shadows, right into the line of the intruder's sight.

There was a smile, wicked—gleaming through the darkness. Evermon wondered how a man like this could have lived in Aradon! Could have been in the employ of his own family! He had known him, before Alindra, at least he had seen him around since he himself was a little child. He realized, in those moments of staring at someone you through you might have known, that most things around Alindra, after a time, changed.

The man circled around to cut off the boy's retreat to the water. Then the man moved forward backing the Prince up to the trees. He crouched, ready to spring. Evermon thought he should pray. He wanted to say goodbye to so many people in his life. Then he thought *'Attack! Throw him off!'* And he did.

The boy's sword came down in a mighty slash and the man easily fended off the blow, laughing at the impertinence of the soon to be dead Prince. The man's massive blade swung sideways and would have cloven the boy clean in two but Evermon managed, somehow, to maneuver his sword and deflect the powerful blow, but he was sprawled backwards by its force.

Evermon then raised four successively quick blows on the man and he withstood each, returned, thrust and slice. The man struck out, lashing wildly and widely, and Evermon ducked and dodged, scrambling out of the way. The soldier swung another crushing blow at the boy's head and Evermon brought his sword up to block it and his pommel was cracked at its meeting with the soldier's blade. The man pressed down upon the youth until the edge of his blade was about to shave what had never been shaven. The man was close. His breath was foul, fetid! His body stank the unwashed stink of sweat and urine. As his dirty, greasy flesh came in contact with Evermon's straining, nearly naked body, the Prince pulled his dagger in desperation and thrust it into the man's side. He pulled out as the man backed away, eyes bulging. Evermon's rusty sword came up to rive him from his crotch up to his pelvis. Evermon pulled it out and then it rang out sideways and sank deep into the man's neck but was stopped by the vertebrae covered in knots of muscle. Evermon sliced, sawed through, withdrawing the sword with a sickening sound and the man crumpled forward missing a large part of his groin, with his head flopping to the side as if it had just come unhinged.

As the man's blood leeched into the ground at the boy's feet, Evermon ran, dagger in one hand and sword in the other, to the river bank where, with only his weapons to hole him up, he threw up everything he had eaten in the last twenty-four hours. He then sank to his knees, his body shivering and shaking. His mind was numb except for one thought—he had just killed a man!

Training in the yard of the Purple Palace had been different. It had not prepared him for this. Being present at the healing of the wounds of his friends by the Circle was different. Even the thought, in fantasy, of overcoming your enemy, being victorious in a battle of strength, was not the glory he felt at this moment. There was no glory. Relief. Not glory.

He groaned and wretched again as his stomach felt as if it was trying to eject itself from his body. He leaned forward, hands on the ground, and dry-heaved, shook, sweated and then fainted.

•• 12th day of 4th Month ••

When he awoke the next morning he pushed himself off the ground, weapons still lying near his hands, and he remembered what had happened to him. He stood, shakily, and waded into a deep pool of the river near the edge where it bent away from the bank and the currents ran slack. He immersed himself numerous times. He pulled off his loinwrap and rinsed it out. He used it then, to rub and scrape his skin clean of the blood, sweat and guilt of the death of another human being.

After an hour of scraping and rinsing he climbed out of the river and dried his wrap by running it around the bole of a young sapling, twisting it tightly and wringing all of the water possible from it. Then he dried himself with it, twisted it dry again and wrapped himself up. He picked up his bandolier, replaced his dagger and sword and without a backward glance he secured his pack and launched his coracle into the currents of the westward flowing River of Sadness. He now suspected how and why the river had received its name.

•• 11th day of 4th Month ••

The Chamberlain, the Dwarf, and Nathan, The Circle Leader of Aradon, had examined every detail of the Room of the Talisman. There were problems. It didn't add up properly. Usually, if people exploded, there was something left of them—some trace—but there was nothing—not even blood on Baladar's clothing. (What little of it was left.) Not that they wanted there to be such evidence or that they were disappointed about it or anything. They were, on the other hand, ecstatic! It meant that Baladar was not dead. That the Queen was covering something up. When wasn't she covering up something? Gladenwreath thought, *'How long would Miraden let this charade go on?'*

They pretended to believe the Queen's grief as it played out over the remainder of the day, their thoughts rarely straying from what had she might have done with Baladar. They would let it generally be known among the population that the boy had been killed in the explosion. However, the Circle members would know the truth. The quandary: she didn't—and wouldn't—kill her own son. She must have banished him like she did Evermon. She must be hiding him somewhere!

•• 11th day of 4th Month ••

The day was warm, almost hot, and Baladar was almost glad that all he had on was his loin-wrap. He felt cooler this way. Everything around him looked purple—that he could have done without. It made him dizzy. He tried to walk and kept running into the edge of the warding, falling back and landing in the center of the bubble, usually on his hind end. As he thought about it he devised a plan. He stepped carefully against the upward curve of the warding in front of him. The bubble responded and he began rolling it forward, under his feet, balancing with his hands against the continuously revolving sphere. He was delighted at this new method of transportation, so captivated that he didn't notice what was happening outside the warding.

A pack of wolves had gathered, eyeing him hungrily. He stopped and looked back at them. Their leader, at least he appeared to be such, howled. The pack charged. Baladar braced for impact.

With yelp after yelp they bounced off the odd purple thing surrounding the man-child. Baladar smiled. His mother had even gotten it wrong here. A punishment had become a protection. He stood, arms crossed, staring at the leader of the wolf pack. He stared him down hard and the wolf whimpered and relented; as most animals will under the penetrating gaze of a human. He led his pack away, howling.

Baladar returned to the revolving walk and his bubble moved forward toward the northern cliffs of a valley. As he got closer he saw a pile of stone and the occasionally crenelated top of a tower or wall. He stopped. *'Mountain Hold, Mother said. Mountain Hold. My father built this place.'* he thought. *'What had Daniel called it? Oh, yes— Twelve Towers!'* He began to explore. Being inside the bubble made it more difficult to walk across the rubble in his warding. After falling several times he had another thought.

He concentrated on the rock that was located just outside the bubble. A large square stone cut out of the mountain. He focused on it and then he was standing on it! Outside the warding! Of course! Why hadn't he thought of it before? His mother didn't know he had this much magic. He could 'pop' in and out of the bubble for his own protection. His mother, in her complete and typical lack of foresight, had provided for him a home. He 'popped' back in. He 'popped' back out. Just to make sure. As long as the bubble stayed up he'd be safe.

Leaving the bubble he leaped from rock to rock—exploring the ruins. As he approached the rear of the pile of fallen stone near the mountain's base he saw an opening in the cliff face. He worked is way over to it. As he stood in front of it, he concluded that the opening was man-made. It was an arch of stones supporting the rock above it. He entered and after a few paces—it was dark. He scrambled back out.

'Light—that's what I need—light!' he thought.

"Light!"

Torches, unseen before, flared to life from the walls of the tunnel. He'd have to thank his mother. She was always calling for light in dark places. *'Too bad she didn't call for Light in her own mind,'* he thought. He re-entered and probed along the corridor. As he neared darkness again he'd call for more light and torches would burst into flame. Then the tunnel forked. He went right. The tunnel ended at a large wooden door. He tugged, he pulled, he yanked. The door remained shut.

"Light!"

A soft, warm glow came through the opening in the door just above his head. He pulled himself up, just off his toes, and peered through it. There were large, long boxes filled with earth; manacles and chains on the walls; a table thing with more ropes, manacles and capstans at both ends. There were pokers and pincers and knives and spades on another table. Baladar shuddered and lowered himself. *'My father was not a nice man.'*

He retraced his steps and took the other fork. It was not as long but it did end at another door. This door was open!

"Light!"

Revealed through the open door was a room full of scrolls, beakers, books, vials—all organized in ranks and shelves— untouched by the cataclysm that had erupted above them. He heard a snarl and a yelp behind him. He ran and slammed the door into the muzzles of several wolves, who snarled and ripped at him through the large low-barred opening in the massive door.

He turned and smelled it. Then he saw it. Papers—shredded. Grass. Branches. Pieces of cloth. All in the corner of the room and as he got closer he saw traces of fur on the cloth. This was their den!

As the wolves snarled at the door he rummaged around with only an occasional backward glance.

Some of the contents of the vials were familiar to him. Most were not. Then he saw the books and scrolls again. They were full of spells, potions, incantations, histories. Hope beyond hope—he had found his father's library!

•• 12th day of 4th Month••

As Evermon floated down the river, the water got deeper. The farther west he traveled the more alive things became. On his right he passed a city. All appeared empty; vacated long ago during the War of the Realms and never reinhabited. The forest had begun to reclaim it. Vines and creepers encrusted the walls, trees sprouted near the base of the battlements and threatened to crack them open with their growing, reaching roots. The once proud City of Zanadon had deteriorated into an unwanted, broken shell. It made the Prince of Aradon sad. Then mad. It's what Alindra would do to his home in Aradon unless he could find his mother and cure his father.

He couldn't bring himself to enter the city so he laid down in the coracle and slept the sleep of the distressed as his little craft floated on.

•• 12th day of 4th Month••

Holder was whistling as he passed from Aradon into western Zanadon's panhandle area. It did not seem as dark as its stories had made it out to be. Her father had always taught her (him) to avoid Zanadon, and she had. It was almost bright—pleasant. Not like Father's description at all. The green of the grass and trees along the road made him feel hopeful. The road was in good repair (thanks to Aradon and Caladon) and he pressed on toward Caladon and its border several hours away.

The bridge over the River of Sadness was too enticing when he arrived there. With the sad castle and the city in the near distance, the Caelith in him took over and Holder sat under a tree by the bridge for a bite of lunch. Bread and cheese eaten in peace and quiet. A boon to the soul. Holder reached into the pack and withdrew his harp, glanced at the sparkling waters, plucked a few notes and began to sing. A boat floating toward him stopped his song. He stood high on the bank and peered toward the little craft below and saw a nearly naked man or youth in the bottom of the little boat.

"Hey, there! Traveler!"

The figure startled and kneeled in the bottom of the boat.

"Hey, fellow Traveler," and he reached his arms over the side and paddled his way to shore. As he stepped out on the bank, holding the coracle above his head, Caelith/Holder's eyes flashed. There was so much of him to see—and she liked the view. Then she thought, *'I'm Holder, now. Control!'*

If Evermon had known Holder was Caelith—that this he was a she, he might have shielded himself behind the coracle out of simple decency, but he strode up the bank and set his coracle down against a tree.

This river stranger was a startlingly handsome youth. Caelith struggled in suppressing her attraction.

"What's your name, stranger?" cried Evermon.

"Holder."

"A Harper?"

"Yes! How...?"

Evermon pointed to the harp in his hands.

"Oh—this—well—yes. And you sir?"

Evermon looked dully at Holder who pointed at his bandolier and two blades.

"Your name?"

"Oh, Evermon—former Prince of Aradon."

Caelith's jaw dropped and Holder choked. Evermon had changed (Oh, how he had changed!) since she had last seen him. Strong. Tall. Handsome—sexy in his loin-wrap. 'Control,'—she thought again.

"Prince Evermon—it's my honor."

"And mine, Holder."

"Tell me—how are you a 'former' Prince?"

"I don't know if I am, really, but I was exiled by my step-mother. She hates me and my family and wants the throne. If I go back it will mean my death."

Caelith and Holder were surprised together. Just how much should she reveal? (Well, not as much as Evermon was revealing!) She decided to play dumb.

"When did this happen?"

"A day or so ago—I don't know—I've lost track of the time."

Caelith was staring at him again. Evermon noticed and shifted his weight and crossed his arms. Caelith jolted back to being Holder.

"Umm" pointing at all the wounds and bruises. "Did she do that?" Nice cover, Caelith!

"No—but she had her guards do it."

"I'm sorry, Evermon."

Oh, how she wanted to tell him who she was but she couldn't—not yet. It might put an end to her quest.

"Come on, let me put some ointment on those sores."

Evermon sat as Holder got the salve out of his pack and slathered it across both the open and closed wounds and bruises.

"That feels good."

In response, Holder pressed harder—rougher.

"Hey!"

"Sorry!" Being a guy wasn't easy. Or so Caelith was finding out.

"What sets you on the road, Holder?"

"I am searching for a position as a Harper. When I find one I will settle down."

"How old are you?"

"Sixteen," she lied. She was eighteen.

"I'm only fifteen. I would have figured you a little younger than I am. Well, it seems that it has fallen to me to cure my father, rescue my mother, find my brothers and restore my Kingdom and maybe even find my cousin Caelith."

Holder choked again. "The Princess of Mirador is missing?"

"Where have you been?"

"Traveling."

Evermon nodded.

"Well, Prince—I think that we can accomplish all of that before tomorrow morning."

Evermon laughed. Holder joined him.

"We?" Evermon said pointedly.

"Why not—merge our quests? You need help and I need a position. Is there a Harper in the Court of Aradon?"

"As a matter of fact—no. So, you're it! By official decree of the King—er, Prince—uh, former Prince!"

"And we'll need something else."

"What?"

"Clothes for you!"

Evermon laughed again.

"No matter who you are you can't wander the world nearly naked!"

Yes—Caelith—no matter how much you want him to! (Shut up, Holder!)

Evermon laughed again. "Right. What do you propose?"

'Propose?' The word flummoxed Caelith for a moment until Holder took over, rummaged through his pack and threw breeches and a chemise at Evermon. They fit! Sort of. Each garment purloined along the way was a gold piece left behind.

"Much appreciated, Holder."

"Glad to do it, My Prince." Holder didn't lie—but Caelith did. What had gotten into her? She had never felt this way before.

"Evermon."

"Huh?" Caelith was confused.

"My name... is Evermon. Not 'My Prince.'"

"Evermon. There's a small hamlet across the border into Caladon or so I'm told. Maybe we can find you some boots there. I'm wearing the only pair I have."

As they walked north toward Caladon on the Western Highway, Evermon was observing Holder. '*Something is not quite right*,' he thought. '*But he's still young, maybe not even sixteen, and he's a Harper, not a farm boy*,' he concluded. He put the conflicting thoughts that had occurred to him out of his mind—for now.

Caelith had always thought Evermon too young for her. Three years between them had seemed an eternity when she was fifteen and he was only twelve. She had liked Galderon, his older brother. Or even Raileon—the oldest. Suddenly, at the sight of Evermon in front of her, he didn't seem as young as he used to seem.

ℳ

CHAPTER SEVEN—
ANSWERS—FINALLY!!

•• 11th day of 4th Month ••

Baladar was frightened. He hadn't known if he could do it. The door was latched but not locked. His purple safety bubble was far away—outside the cave and across the ruins and scree. He had placed all the scrolls safely, he hoped, in a large cabinet so they would be protected from further use as wolf-den lining. He had one scroll tucked into his loin-wrap. He would study it tonight; if he made it out of the room safely. It was time. The wolves were resting. He eased the latch on the door up, quietly, and he 'popped' leaving the door to swing open. The wolves clamored into an empty room while Baladar found himself safely, happily, successfully, surrounded by purple.

He summoned food and surprisingly, it was in his hands. As he took his first bite of the beef he felt guilty. He wondered if the meal had come off some family's table. As his hunger drove him to eat, more than guilty—he ate, thanking in his heart whoever provided the feast. He settled down on the large flat rock and pulled out his scroll as he vanished the empty plates away—hopefully back to the family that they had come from. He didn't yet quite understand how it worked. He was just glad that it did work! He was going to enjoy this very long scroll about wardings.

•• 11th day of 4th Month ••

Alindra was stuck on the throne of Aradon handing down unpopular decision after unpopular decision. (Isn't this what she wanted all along? Power?) Nathan and Gladenwreath smiled behind their hands as the petitioners scowled at the Queen as she entrenched herself deeper and deeper against all comers. The 'advisors' chose to not interfere with her self-destructive methods. She obviously had no talent for leadership. Just a thirst for power. So typical of those who seek office. So the 'advisors' themselves followed the advice of a wise, old man named Miraden: they watched, they waited, they reported—they enjoyed the discomfiture of Alindra, or whatever her name was.

•• 12th day of 4th Month ••

Holder and Evermon, brothers in their quest, marched on Caladon City. It was much easier going now as Evermon sported a pair of new boots that Holder had purchased for him. (She could do that at least.) They trooped along laughing, exchanging dreams (Holder had to be careful here), extolling the virtues of their freedom.

They passed easily through the gates of the city and Evermon looked for the home of their Circle leaders, Twm and Bronwyn. Now, Evermon was fairly tall and fairly strong underneath his new clothes but as Twm opened the door and towered over Evermon, Evermon with all his gifts, felt small. (But he would never be small in Caelith's eyes.) Twm smiled and welcomed the exiled Prince.

After feasting on Bronwyn's excellent cooking Evermon was talked into seeing Miraden, but Holder (Caelith) was not a big supporter of that idea. She was certain her grandfather would recognize her. She only gave in to the plan to transport to the White DragonMount because she would have to reveal who she was to stop them from going there.

With tomorrow's activities planned out they settled down to sleep. Holder took the bed on the right and Evermon the one on the left. Evermon slept in his loin-wrap. Holder, fully clothed, turned over and faced the wall just as she had done the previous nights. Well, she had faced a tree, but at least she was turned away from Evermon—too great a distraction.

The Prince dreamed of the possibilities of finding his mother and curing his father. Holder dreamed of Caelith and Evermon together. Would you care to bet on who it was that got a better night's sleep?

•• 13th day of 4th Month ••

With the morning sun came a howling and a snarling outside the purple warding. Each wolf approached the purple thing and lifted its leg to let the man-child know how they felt about him, then ran away. Baladar laughed and stretched, but was interrupted by the strong smell and had to wrinkle his nose.

He walked his warding over to the creek about a hundred arms away. He walked it right into the water and sat there rolling it a little bit at a time, until the worst of the smell bad been washed away.

Now he could try what he had read about last night. He checked for the wolves. None. He 'popped' outside his mother's warding. He concentrated—focused on his hands—a small purple light glimmered in his palm. He worked feverishly to enlarge it. Knuckle by knuckle it grew bigger until he was standing inside it just touching the top and bottom with his head and feet. Then he extended his arms out to the sides until his hands touched the bubble.

He was tired. This was work. Taking a deep breath, he continued.

He began to maneuver the bubble; to shape it. It began to collapse around him. He kept going until it fit tightly over his skin and loin-wrap. It became... like a second skin. It felt... spongy... clingy... wet, almost. He walked into the water again and pushed his other warding back to the ruins. As he reached them he heard a yelp and a howling of many voices.

Soon be saw a short trail of five wolves as they came back to the tunnel and went inside, ignoring him completely. There had been six of them. One of the cubs was missing! This would be a good time to test his accomplishment. He went for a walk in the direction of the yelp, toward where the wolves had come from. It wasn't long until he saw a wolf cub struggling on the ground, its paw caught by a wire snare.

The noose was tight and it had already bloodied the lower part of the cub's leg, rubbing off the fur as the cub struggled against it. When the cub noticed the man-child it snarled and yapped. Baladar kneeled down and looked the cub in the eyes. After a while the cub quieted down as Baladar knelt, waiting patiently. He extended a hand. The cub nipped at him. His gaze bore into its eyes again. The demeanor of the cub changed drastically. His ears perked up instead of laid flat back along his head. It settled down on its haunches, tongue lolling. It yipped a little bit as if saying to the man-child, *'Give it your best shot!'*

Baladar approached and calmed the cub further as he disengaged the wire from the flesh of the cub's paw. The cub licked Baladar's hands as he gently eased the pressure on the loop and the cub was able to withdraw its paw.

It began to limp away. Baladar followed. The cub made very slow progress. Baladar went around front and looked into the cub's eyes again. The cub settled, prone to the ground. Baladar went to its side and lifted it into his arms. He carried the cub back to the ruins. He entered the tunnel.

"Light!"

The cub was startled but stayed in the boy's arms. He walked down the corridor—as far as he dared. The wolf family appeared out of the dark, snarling. The boy stopped and stared at them. He set the cub down and began to back away. The leader launched himself at the boy, took him down to the floor of the corridor, and reached forward, muzzle open.

•• 13th day of 4th Month ••

"Baladar is missing also."

"Not dead, but missing?"

"Yes, Miraden. Alindra faked his death; we are sure of it," admitted Nathan.

"Where do we find him?"

"We don't know but the Circle is searching for him now like it has been searching for Evermon and Caelith."

"Poor Baladar," came from Evermon. "I'm sorry Caelith is gone."

Did Caelith feel strange, uncomfortable, even guilty just sitting there in the presence of her great-grandfather? Sure, she did! Was she about to disclose her identity? Not on your life!

"I know she is safe. I just don't know where."

Holder gasped and recovered. Miraden gazed at him intently. Caelith didn't see a sign of recognition in the old man's eyes.

"My Prince, I have found a map to the Waters of Life. If you will lead a party there I am sure that it will be a profitable trip."

"How many?"

"Four or five should be sufficient."

"Holder, you game?"

"Ummm, of course!"

"May I come, too?" asked Nathan.

"I think that would be good."

"And me!" said Gladenwreath.

"I ask you not to ask, Noble Dwarf. I have another quest for you to lead if you are willing?"

"I will always do as you ask, Miraden."

"I thought so. Thank you. As for a fourth—I suggest, Alan."

Nathan was incredulous. "My son?"

"Yes. You may need a healer and Elias is busy with other matters now."

"Alan's perfect."

"Yes. He is. Good. Then the four of you will go."

"What about Twm?"

"Twm also has other business with Arik in the Northern Reaches. There is much happening in the Realms right now. Send for Alan immediately. We will outline our plans after lunch. Twm, would you see Gladenwreath back safely to Aradon? I need him to continue spying on Alindra. In a few days, Noble Dwarf, your own mission will begin.

•• 13th day of 4th Month ••

Baladar laughed as the wolf licked his warded face. It worked! He tentatively put out a hand and scruffled the fur about the wolf's shoulders. He couldn't really feel it, due to the warding, but he was touching it. The wolf backed off and let the man-child up. Baladar continued to pet the wolf as the she-wolf licked the paw of her cub. As the wolves withdrew to their den, Baladar watched and then 'popped' to the other end of the fork in the tunnel.

He saw the locked door. He stared at the door and its locking mechanism. With his mind he twisted and turned the tumblers of the lock—he didn't know how but he could actually see them in his mind—he just could—and the sweat dripped off his body and ran to his toes, making his feet sloshy inside the personal warding. The lock clicked. He pushed open the door to the torture chamber.

"Light!"

Something toppled into him, knocking him to the floor.

•• 13th day of 4th Month ••

"Deep in the Mountains of Caladon, near to the borders of Colabos, lies the Temple of the Ancients which guards the Valley of the Waters which leads to the Well of the Waters of Life. Three magical enchantments bar the way to all but those equipped with the solutions to the riddles that will be proposed. The book says this:

"Enter the temple but beware the Opal;
Exit the temple but beware the rock;
Pass the rock and discover a key."

"So what are the answers?" asked Miraden.

"The Opal," said Alan.

"The rock," said Nathan.

"The key," said Evermon.

"But what are they answers to?" asked Holder.

"Three riddles—physical or verbal, the book doesn't say. Find the Temple and you will find the entrance to the Canyon of the Waters. It lies in the Valley of the Path Once Found. The temple leads past the rock to the Waters of Life.

"How do we get to the Temple?"

"The path is hidden through the Shifting Forest. At each opening of the forest you will be shown two paths. You must choose the right one."

"Which is the right one?"

"You must choose. The book does not say."

"What if we choose wrong?"

"You will have to retrace your steps... or maybe... don't choose the wrong path."

"But?"

"Choose the right path. That is all my books said. Nathan, transport them to Caladar. From the city you will have to walk to the point where the road disappears into the woods.

"Yes, Sir."

They prepared to go. Miraden had filled their packs with food and supplies. It would not be an easy journey. Miraden called Evermon to him.

"Watch out. You are in charge."

"But Nathan is older and..."

"It is your quest, after all. You are the Prince. Look after Holder. Protect her... him."

'What a strange thing to say,' Evermon thought. "I... will... Miraden."

•• 13th day of 4th Month ••

Baladar was frozen to the ground in fear. He couldn't move. Well, he wouldn't move. He wouldn't even open his eyes. He didn't want to touch whatever was on top of him so his hands spread out to his sides, pressed against the floor; trying to escape downward through the stones.

Whatever it was hadn't ripped his head off. It hadn't bitten him. It hadn't raked him with its claws. It didn't even smell bad. Wait! Could it? He was warded! He opened his eyes then closed them again. He used his warded hands to slide the rotting corpse off of him. He only opened his eyes again as he sat up and away from the mass of rotting flesh, bones and rags.

Curiosity is a funny thing. It drives us. Especially when we're young. Yet it's perfect. Healthy. Until it puts us in danger. Curiosity must be tempered with wisdom. So why, when we are our most unwise, is curiosity the bigger part of us? Well, Baladar could use his wisdom now and it backed him out of the room as it finally overwhelmed his curiosity. He pushed the door shut and let out a huge, deep sigh. Maybe he'd go back in there, sometime. Maybe he wouldn't! He walked out of the tunnel and into the sunlight. He scrambled over the ruins and climbed to the highest point on the tumble of rocks.

It really must have been something, this mountain fortress. Even though he didn't like him, his father must have been some Sorceror!

•• 14th day of 4th Month ••

Aloshtu, Prince of Plateau Taradal, and his younger cousin, Serrantu, the former Jinnie, had just finished praying at the Temple of the Dalic Oracle near Taratown on Lake Nock. They were concerned about what was happening in the Realms and they had come to the Temple to see if they could find any answers.

Almost all of the Circle members of the Realms and Reaches were on some type of a quest at the moment—looking for Evermon, Caelith and Baladar. Friends of the Circle were in trouble and the Circle had gone into search mode.

As they stood from the altar they felt more confused than they had when they knelt down. The message they both had received was—odd. They were to proceed into the part of the Northern Reaches just over the Tara River. They were to search the valleys there. They 'popped' to Solah City, Kalaal and Dalarra's home, and picked up Kalaal. Dalarra and the children would be searching elsewhere. They swept Kalaal away and 'popped' to the borderlands.

There at the southern edge of a range of tall mountains that extended west, north and east of their position, they began their series of transportations until they recognized the valley that the Creators and Dal had shown them in their vision at the Temple. The view was almost right; almost matched the pictures in their minds. They then turned east following the circuitous valleys. They saw bear, wolves, and smaller animals. What they were hunting were deer, and three humans. "The deer in the south, where Aloshtu and Serrantu lived, were small and scrawny, (the humans weren't) while their northern cousins were large and hardy, providing meat for months. The deer were conspicuously absent. The wolves were plentiful—maybe too numerous.

As the valley opened up into a long narrow canyon they heard a snarl. That was no wolf! They each nocked arrows into their bows. There were crashes, creaks, snaps, all coming from the trees on the slope to their left. They found cover behind a boulder, bows ready. They threw up a red warding as the crashing got closer but it wasn't just coming from in front of them now. The slopes behind them resounded to the movement of a very large animal—or possibly animals.

•• 14th day of 4th Month ••

Holder looked around him and saw the company he was with: The Prince of Aradon, The Circle Leader of Aradon and his Aradonan son. There was also, unknown to the rest, Holder, the Harper—Princess of Mirador. So, Holder asked for a few hours of their time before they arrived at Caladar to begin their quest. He wanted them to meet a very special family of Aradon.

Choruses of "Holder! Holder's back! It's Holder!" greeted the arrival of the four travelers at the gate of the farm of William and Tildy. She hadn't really thought about it, but this was going to cement her identity in the minds of her companions. Eleven excited children surrounded the group and dragged Holder away from his companions leaving them to wonder what it was that they had done or not done. What had Holder done? A very chagrinned farmer stood in front of them, hat in hand, so to speak, and apologized to them and invited them inside.

Holder, with help from the children, explained the history of their relationship. It had been a sudden and a permanent friendship. Holder, after all, appeared not too much older than the oldest of the Farmers. So it seemed to all that it was natural that a quick bond could be formed. When the stories were done, the songs began because the stories were told over a mid-day meal that would send the travelers on their way.

"How come you won't stay the night again?" asked a saddened Little William.

"We are on a great quest for Miraden and Daniel and the Circle of Light..."

"The Circle of Light? Whoah! I'd like to meet the Circle of Light" one of William's older brothers exclaimed.

There was laughter among the four travelers that elicited strange looks from the family.

"But you have," Nathan smiled.

"When?"

"I don't remember it."

"We haven't ever."

"Oh, but you have—you are. I am Nathan, Circle Leader of Aradon and this is my son, Alan, also a Circle member."

The children were hushed. Farmer William and Tildy were bemused, as reluctant smiles creased their faces.

"Whoah! Real Magicians? Here! Whoah!"

"And don't forget a Prince of our Realm," Holder said, pointing to Evermon.

"The children stared at Evermon as if he had suddenly turned into a three-legged Ogre with purple skin. Evermon shifted and smiled. The children breathed as one.

"Whoah!"

"And Holder!" Little William added.

The four travelers laughed. They had, not one of them, realized their celebrity status amongst the young citizens of the Realms until now.

"I am afraid that we," said Evermon, "are no more than yourselves—Citizens of the Realms. We each have our jobs—our positions—our duties—and there's not one of us here who is not important to the safety, or the future, of the Realms. Without this farm our people do not eat. Without Nathan and his family we have no jewelers. Without Holder, no songs."

"And without you—no Kingdom!" Little William interrupted.

"Exactly! Each of us makes our contributions. Without any one of us the Realms would be a little poorer."

The children were silent. The parents and the travelers smiled at each other. Soon, it was time once again for Holder to depart.

There were no tears this time; no moping. For they knew that Holder was a man of his word. He would return and so would the others.

As the family cleared the supper dishes, after saying goodbye to their visitors, the simple and functional candelabra over their table began to flutter. Alan had returned, cloaked in invisibly, to the family because he had an idea; one of his fellow travelers had endorsed it whole-heartedly. He had snuck through the open door and then used a hover charm to float over the table, near the ceiling. As he held on to the candelabra to keep himself steady, he dropped eleven gold pieces—one by one—to the delight, the surprise, the astonishment of the family below him.

William and Tildy sat and wept—grateful but overwhelmed at the generosity of others. It was simply their own generosity that was being rewarded.

The children had each retrieved one of the gold coins and had dutifully brought it and placed it in front of their parents. As a family they bowed their heads and blessed the Creators for their good fortune.

A pleased but very humbled Alan smiled in his invisibility and floated out the door. From a few spans outside the house he 'popped' to the trio of friends waiting for him down the road. Friends he would share his humbling experience with as they traveled to Caladar and beyond to the Shifting Forest.

•• 14th day of 4th Month ••

It was a dreary morning as clouds covered the tops of the mountains and rain beat down on their slopes and valleys. The din created inside the protective warding Baladar's mother had given him became loud, like rain on a metal roof. Baladar himself paced and the warding rolled with him. Then he thought of the potions and ingredients and the books and scrolls. Maybe it wasn't too early to return.

Baladar wanted to read more; had to read more! He figured it was something that was sort of due to him—kind of a legacy; although he really wasn't familiar with that word. He determined to enter the library—despite the wolves. He 'popped' to where he had left the cub yesterday and walked forward, slowly. He heard the wolves in their room; his room. He stopped. He took a deep breath. He almost turned back. He gulped and crept through the door. The wolves were on their feet immediately. They each walked over to the frightened man-child and sniffed him and walked back to their den in the corner, satisfied that he was not there to harm them. He walked over to the cabinet and took the scrolls over to the table, followed by the books. One scroll was brightly colored and it stood out from the rest. He unrolled it placing a beaker on each corner. It was a map!

He was hungry; He summoned food. He hoped it was off Alindra's own plate, this time, at least that's what be imagined when be had pictured the food in his mind. As he ate he turned melancholy. He missed Evermon and life at the castle with Gladenwreath, Nathan and Jayden; and a small part of him even missed his mother—at least the mother he used to know—the mother be had had all to himself during all those years at the Purple Lake. Why had he wished for change? This isn't what he had asked for! (Is it ever?)

As he looked at the map, brushing off the crumbs of his meal, he saw five prominently marked places. The first was labeled: 'Castle Norstok' in the far Great Northwestern Reaches; then there was the 'Castle of the North' which his mother had talked about so often, where he was born; then he found 'Mountain Hold' and scrawled next to it in a smaller hand was 'Twelve Towers. So that's where it was located! No wonder it was so hot here. He wasn't too far from the Great Eastern Desert! His original Taradal homeland. He grew homesick all over again, but knew he would never be accepted there. The stories his mother told him had made him think that he could never show his face there after what she and his father did to the Taradal peoples. He didn't fit in anywhere!

A tear dropped on the parchment in front of him. When he brushed it away, he found 'Pine Island,' marked.

"I've heard of that place, too!"

The wolves jumped at the sound of his voice and looked at him.

"Sorry!"

A whine came back at him as they settled down again that seemed to say don't do that again.

Above Pine Island there was another marking—another castle. 'Castle of the Rock.' It was in the middle of the Northeastern Bay near Troll Island. Its lettering was the only one done in silver ink. All the others had been in black.

He re-rolled the scroll and placed it in a special place on the shelf in front of him. He looked at the stack of scrolls and parchments around the table and perused each briefly, separating them into piles of: spells, potions, enchantments and—terra magic? He read along in that one until he understood that Terra Magic was used the elements of earth, water, air and fire to construct whatever it was that was desired. He thought that that was only for the Elves and not for the Dajinnie peoples. It looked like his people were thieves in every sense of the word.

"This must be how Twelve Towers was made!"

The wolves startled again. He had to stop speaking out loud.

With the papers sorted he began opening books. Almost all were histories: the Realms, the Reaches, Dajinnie tales—he put that one aside. He might be able to find out who he really was. There were books about Elves, Trolls, Dwarves, Faeries, Nymphs, Dryads, Sprites, and a race called the Skwatwael. That must be Kwuktw's people! There was a also a big book about Dragons. He put that with the Dajinnie book.

Next he found a book about Castles and Fortresses. He placed it next to the map with the special markings. He found a book full of strange drawings of machines with wheels, wings, fins, sails, oars—it was labeled "Mobility Machines." Some of the drawings he recognized but most he just couldn't figure out.

Then he found a white book. Emblazoned on its cover was "Dal and the Creators." He had been taught that Dal was greater and separate from the Creators. He sat spellbound as the stories which he had been told all his life were revealed as only fairytales. The truth in the book began to ring true to his heart. Evermon and his friends had changed his life. Dajinnie magic was condemned as Dark Magic. His father had been the darkest of all Dajinn. Why, then, did his father have this book when it contradicted everything his father had believed in?

His father had killed thousands and planned the deaths of thousands more.

His father had left his own son alone.

He folded his arms over the book and laid down his head and sobbed. His strange noises alarmed the wolves at first but as one approached the boy, he nuzzled Baladar's leg and whined a bit.

Baladar's arm moved down and his fingers entangled themselves in the thick fur of the cub's neck. After a minute or so Baladar raised his head and looked at the wolf, who whined again. Baladar went to his knees in front of the wolf cub and scratched both sides of the cub's neck with both his warded bands. Then he looked down and found that it was the cub that he had rescued—the paw was healing. He looked deep into the cub's eyes and the cub licked his face. He giggled and threw his arms around the cub's neck and hugged it to him. The cub endured this strange man-child ritual. In Baladar's world there was nothing like a boy and his dog, so Baladar released his personal warding. The purple disappeared!

•• 14th day of 4th Month ••

As the rocks tumbled and the branches cracked, the three hunters steeled themselves against the attack from more than one direction. They raised three purple wardings inside their red warding. The woods grew silent. Their warding suddenly shook as it was struck from above and a shadow passed over them and disappeared again. Their warding was rocked by another blow. It seemed darker outside than it should be, but they could see nothing that blocked the dim sunlight. There seemed to be shadows all around them. They unstrung their bows and placed their arrows back in their quivvers. What they were facing, would not be beaten without magic.

Aloshtu 'popped' out of the warding to about one hundred arms away. He looked back and saw huge shadows on the ground around the warding. One shadow peeled away and moved across the ground towards him. It moved quickly. He shot a bolt of lightning at the air above the shadow and it was absorbed as if there was something there. He shot again and again and the shadow stopped moving and a striped, furry body began to reveal itself. It was a tiger, like those in the south—but it was huge. Aloshtu, at a span in height, didn't quite come up to its shoulder.

"Aloshtu!"

He turned and saw several shadows heading in his direction and he 'popped' back into the warding. Howls were heard and shadows stopped and turned and once more surrounded the warding with the three hunters in it.

Even though the warding shuddered against the invisible blows, they had no doubt that they were strong enough to stand up against the magically weaker creatures. Serrantu proposed an idea. The three in the warding disappeared. The warding continued to shudder.

Pop!

Serrantu fired lightning at the air above the shadows. A purple tiger-shape appeared out of nowhere attacking the bubble he had just left. The purple tiger turned and saw nothing. It growled. It sniffed the ground. The now invisible hunters were quick—moving all around the perimeter of the area containing the tigers and their warding. The others stopped attacking the warding and turned to the space around them. They paced. Kalaal 'popped' into the warding and dismantled it. He continued to 'pop! around the area of the tigers leaving his spoor but no other sign of his being, except the occasional footprints standing side by side. The tigers became enraged at being able to smell but not see their prey. He raised another red warding along the inside of the perimeter shield wall that the three had erected. The red began to visibly surround the tigers as it adhered to the inside of the outer shield. They roared and attacked the movement of the leading edge of the color as it was erected. From their footprints and the pitches of their roars it was determined that there were five tigers inside the enclosure with only one of them visible in its purple warding.

They figured that two adults and four cubs had originally attacked them. There must be only one adult left, for only one warded shape was visible. Magic is usually not a gift given to cubs and children. So, the father, or the mother, prowled, frustrated at not finding their prey.

The red warding completed itself in a gigantic dome. Kalaal 'popped' out to his brothers. They uninvisified and the tigers leapt at the wall and sizzled their faces and paws. A howling was sent out loud enough to raise all the tigers of the continent to come and destroy these puny humans, but the five remained alone as the red warding began to shrink. The adult's purple warding shimmered and went out as it contacted the shrinking red. Then all five

C. MICHAEL PERRY

remaining tigers burst into view—magnificent, beautiful, overly-large and very dangerous animals. What could the hunters do to enclose the animals yet keep them alive, healthy, and separate from the world? They decided to reverse the direction of the shield wall. They would cover the valley with it. Nothing could get out and nothing could get in.

They reinvisified and continued the wall's expansion. As they came upon animals that were outside the shield they 'popped' the creatures inside. They worked all afternoon to cover the valley twenty leagues long from pass to pass and two leagues wide from peak to peak. They had pushed themselves out of the valley—eastward. They had tired themselves out of all energy. Aloshtu knew what to do. He summoned chocolate and they feasted on several bars a piece to renew their energy and rebuild their magical powers. Then they fell asleep in a double-purple warding.

•• 15th day of 4th Month ••

Baladar was running—fast. He flew over the rocks and logs as quickly as his almost-ten year old feet could carry him. There was yelping behind him. He looked around. He 'popped' to the uppermost stable limbs of a nearby tree. Then he nestled himself into a notch and waited.

The wolfpack bounded into the small clearing—yelping and snarling; not seeing or smelling their quarry. The cubs were leading with the parents running guard at the rear. They found the spot where Baladar had stopped. They circled. They whined. They howled.

Baladar laughed and yipped back at them from his safe height in the tree. They looked up and howled again. The boy 'popped' into their midst. The cubs licked and yipped gently at their new friend.

"Boy! What are you doing?"

Baladar startled. The wolves turned, teeth bared and growling, to see three men in black, downwind, inside purple things with sticks aimed at them.

"Put your bows down. These wolves are my friends. They will not hurt me, but they could hurt you if you don't act quickly."

The three hesitated.

"Please, put them down before the cubs charge you and get hurt."

The three complied.

The boy turned and looked at each wolf in the eyes. He ruffled their furry necks and they whined, licked their gums and stood down.

The three men were amazed.

"You'll pardon us if we keep our warding?"

Baladar shrugged, "If you each had a personal warding, it would be easier."

The three looked at each other and nodded. A purple film began to grow around their bodies covering, clothes, bows, hair, skin. Baladar was amazed. He had to build a regular warding and shrink it. These men could create the personal warding on their own skin. The exterior purple warding released with a pop which startled the wolves. Still, they watched as their man-child walked up to these strange men, then turned and motioned them to return to the cave. The wolves took off. Baladar extended his hand to the three.

"I am Aloshtu."

"I'm Serrantu."

"And I'm Kalaal"

"I've heard of all of you. You're legends. At least Evermon thinks you are!" The next three questions came out in a jumble:

"What do you know of Evermon?"

"Where is he?"

"Who are you?"

Baladar turned to each man in turn and replied to his question. "He's my brother. I don't know. I'm Baladar."

The three were floored—with delight and surprise. "The Circle is looking for you. Your brother has been found."

"Where?"

"He was with Miraden. He is now on a quest with several others."

"So, you are Alindra's son?".

"Yes," was said with his head bowed in shame.

More questions came at him than he could answer.

"Wait! Come with me. I want to show you something."

Baladar started off and the three Taradal followed. He led them through the forest and back to the ruins of Twelve Towers. He walked all the way. He didn't want anyone to know the extent of his magic powers—yet. Just in case he needed them for surprise. He and the three scrambled over the ruins and entered the cave.

"Light!" he whispered.

The torches were flaming as the three entered. Baladar led them down the corridor to the library. The wolves had not yet returned. Baladar was puzzled but not worried. At least they had left when he asked them to.

"My mother banished me here but I don't think she knew that this part of it still existed. She hoped I'd die. This is what is left of my father's magic and these are his writings,"

"Who was your father?" came from Aloshtu.

"Dajinn."

Serrantu unsheathed his sword. Aloshtu and Kalaal restrained him. They knew only too well the consequences of rash actions to thoughts of the moment. Serrantu put it away. Reluctantly.

"You can hate me if you want to. But you can't hate me as much as I hate being my father's son!"

"Are you a Dajinn?"

"No."

"A Sorceror?"

"No…" Well, now he had to tell. "I am a magician and an alchemist."

"But…?"

"I do not like my father or what he did. I do not like my mother, either. Evermon is my brother."

"Evermon said you were a lot like him."

Baladar smiled, relieved that there was someone who believed in him. "I thought that we could take all this back to Miraden. It may help him find the Queen and the Princes—maybe even cure the King."

Smiles brushed across the faces of the three hunters. This boy seemed unspoiled by Alindra. He was definitely not like his father.

How was that possible? Because his father, Dajinn, had never had much, if anything, to do with the boy.

They packed all the beakers and vials and bottles in the cabinet and placed the parchments, Scrolls and books carefully and orderly in the large trunk; except for the map and the book about the castles. Those Baladar tucked under his arm.

"Why?"

"Miraden needs to see these first."

Aloshtu held Baladar's hand. Kalaal touched both the cabinet and Aloshtu. Serrantu touched the trunk and Aloshtu. Aloshtu 'popped' them all to the White DragonMount.

ML

CHAPTER EIGHT—
PLOTS AND PLANS

•• 14th day of 4th Month ••

If one discounts Pine Island, Slipper Isle, The Rock and Troll Island (only half the land area of the Northeast Reaches) there is nothing left of note in the region; and some of the remaining locations may not be noteworthy either. Even the cities in the Northeast are diminutive when compared with any others on the continent. Twelve Towers was built by non-native Northeasterners, so its significance is lessened. Daniel knew that all lands must come under the influence of the Orb and Sceptre someday; that now was the time for the Northeast Reaches. Miraden was positive that the Northeast held the key to several of the mysteries surrounding Alindra.

Not that there wasn't great beauty in the region. Its mountains, in the borderlands to the south were stately and picturesque and filled with live game. The silver ribbon of a river that crossed the Reach from west to east opened out into a spectacularly glistening bay.

But it was colder here. The growing season was shorter and at least half of the plains were infertile and tundra-like. South and west of the river, food could be (and was) raised in abundance—like on the great southern plains of our own Canada—but few people, if any, lived there and only certain areas were farmed.

There were two towns on the river. Porthold, at the eastern end of the river delta, was a small and clean town with no more than four-hundred year-round inhabitants. It was on the Taradal trade route and seal skins and oil were the primary trade goods.

DANIEL LIGHT AND THE EXILE OF ARADON

Halfway across the Reach, in the center of the vast plains and farmland, was Midhold with slightly less than four-hundred residents. Most were involved in growing, processing or selling the grains needed to feed the entire population of the Reach. Northport was a small fishing village of a hundred or so persons, isolated in the far north in the delta of another river that came out of the mountains of the Northern Reaches. They traded with other ports along the northern coastline of the continent and with Porthold which, in turn, supplied them with the necessities of life in exchange for their more than bountiful supply of fish.

Aside from the loose interdependence between these three communities, there was no other indication of even a sense of nationality, of country, or of Kingdom. Each city did their own thing with small aid and cooperation from the others. No one settlement stood above another. There was no central government.

That afforded them their isolation from the rest of the continent (and the world). To have less was to be ignored by the other peoples of the world. They had the rights to pursue their lives in peace. Life was simple, uncomplicated—dull.

A fourth city, Southold, on the Taradal Bay, was merely an extension of Dalport in the Taradalnock Lands and populated mostly by disenfranchised Taradal and Realmer, alike. No structure existed. No link to other settlements. No interest inside or outside for anything Southold-ish.

Then on a beautiful bright, Mid-April morning the Emissaries came to each town. Daniel had sent Bentar and Irala from the Taradalnock Lands to Porthold; Lars and Gilda from Burgenvaria to Northport; and Ivor and Juliet of Caladon to Midhold. Their purpose was to learn what they could from the people, and to introduce themselves to the citizens of the Northeast. There were two cultures at play here; descendants of the Realms in all communities and a very few Taradal at Porthold—mostly transplants—those who had stayed behind as the trading ships left port. The people at Midhold were welcoming, but wary. They were a crossroads of sorts as the main road leading out of Caladon and Balador northward split to send its travelers to Midhold, and they hadn't always had good luck with strangers and travelers. The people in the ports were open, well, more so, as they had had dealings with outsiders throughout their long history and had developed a trust that comes only through familiarity.

But just where did the original Realmer settlers come from? And when?

The families were old; children, grandparents, great-grandparents, as far back as storied memory allowed, had been raised in the same areas, the same towns, even the same houses—all outside the Realms.

The stories of Midhold, told to Ivor and Juliet, seemed to date back to just after the Great War. Little, however, was remembered of their actual origins.

Ivor and Juliet, filled with wonderful stories, but still frustrated, took to the air in flight. They wanted an overview of the area. They had not been around when the Circle had done their original fly-over of the Northeast. They left the ground at Midhold towards the north and spiraled out, moving clockwise around using the city as their center. On their second pass around to the south they saw a low hill topped by, well, it was too small to be a castle, but it was a man-made building of some sort.

They drifted out of the air to stand in front of a cube of a structure. It was built out of square and rectangular blocks of worked stone. The joints were precise and it was ornately decorated with stone filigree—the workmanship was superb! What puzzled them was the writing—the seemingly endless inscriptions on every wall. The building was an actual cube with measurements of ten spans in each direction. Every knuckle of space on its wall was covered with... words—well, runes—but in a language which neither Ivor or Juliet could decipher.

A call went out to the other two pairs of explorers to come as soon as they were able.

Northport hadn't taken much time. They were a simple and happy people in a very small community. They welcomed outsiders but had no desire for change. Their stories? They were only of the great fishermen. Nothing historical. Nothing to tie their fealty to their ancient fathers. Life on the northern coast was harsh and all their time was taken up with the activities that taught them and helped them to stay alive in this cold environment centered around the sea. Anything that had no direct connection to the source of their sustenance (the sea) was forgotten or ignored. So, Lars and Gilda were soon at the strange cube of a building trying with the others, and without much luck, to decode the inscriptions.

Porthold also cared little for its history away from the sea but Bentar and Irala had made valuable contacts and had ingratiated themselves to the Portholders. With a promise to return, they excused themselves and joined their associates at the cube.

The language there was not Taradal in nature, which both read and spoke fluently, so Daniel was summoned. He and Tilly arrived hand in hand.

It didn't take long and Daniel recognized the words etched into the stone of the monument to the Ancient Ones. The language was that of the Creators. Daniel found a date of 400. Over 2000 years ago! He also found a very disturbing name. In bold but ornate letters, over the only door, was the name 'ORTHON' as the Creators would have written it. Why would the Creators provide a tomb for the evil son of Tophet? The answer is that they didn't; which Daniel found out soon enough. The Creator's language had been spoken by the Ancient Ones. Daniel knew that. It was only with the creation of Men and Dwarves that the language had begun to change to New Speak.

The runes told of the great deeds of the evil one. His power. His glory. Around to the south side of the cube, lists were found. Lists of Orthon's descendants. There were many and Daniel was disturbed by that. He was never known to have any wives. Ah— they were not wives! They were concubines! Seventy-two names were listed—both concubines and their children. Daniel startled at one name in particular, but held his tongue for the moment.

On the door Daniel found the words that would open the door. The door had also relinquished the curious fact that all those named on the walls were buried inside.

Daniel spoke the ancient charm—"T'lithaldar Elach'ta R'istha, Meral'k."

There was a thump; a blast of dust from around the door; a rush of stale air as the door withdrew into what Daniel and the

Circle came to know as a reliquary. A depository of bones and other relics. Jars, urns, crates and boxes—all ossuaries—lined one wall of the structure, all sitting on shelves. Individual crypts lined the other three walls. Names were emblazoned across each seal. One could only surmise that those with crypts were in favor with Orthon when they died. Those without...

Each vessel, nonetheless, was inscribed with a name. Seventy-one names. Seventy-one ossuaries. Orthon's name and the name of that one other did not appear on the inside of the building as it had on the outside.

In the center was a plain cube of granite—no carvings—no inscriptions. Until Daniel blew the dust away and saw the faint outlines of two human hands etched into the top of the stone. At first Daniel thought it was an altar of sorts. The handprints gave him another idea. He placed his hands in them. The thumbs were wrong; they pointed outward, not inward. He crossed his hands, wrist over wrist, and fit his hands into the prints. There was another thump. The cube began to descend into the floor. It was a large space, about six arms on a side, and as it reached the level of the floor Daniel motioned the others onto it and they crowded together on this ancient elevator as they disappeared through the floor.

As the stone reached the level of the floor below, the darkness almost complete, the stone stopped with a thunk. The halting of the cube stirred up dust long undisturbed—and the eight coughed.

"Light!" Daniel called.

Nothing.

"Chal'kta!" and the torches blazed on all four walls of the lower chamber. Daniel stepped off the cube and it started to descend again. He jumped back on and it stopped a few knuckles below the level of the floor of the lower vault. They would have to explore from their present position on the stone. It wouldn't be difficult. The room was small. Much smaller than upstairs. There was only one name that shouted to all of them from the wall at their left:

ORTHON

Miraden's nephew. One of the instigators of evil in the ancient world.

By the wall opposite Orthon's ossuary was a collection of gold, jewels, couches and jars. Orthon must have expected that he would either come back to life here or that he merely had to wait here for the world to return to him. Centuries of dust covered the forgotten articles under the flickering light. Unremembered Orthon was not going to return. He was definitely waiting behind the stone slab of his reliquary.

"There are seventy-three total names, including Orthon's, on the outside of the T'lithaldar..."

"The what?"

"Sorry, the tomb -- 'the place to stay at rest', but there are only seventy-two ossuaries inside, including this one."

"Whose name is missing?"

"Accosta's!"

•• 14th day of 4th Month ••

There were six trusted guards in the room with her as she enchanted two more men, seated naked before her. There had been seven and one had disappeared—she knew not where. She had searched the Realms and Reaches for a long time for suitable subjects for her secret band of enforcers. The greatest requirement for their service was that she could control them and that they were strong, physically. The two newest had been murderers, rotting in a prison in Norstok. They would be perfect. They were undergoing the painful initiation that Alindra had devised. A spell that turned the heart and mind, physically changed them, and gave them over to her control with absolutely no promises in return. Evil exacts all but gives nothing back. Exacted obedience. They would live now only to serve Alindra.

As their young bodies shook and their eyes, nipples and navels oozed with blood, the darkness entered their bodies and took hold. It had taken Alindra ten years—all of Baladar's life—to find these eight men and convert them. There were that few among the dungeons of the Realms and Reaches. They could not expose her nor could they disobey her. She owned them—mind, heart and soul… and body.

As the spell ended, they collapsed onto the floor, rolling off the bench. She wiped the blood from around their eyes, nipples and navels—hands and fingers lingering over their young bodies. Tonight she would consummate her relationship with these pawns barely out of their teens. As she had with the other six already in her service. As she would with any she might find in the future. There was no end to the Darkness of Alindra.

•• 14th day of 4th Month ••

"Orthon's daughter?" Miraden exclaimed. "I knew there had to be a connection! And Accosta is Alindra?"

"No doubt, Grandfather. Between the tomb and Baladar's information—I am convinced."

"And many more wives and children?"

"Well, not wives—but children, yes! All of them dead."

"This must change our approach. She has greater powers at her command than we suspected."

"Powers, yes, Grandfather—but the knowledge to use them— no. We have seen that lack of knowledge through the Portals and the Arikkans. She must be seeking that knowledge but I think there is nowhere for her to find anyone or anything with that knowledge."

"Except Dajinn."

"Yes, and Tophet. Could there be more Dajinnie?"

"I am afraid so, Daniel. But we cannot know where unless the Creators know and tell us; or unless we stumble on to them."

Daniel left for the Crystal Castle; troubled but informed. Miraden went to his books. After study, not entirely futile, there was a shimmer in the room.

•• 14th day of 4th Month ••

The Emissaries returned to Midhold to spend the night at a local inn; soak up the local culture, expand their knowledge of the Reach. As they settled into three of the six total rooms (the people here never expected too many visitors at one time) they were pampered and spoiled by the grateful Innkeepers.

"Not many people even know of Midhold, let alone stop here."

Why else would you come unless you knew someone or had business there?

The town was surrounded by a stockade of sharpened tree boles stuck upright, into the ground. It had wooden gates at each end to access the road. The houses and stores lined the two main thoroughfares with six or seven other streets where the townespeople lived. Small, compact—easy to get around in.

Midhold also lay within a day's journey by horseback from the area of Mountain Hold. Several unsavory characters (good prospects for Alindra, but, in reality, too old) entered the Inn that evening dressed in rags and wolf skins. Their horses carried fresh pelts. Traders. Trappers. Beasts. Lower than the animals they killed. Even the Midholders had as little to do with them as possible.

They complained of the few wolves left in the wild.

"Well, maybe if you took fewer there would be more for everyone!"

"The best valley we found" one trapper continued, unperturbed, "is west of the old hold there. But we couldn't even pass into it. Warding of some sort! Enchanters! They think they own the world! We found wolves in the Hold Valley, though, and eastward. These came from eastward." He fingered the pelt he was wearing. "We lost most of our snares in the Valley of the Hold." They spoke to the obvious Realmers in their midst with contempt. "Probably those Enchanters again."

They approached Ivor with their new pelts.

"Thank you, no. I prefer the fur on the animal."

The trappers looked around, shoving the pelts towards those still at dinner. All turned away from them. The trappers scowled and re-tied the pelts to their horses. They came in and threw a few coins on the table for their ale, tipped their tankards back all the way leaving the creamy foam to encrust their untamed beards and mustaches. Then they walked out into the night, mounted their horses and headed north—clearly getting the message that they weren't wanted at Midhold.

As the Circle finished their business in Midhold and cemented certain relationships there, they all 'popped' to the eastern fort on the lone point guarding the bay that overlooked Pine Island. It had been magnificent—once. The walls were still crumbling and cracking from the ice and water of the harsh seasons there; freezing and thawing. It had been substantial once and most likely was the home of Orthon and his 'family', for a time.

As they wandered through the keep at the center of the star-shaped fort they found remnants of opulent living. Far and away above anything that the citizens of this Reach enjoyed now. Sumptuous but tattered drapes and rugs, dilapidated furniture and other detritus of those who lived in their own excesses at the expense of others.

They found a library empty of all that would make it a library. The collection had probably been split between the Fortress of Fear and the Mountain Hold years ago. Despite the efforts of evil ,that collection would soon be reunited and complete—and in the hands of Miraden.

•• 15ᵗʰ day of 4ᵗʰ Month ••

Alindra, sated, rose from her bed. She dressed, then gathered her band of assassins around her. She gave them their assignment. Their target was The White DragonMount. They were to destroy as much of it as possible while taking out the meddling Enchanter Miraden. She equipped them with vials of Baladar's potion, bows and arrows, shields and a generous dose of her hatred. Each of them mimicked her moves and her moods. She was in her element now! No more pretending—no more potions to put on a false face and demeanor. She was Alindra no more—she was Accosta again—as she was born to be! She was her father's daughter and she would destroy the man who had taken her family, position, and power from her. Because now, she had the magic, the power and the opportunity! What Dajinn could not do; what Tophet and his daughters had failed at doing; what Sorcerors and Werewolves and Necromancers and Dwarves and Vampires had been incapable of—that is where she would succeed. The greatest of all the Forces of Light, the last surviving Enchanter of the Creators would die—not by her hand—but by her design!

ᙢᒪ

CHAPTER NINE—
SURPRISE AFTER SURPRISE

•• 15th day of 4th Month ••

The shimmer appearing at the White DragonMount soon filled with the forms of Aloshtu, Kalaal, Serrantu, a cabinet, a trunk and a boy. Miraden looked up from the book he was almost buried in. He welcomed his Circle friends and they introduced him to Baladar. He was most pleased and Baladar was charmed by the old man. Baladar handed him the book and map in his own arms with great respect.

"These should help in Aradon, Sir."

"Your mother's?"

Baladar shook his head. "My Father's. My Mother never told me much about him."

"Accosta?"

"No, Alindra."

"Her name, with Dajinn—your father, used to be Accosta. She is the daughter of my nephew, Orthon. Which makes you my great-grand-nephew and Orthon's grandson."

Baladar looked up in fear at the old man, searching for some slight sign of condemnation, or at least disapproval; but he found none in the kind face and gentle eyes of the Enchanter.

"How old is she?"

"Over two-thousand years old."

"How old are you?"

"Nearly, three-thousand."

"But you don't look a day over a hundred."

Miraden laughed. The others in the room joined him. "A Enchanter's life is charmed. But as old as that? Are you sure?"

"Well, I don't really know. Even Aloshtu is beginning to look old to me—Sir."

There was more laughter.

Miraden, holding the book and the map, motioned the boy over to the table where he had spread out the items. He urged Baladar to lead him through what the boy had discovered and the old man was alternately concerned and overjoyed at the information available. Baladar, after all, was only almost-ten and his ordeal at Twelve Towers had tired him out completely. He fell asleep with his head on the table as Miraden asked him a question. Miraden picked him up and laid him in Elias' old bed with a protective warding over him so that Alindra... Accosta... what's-her-name, couldn't find him, if indeed, she wanted to. She certainly had the power to do so; but why take chances?

The three Taradal told Miraden of their own discoveries and also of what Baladar, had told them of himself.

"He is of my blood," the old man said.

"But is he a danger?"

"I do not know. I can't see how he could be after all he has come through, seemingly unscathed."

The hunters nodded. They too, wanted Baladar to be free of the evil that had plagued both sides of his family.

"How could Dajinn's son be anything but a Dajinn?" Serrantu reasoned, looking between Kalaal and Baladar.

"How could Accosta's son not be like her after being raised by no one else but her?" was Aloshtu's question as he looked at Kalaal.

Kalaal just looked right back at all of them and smiled. For he, too, was Accosta's 'son'. He had escaped her without permanent harm. It was certainly possible for Baladar to have also done that. There was something about Accosta—something disingenuous— that repelled, you; that said to you that something was not right about her. Children know this; can sense it—innately.

The known events of the Baladar's life, as calamitous as their import was, as confusing as those events were, showed that a clear light was left in the boy.

"I will test him."

The hunters nodded again. "If we can help in any way, we will. If he has broken the curse of his blood we want to celebrate with him as he is also one of ours!"

Miraden smiled and the four dug into the extrapolations between the marks on the map and the information in the book.

They, too, soon grew tired, as the boy had, and retired to the extra beds in Daniel's old room while Miraden crept into his hammock hanging near the wall of his laboratory.

He was pensive. He tried to wrap the wisdom of nearly three-thousand years around the problems, challenges, doubts and events of the last few years. He tried to bring his immense reserve of knowledge to bear and he became not less certain, but certainly, not more sure.

As he slept, he was called, and his great-grandson spoke to him for the first time from Colabos.

"Grandfather—simplify!"

Miraden stirred.

"You know too much—simplify!"

Miraden tossed.

"The only way to eat a Curelom is one bite at a time."

•• 16th day of 4th Month ••

Alan was lagging behind. This was his first quest, he was only fifteen—well, so was Evermon! Alan, however, had never been out of Aradon and Evermon was used to traveling all over the Realms. Alan was just busy taking it all in. There was nothing wrong with him physically or mentally. He was just being observant. He was on overload. Evermon was certainly not noticing everything around him—as he should have been doing. Miraden had said he was to watch and protect Holder before they had left a few days ago. Now, here they were approaching the entrance to the Shifting Forest and he was still studying Holder; taking stock and having the pieces not add up. What was it about the Harper that intrigued him? A thought flashed through Evermon's mind but was quickly dismissed. If he was certain of anything he was certain of the fact that he liked girls. Boys as friends and comrades were just fine. But that was where he drew the line. He had often watched the castle maids as they bathed. He knew he liked what he saw. He had enjoyed his spying for much too long and far too often as he hid behind the wall near the pool—young and unseen and unsuspected. He may be a Prince—full of promise and strength—but he was still a young and curious male. He knew it wasn't simply curiosity that drew him to the maids. His body told him many things that he was sometimes embarrassed to admit to himself, let alone others.

There was still something about Holder that puzzled him—drew him in. He had to know because he really liked him.

Nathan had already found the puzzle at the opening of the forest while Evermon was daydreaming and not noticing things. Each time Nathan stepped up to it, it opened showing two paths, just like Miraden had said it would. Then he stepped back and it closed up. Each time he approached the opening the paths seemed to lead to different destinations.

"What are you doing, Dad?" inquired Alan as the others came up around them.

"Watch."

He advanced again. The paths opened. He retreated and the paths closed. He repeated the exercise to discover different paths each time. After about fifteen minutes Holder spoke up.

"There is a pattern—have you noticed? There are seven pairs of paths. After the seventh one passes the first one repeats again and so on."

"Which pair are we supposed to choose?"

"And which of the two do we walk down?"

"Miraden said only to choose the right path."

Alan spoke—"I don't think that he meant that we should choose only the correct path." They all looked at him. "We should choose the path on the right—The Right Path; and he laughed a goofy-teenagery-boy-like laugh. The rest joined him, leaving out the goofiness, and patted him on the back. There can be wisdom in youth. After all, Miraden had been told to simplify.

"So, which pair of paths?"

"We had no specific instructions about which pair so I don't think it will matter," offered Evermon.

They all agreed. Alan stepped forward and the trees opened up. A path of clear, bright green extended to the left and a path of shadows beckoned them to the right. Alan stepped to the right and the others followed and the trees folded closed behind them. The path was cool and as they stepped out of the soon-to-be summer heat they felt a peace. If nothing else the shade would help them endure the walk.

•• 16th day of 4th Month ••

Miraden laughed in his sleep not aware of the three rocks that came sailing in through the opening of the White DragonMount. They hit the right side of the corridor and exploded, causing the roof of Elias' old room to cave in, the arch to the laboratory to collapse and other doorways along the right side to be weakened and fall. Serrantu, Aloshtu and Kalaal were in the arch of Daniel's room, on the left side of the tunnel, hiding in the smoke, having been blasted out of their beds.

Three bolts of lightning penetrated through the dust as they shot towards the cave's opening. Two screams were heard. The three hunters ran through the tunnel and witnessed eight men disappear into a Dark Portal just spans away from the entrance to the White DragonMount. The Portal went black and inert, then vanished into invisibility. Lightning flashed again and the Portal reappeared, shimmered and exploded leaving tree limbs and rock dust settling to the earth.

Aloshtu looked down the path leading from the cave where he had almost tripped over a human arm. One lightning bolt must have hit true. Then Miraden nearly 'popped' on top of the three Taradal.

As they steadied the old man, who was visibly shaken, he asked: "Where's Baladar?"

•• 16th day of 4th Month ••

Accosta was waiting at the Portal of the Castle of the North as her assistants, one armless, another limping, appeared in front of her. The lightning had cauterized the stump of the arm so that there was no blood, just the stump; and it had charred the flesh of the limper's leg. She 'popped' them to the castle. Her laboratory was empty—destroyed by the Circle, no doubt! She 'popped' to her cabin at Purple Lake and combined several ingredients and bathed her young men's wounds in the restorative balm.

She loved to play the 'healer,' but it wasn't for the healing itself.

"We only had time for three of the rocks but the right side of the cave is demolished."

"Who shot at you?"

"We didn't stay to find out."

"And Miraden?"

"We don't know."

"You don't know?"

They were silent. Tense. Cowed.

"He knows someone is after him now!" screamed Accosta.

"But will he know who?"

"Or when we will come again?"

"I don't see how he can, My Queen," spoke the armless one.

"We will try again and again. You will succeed in killing the old fool!"

•• 14th day of 4th Month ••

"Please, Miraden, help me! I'm scared."

The rock and earth pressed tightly around the boy in his bubbled warding. He felt like he couldn't breathe. It wasn't like shrinking his warding. He couldn't see anything!

"Focus on the sound of my voice!—See me in the corridor. You have been here. 'Pop' to me!"

Pop!

Baladar had made it out without a scratch on his body. His mind and emotions, though, were considerably rumpled. The warding Miraden had placed had indeed protected him from Accosta. She fortunately or unfortunately, hadn't had a clue that he was even there. The boy clung to Miraden, who comforted him and eased his anxiety.

"The room filled with rock. I couldn't see! I couldn't breathe!"

Miraden picked the boy up and with the three Taradal 'popped' to Dolah Tok. He would ask the Elves for sanctuary.

As Baladar listened to the description of the attack on the cave; as he learned of the explosions and who had engineered the raid—his mother—he began to cry. Aral, the Elven Hegemon, turned to the boy, noticing how upset he was.

"Baladar, do you know something, anything that will help us?"

Baladar nodded. It was hard. Oh, so hard!

"What is it?"

"The explosions...?"

"Yes?"

"I know how it was done." *But I can't tell you!* remained unspoken.

"How do you know that?"

A breath. A sigh. A biting of his lip. "Because it was the last thing I invented before my mother banished me. She must be using my invention."

He told them about the cabin and the lake; his talent at alchemy; the mixture in the vials and what it does when it dries and comes into sharp contact with other, solid things. He told them of his tests.

"Take us there!"

Baladar, Miraden, Aloshtu, Serrantu and Kalaal joined hands. Baladar had never taken others with him before. He was nervous but he soon felt the shared power of the others rushing through him. It gave him confidence. He thought of the shore by the lake in front of the cabin.

And they were there!

He had done it! Even though Miraden and Aloshtu were standing in the lake instead of beside it, they were there.

They slogged out of the ankle deep water and dried themselves off with magic air. Then they proceeded into the cabin with Baladar in the lead. The boy showed them the potion in the vials. Miraden worked quickly to enward it all with three purples. Then he levitated it all out onto the lakeshore. He, Aloshtu, Serrantu and Kalaal began to tear the cabin apart, piece by piece. Baladar stood there, stunned. Even Enchanters could destroy! He had only witnessed Sorcerors and Sorceresses being destructive. The Enchanters left the chimney standing. Miraden looked down at Baladar and nodded his head toward the standing column of bricks and stones. Baladar pointed to himself and Miraden smiled.

Baladar threw his hands towards the chimney.

Nothing.

Baladar tensed. He could not fail! This was a test. He thought of Alindra. Which made him think of Dajinn. Both of them had thrown him away! In his rising anger he struck out his hand towards the chimney. It cracked, shattered and exploded. It vanished! There was nothing left of it but dust in the air. No large chunks—no little bits—just powder. The five Enchanters watched it, astounded as powder settled to the earth.

Miraden looked at his Circle members with considerable alarm.

•• 16th day of 4th Month ••

Accosta focused her thoughts and energies on her cabin at the lake. She called the vials of explosive compound to her. Nothing appeared on the table. She tried again. She could not see them! Why were they not here? One more try! Nothing. She screamed as she 'popped' to the cabin and her scream continued with her across the leagues from the Castle of the North to the Purple Lake of Aradon where she stood in front of a gaping blackened hole in the ground. No cabin. No potion. No nothing.

•• 16th day of 4th Month ••

Miraden and Baladar returned to the cave to pick up the items they would need to unravel the puzzle that plagued them. They called the books, maps and scrolls through the rubble of the door to Miraden's lab and sat them on a table in a room next to Daniel's—nearer to the cave entrance. The three hunters went straight to Dolah Tok to confer again with Aral and the MerElves.

Miraden decided that he had better talk to the boy privately before others raised damaging questions. Why did it always fall to him to lead boy-Enchanters into adulthood? He had done this very same thing with Daniel, Elias, Timothy, Arik, Boncaster—and others—but never with one so young and so powerful as Baladar.

Baladar was worried as he stood in a nearly empty room containing only books, scrolls and a table. Miraden had told him to stay there while he put a warding over the mouth of the cave—and stay there he would. Frightened. Alone. When the Enchanter returned he looked stern but not unkind. Baladar couldn't imagine Miraden being unkind, but the boy was still worried.

"I need to be blunt with you, Baladar. You have a more than impressive ability. No one I ever knew has ever been so young with so much power—not even Daniel. The power in you comes from both sides of your family."

"But they never knew."

"Never knew what?"

"That I had any power."

"You have had no training?"

"None—except the alchemy I learned from my mother."

Why must our children, gifted or not, go unnoticed in a world bent on self-possession?

Miraden considered for a moment and proceeded. "I am going to tell you something anyway. You made a mistake today—a very dangerous one."

Baladar blanched and tears began to fill his eyes. "But... I..."

"Now, now. It's something that you can learn not to do. I hadn't realized how little you knew about your magic."

"What can I learn not to do?" The eyes of the boy were bright with hope.

"You used your anger to destroy the chimney. I felt it in you."

"It worked," he said sullenly.

"Yes. It did. And it always will."

"You and the others tore the whole house apart!"

"Yes, we did—but how did we do it—and why?"

"You just did it."

"I sensed your anger at your parents—it was most alarming, Baladar. You used that to motivate you. We must never use anger to gain the power to work our magic. Or else we can become like Dajinn—or Tophet."

Baladar almost said something. He almost reacted out of pride and anger. Almost. Instead, he did a most unchildlike thing. "Then how did you do it?"

Miraden smiled in amazement at the ability of this boy. "Accosta and your cabin were a threat to our safety and to the well-being of everyone in the Realms and Reaches. We called on the power of the Creators—of Dal, if you wish—to remove that threat. To protect us."

"And I used my hatred to try and destroy her."

Miraden was astounded. This little boy had grasped immediately a very difficult concept. "Very good, Baladar. I knew you were bright."

"But I still did wrong."

"Doing something wrong doesn't mean that you are not bright. We all make mistakes—before we know about something. Even me."

Baladar looked up at Miraden. "How could you make a mistake?"

"I made one today. I asked you to do something for which you were not prepared. I should have prepared you first."

"So we both failed your test, huh?"

"Yes, Baladar, we did. And I will never ask you again to pass a test I have not prepared you for."

Miraden placed his arm around the boy's shoulders and they 'popped' up to the shores of Salah Mal, the lake over Dolah Tok. They walked in silence in the warm Spring air and Baladar thrilled to the feeling of confidence that Miraden had in him; the sensation that someone alive cared who he was; even 'that' he was. He had never had a father who was a real father to him; his own dying before he was five. The boy, astute and eager, figured that even if he hadn't died, Dajinn would never have been a true father. He looked up at Miraden again.

"Where does your power come from if not from what you feel?"

"What do you feel when you transport somewhere or create a warding?"

Baladar thought. "I feel I have to... I just have to do it."

"Why?"

"It's important to me."

"Yes... ?" Miraden encouraged.

"There's more?!" Baladar asked in consternation as he contorted his face, perplexed.

"Yes," Miraden laughed.

Baladar knit his brows and struggled with the concept Miraden was seeking from him. "Because... because it was the right thing to do?"

Miraden smiled. Baladar looked up again, not having heard an answer from the man. When he saw the light in Miraden's eyes he knew he had answered correctly. They walked on in silence again until they came to a particular spot Miraden had been searching for. They stopped. "There is always a right time, also" was Miraden's advice.

Baladar looked out at the bright, blue waters of the Mal, the lake. He was filled with wonder... and millions of questions. Could Miraden ever answer them all?

"Who does Evermon pray to?"

"I would assume, the Creators. Why?"

"He prayed every night. He was going to teach me but we got—we got banished." Silence. "Evermon is good, isn't he?"

"As I understand it he is very good, but not perfect. No one is perfect."

"Even you?"

"Even me."

"I want to be perfect. Can I?"

Miraden looked at him, surprised. "It is the Creators fondest wish for us."

"So praying is kind of like magic, huh?"

"Yes, Baladar—it is exactly like magic. It is the magic we ask the Creators to allow ourselves to work within us."

And with that he happily took Baladar's hand and leaped up into the air, hauling the screaming boy with him, no longer earthbound.

"Miraden—I can't swim!"

They hit the surface of the water. Baladar was in a panic. They continued downward. Miraden squeezed the boy's hand in reassurance. Baladar tried to hold his breath. Miraden shook his head. They sank and sank—the bright blue becoming deeper and deeper—richer, fuller.

Then Miraden moved his free hand and they slid from the water into the air beneath it and Dolah Tok shone up at them in all its brilliance; the golden Palac below, where Aral, Aloshtu, Kalaal and Serrantu awaited their arrival. Baladar felt free. Empowered. Good. Miraden felt a wave of reassurance wash over him as his feet touched the Palac and they were welcomed by friends.

•• 16ᵗʰ day of 4ᵗʰ Month ••

The throne of Aradon was empty. No King. No Queen. No Princess. No Second Queen. It had been five days since the double disappearance of Evermon and Baladar. Now even Alindra was gone.

Gladenwreath and the Chamberlain were meeting with the Circle Council of Aradon—minus Nathan. Aradon needed a Prince Regent. King Emeron's brother, Evermon's uncle—the current Ambassador to Caladon—was Alfrond, the only one with the right to hold the throne until the return of the rightful King. An epistle was sent and Alfrond and Elayda, Testra and Palanca, came home. The citizens celebrated their return. Well-loved and sorely-missed, Alfrond spent the next few weeks undoing the damage of Alindra.

•• 19ᵗʰ day of 4ᵗʰ Month ••

Gladenwreath, Kwuktw and Sean (Elias' older son) were summoned to the crumbling halls of the Castle in Zanadon by Miraden. The Dwarf, in full armor, was a startling contrast to the Skwatwael Prince in his simple white chiton. Sean was somewhere in the middle dressed in his sturdy hunting clothes.

Miraden had unfolded what he had found out about the prison of the Queen of Aradon from the ancient books; discovered only through the assistance of Baladar with his books, scrolls and maps and Aloshtu, Kalaal and Serrantu. Estrella's book proved itself to be especially useful.

"The directions must be followed; you cannot backtrack. It is very clear. If you get lost you must start over at the border of

Caladon."

The Dwarf huffed; as if he could get lost!

"The three of you—all travelers—must begin and end together."

"So that's why we can't just 'pop' to the Rock?" asked Sean.

"Precisely. The path to the Rock is part of the key to accessing it."

"Do we have a time limit?"

"None. As quickly as you are able will be sufficient!"

"Miraden, I am ready for the directions—I am anxious to be off."

"I understand, Noble Dwarf."

During trials, quests and service Dwarves were the most patient of beings, but when they were unoccupied—they were the least impatient.

Miraden looked at the three and then read from the scroll in his hands. It was penned in Old Speak, and he translated for the others.

"Follow the Polestar north until the stars of the Archer bisect, at a right angle, the line drawn between the Polestar and the horizon."

The Dwarf nodded.

"Then follow in the direction of the Archer's pointing arrow until the Bear comes over the horizon at midnight—you will then be far beyond the borders of the Realms of the Crystal Orb at this point. From there, under the belly of the Bear, you will see the Ice Castle. Step from that spot and it will vanish. As you step from the spot there will be a cairn. Solve its riddle and proceed."

"What riddle?" asked Sean.

"It does not specify the riddle, Master Matthewson."

Gladenwreath, the most talented of all the navigators of the most accurate of the Dwarven Clans of navigators grunted his understanding. With a handshake and a nod each of those on the quest bade farewell to Miraden.

•• 20th day of 4th Month ••

Accosta was desperate. Something had to go her way. She and

her crippled but elite guard planned something bold. Without warning they blew up the Rooms of the Talisman in Mirador, Panador and Caladon and took possession of the Frosted Flask, The Blood Rose and the Golden Sceptre. With these actions they incapacitated the Dwarves of the Realms. They didn't obliterate them—there was not enough time. For magic is one thing and explosives are entirely another. Even most magic has no guard against explosions. The Realms reeled from the shock of the loss of its Talismans and the injury of the Dwarves. The power of the Orb was not destroyed, but it was surely weakened. Accosta was exultant because she had done alone what all those before her had failed to do with armies and treachery.

"If I'd known that it was going to be this easy, I would have done it this way years ago!"

•• 21st day of 4th Month ••

The Circle went into action from every corner of the continent. This was a monumental attack and very unexpected! Everyone in the Circle knew who had done it. Accosta had been frustrated at being denied Miraden—her prize. Now he was in hiding—and no one knew where. He appeared at certain places but no one traveled with him who hadn't come from his hiding place. There were so many places for him to hide. She would find him, eventually. Until she did she would be playing a shell game of her own. She had resources. Wherever she went, the Talismans went with her. She had magicked together a chest with black lining. It had room to display her trophies: the Frosted Flask, The Blood Rose and the Golden Sceptre—all looking equally splendid against the background of black. With a flip of the lid she was packed and could travel anywhere.

She used the three Northern Reaches very much as her husband had used them. She shuffled from one castle—one new cave—one forest glade—to another as her base of operations kept shifting. She could always be near a Portal. She could strike at will and return to hide or seek a new lair as she had prepared dozens for this very eventuality.

She also learned of the existence of the Talismans of the

Southern and Eastern Reaches. She went, after them. All, except for Plateau Taradal, had never revealed the location of their Talismans let alone the general knowledge that they even existed. The populace had no knowledge and she had no leverage to learn their secrets. She did know of the Morphalls and the Alimorphs. It had been well-touted—the addition of the first Out-Reach to the Realms in thousands of years. She soon found the home of the "Dagger of Fire."

The Circle, now on full alert, patrolled, scouted—searched the continent. Nothing south of the Northern Reaches could hide her. Too many loyal Realmers, and those pledged to support the Crystal Orb. So by finding nothing the Circle had narrowed the search area: The Northern Reaches—all three—became the target for the members of the Circle of Light.

One hundred and forty-four Circle members, except for a few from Caladon and Aradon who were on other equally important quests, took to the skies over the north. Then, with the Circle busily distracted, Accosta struck.

Accosta spent hours in front of her mirror perfecting her disguise. With every imperfection found she raised her wand and tweaked the errant physical feature or article of clothing into place. She became an old Taradal woman. Her raven hair now greyed and frazzled. She would approach the Morphalls in their cave asking for a blessing from the protectors of the Talisman. Something that pleased them immensely to be able to provide.

As she penetrated the Room of the Talisman, deep in the mountains of the central plateau she distracted she six Morphalls on guard and 'popped' her accomplices to the arch of the room's entrance. They appeared behind the Morphalls who scattered as the eleven rocks coated with the potion Baladar had called 'Poof' exploded against the walls and pedestal where the Talisman was held. The Talisman flew into the air at Accosta's command but Tonar, ever watchful, grabbed it and, with his fellows, turned to a being of Light and fled the room. Accosta was left empty handed and missing two more of her elite guards as they laid on the floor of the cave burned to a crisp and smouldering after the Dagger itself had shot fire at them from Tonar's hands. Accosta 'popped' the six survivors to the Castle of the Rock—her Ice Palace. She still had the Talismans—the three she had already stolen. The magic of the Realms would not function for too much longer. That could only mean that her power and influence would increase.

What she didn't know was that there were six other Talismans holding the fabric of the Orb and Sceptre together—seven if you counted the missing or hidden Gentle Jewels.

ML

CHAPTER TEN—
SEARCHING BUT NOT FINDING

•• 21st day of 4th Month ••

Accosta spent some time strengthening the wardings around her Ice Palace they had been built into the very fabric of the palace since its very inception by the original builders. These were wardings no Human or Enchanter could break. She was pleased that her Dark Magic had fortified what she counted as her finest creation.

The original warding had invisifed the entire structure. If you could see it; if you were able to gaze upon its wonder you would believe you were in another world. It was composed of tall, fluted columns of white marble and limestone, each nestled next to the other, co-created with Estrella, Miraden's sister and Accosta's aunt. Accosta had now topped them with graceful spires of clear, solidly frozen ice. Not what you would expect from Accosta, because it was quite strikingly beautiful. The Rock would be cold throughout the year now, as a warding that kept the island frozen and so cold that the Ice Palace would remain intact had been fortified by the Sorceress.

If you were to stand on Slipper Isle, or Pine Island for that matter, and look across The Rock towards Troll Island you would see nothing but a bald hump of stone arching out of the greenish-blue waters of the northern ocean. You would miss the most astounding creation on the entire continent. How like Accosta to hide the beauty around her. There had to have been beauty in Accosta's heart before she helped create it—eons ago. But then she must've poured it all into the creation of this palace, leaving behind a soul—colder than the ice that made up her palace spires, and emptier than the Rock itself appeared through its warding.

Once inside the grand and graceful ebony doors of the outer entrance your eyes are drawn upwards again with the elegant vertical movement of the fluted column motif which was duplicated, in reverse, on the inside of the structure. One room seemed to flow into another with large open archways leading off a central, circular hall and above everything the endless spires of ice, translucently refracting the sun's rays to the floor of the palace.

To think that this place was used only as the prison of a Queen. How contradictory! How anti-useful! Not so strange when you understand that Accosta was a woman of contradictions— Alindra had been one of those—and she certainly had little use out in the world of the Realms.

Due to the safety she felt here, she placed each of the three stolen Talismans, and the receptacle especially designed for it, in a separate room off the central hall. As they seated themselves in their new homes they began to sing. Red and gold and white lights danced, merged and played through and on the flutings of the palace itself. This was, after all, a Palace of Power. That had been Estrella's intent.

With her six remaining guards at the door, the only ingress or egress to the palace, also limited by the several wardings; she felt that she was safe from intrusion. She entered a room that was nothing if not the inside of a conch-shell spiraling downward into the rock. It was pearlescent and pink. She glided down the ramped walkway, still caught up in a world of her own making—a Queen of grace and power—holding on to the ebony handrail, until she arrived at what looked to be a block of ice several hundred arms below the level of the floor of the main hall.

As she reached the bottom she walked to the block of ice and the waters in the floor leaped up to bar the way in front of her. She raised her hand and the waters calmed back down into their pool. She stood and looked at the ice cube as it hovered above the pool of water over its own little island. A smile creased her face as she was reassured that it still held the frozen form of the Queen of

Aradon.

Somehow, through Accosta's magic and the casting of the spell of suspension, the Queen's life-force had been magically tied to her own. There is always a sacrifice required for the use of magic with this magnitude of power. It had also happened with the King and the Prince. She could not kill them without losing most or all of her own life-force. She had at first tried to put the Queen to death but almost died herself. Dark Magic demanded a way to keep the Queen alive but not necessarily aware. So, Accosta had frozen her in a blast of ice, placing her in a suspended animation and preserving both their lives.

As Accosta looked closely at the frozen Queen, she noticed something she had not seen before. Queen Rose of Aradon was smiling and her eyes were open. It was most unsettling. The eyes in the ice didn't follow her when she moved around—they just stared straight forward—but they were still disturbing to her.

She couldn't bear up under the gaze of those piercing eyes. The guilt over a King, a Queen, and Princes—a son—all weighed too heavily on that very minute particle of goodness still within the heart of Accosta. It was enough to make her look away and 'pop' back to the top of the spiral walkway.

She moved to her laboratory and summoned from each of her castles every ingredient and useful item she could remember. She emptied out her castles. Here—she was safe. She consulted her scrolls and began weaving spells as wisps of blue, black, red and orange smoke intertwined and made fanciful shapes of Darkness in the brightness of the Ice Palace room.

•• 22nd day of 4th Month ••

Circle members scoured the Castle of the North but it was empty. They swarmed over every speck of space, through all levels and every room of the fortification, finding it empty and Accosta-free. Feeling safe, they enwarded it with a series of fifteen powerful colored wardings making it absolutely impenetrable to anyone without the proper warding reversal.

•• 22ⁿᵈ day of 4ᵗʰ Month ••

Accosta whirled the smoke, shaping it—moulding it. It took on a slightly human outline as she spoke the incantation:

"Callad-asta-dalar-genille-dajillat."

The smoky forms became a whirling reality of Darkness—Wraiths. She had called forth a spectral, ethereal army of sword-wielding Wraiths with which she would populate her palace.

Two of her guards were magicked into her laboratory after collecting cages and crates full of animals from nearby Pine Island. These animals she magicked into Demons—small, red and unbelievably vicious. They were held behind bars in a room off the central hall. If the front doors were ever opened without the proper spell being spoken the bars would disappear and Dal help the intruders—whoever they were.

With a room full of Demons, a palace full of Wraiths and six loyal, young guards, Accosta now felt invincible. She was surrounded with everything she had desired—youth, beauty and power. Yet, other than the Queen in the dungeons below, the Ice Palace was an empty space.

•• 17ᵗʰ day of 4ᵗʰ Month ••

The shadowy path in the forest was basically unremarkable; until the questers came to a writhing mass of snakes coiled across their way. As they stepped to the side of the path to skirt the cadre of serpents, the trees seemed to reach out and push them backwards onto the path again. They were not going to get around this.

"Well," Alan said, "if we can't get around it, the only thing left to do is to go through it!"

"You're crazy as a Dryad, Alan!"

"No, Evermon—I'm not. It's the only way."

Evermon looked at Holder who looked at Nathan who glanced to his son. They all shrugged their shoulders, deferring to the wisdom of the lad, and stepped forward expecting to be bitten and constricted by the fangs and coils of the snakes before them. Instead, Alan, in the lead, giggled. The others rushed to him and he responded:

"It's all right. It tickles."

They were all feeling it now. It was only an illusion—to test them. They came to the sudden and stunning conclusion that the Right Path would never harm them! No matter how dangerous it looked.

•• 19th day of 4th Month ••

The Dwarf and his companions had spent the day along the River of Sadness and the River of Fear. They had passed the Fortress of Fear and had found the road that led north through the Forest of Fear and into Caladon. The passage through the Forest of Fear was no longer fraught with evil dangers. They saw animals, normal and healthy—along with a very few aberrations, but nothing troubled them and they certainly bothered no one.

As darkness came upon them they had reached Havenwood to stay with the Arik Archer family. Arik was off on another quest (told of in the next volume) so they missed him. Early the next morning they arose and proceeded to the border between Caladon and the Great Northwestern Reaches. Here they would stay until night time when they would pick up the sign of the Polestar. From now on they would travel at night and rest during the day. Gladenwreath was excited.

•• 21st day of 4th Month ••

While Gladenwreath's party was moving out of Zanadon, Miraden was presenting a magic puzzle—a conundrum—to Baladar. The boy was locked and chained, tied, gagged, enwarded and cursed with a spell of silence as he hung, upside-down, suspended in the center of a locked dungeon in Zanadon, in only his loin-wrap. Miraden sat placidly outside the locked cell door.

He first heard a lock click and a chain come clanging to the bottom of the warding. He turned and through the barred window he saw the rope around Baladar's ankles and legs un-knot itself and slowly unravel, rapt concentration on the boy's face. The rope continued to unravel like the wrappings of a mummy from around his body and soon his legs were free.

The rope around his arms and torso loosened and began to fall away. Baladar worked his hands and arms. His wrists were still bound. Miraden saw the sweat on the boy's body, where the lines of the ropes had left a slight impression across his skin; he was really working. Then a rope dropped from behind the boy, crumpling to the bottom of the warding.

Baladar squirmed in discomfort as the chain that supported him, that had been wrapped around his loin-wrap at each hip, tugged even more tightly and bit into his hips. Miraden smiled and sat down again. He heard a popping sound, a small 'snap.' All of a sudden a gag was wrapped around Miraden's own mouth and head. He startled and stood, peering through the window at the giggling, smiling, ecstatic boy standing on his bare feet in the locked cell.

Miraden was amazed as he reached up to his own mouth and took the gag away. The boy had powers over cloth, metal, rope, locks. He could 'pop!' He then heard a click, click, whirr of the tumblers in the lock on the cell door and the beaming boy stepped through. He reached out and hugged the administrator of his test:

"Thank you, Uncle—that was fun!"

Fun?!? Miraden was floored. The boy, in addition to all the other magic defeated, had subverted a silencing spell!

"How?"

"I don't know. I just saw the warding around my vocal chords and unwrapped it like I did the ropes."

Miraden kneeled down and hugged the boy to him. He would need no more tests! Baladar was a walking miracle and would be trained and guided in the proper use of his immense gift.

•• 17th day of 4th Month ••

Evermon's party approached a bend in the path. As they rounded it they saw no path in front of them. It just ended.

"I guess it's time to choose again. Holder?"

Holder stepped forward and the foliage parted and pointed away from them in two directions. Again, the left path was bright and sunny—birds and animals in abundance. The right path led through a dark and dismal swamp. Holder apologetically pointed right and the group, somewhat morosely walked on.

•• 21st day of 4th Month ••

The Polestar was bright and unmistakable in the northern sky. Gladenwreath saw the Archer, down lower on the horizon. There was no right angle—yet. They walked forward, the first step on a long journey. Gladenwreath looked over at the near-nakedness of the MerPrince.

"Did you bring anything warmer?"

"I have no need. I can shift my body's temperature to meet the cold or the warmth. I only wear this to spare you and the others the sight of my nakedness."

"Thank the Creators fer that!"

And they walked on—straight toward the Polestar.

•• 21st day of 4th Month ••

The fire was in the grate. The Enchanter and his apprentice were reading from large, bound volumes as the moonlight streamed through the tower window of Castle Zanadon. They were still in hiding.

"Miraden?"

"Yes, Baladar?"

"I found something you're not going to like."

Miraden peered over the boy's shoulder at the manuscript he had been reading, following the boy's finger as he outlined the troubling text.

Miraden tilted his head and looked at the boy. "I didn't know you could read Trollen! How can you read Trollen?"

"I don't know. I just can. It says that the warding of the Ice Palace cannot be broken by Human hands. So whose hands can break it?"

Miraden pondered as he perused the manuscript. It was an ancient writing and only that one phrase was in Trollen. The rest was in New Speak. "Maybe the one that can read it can break the warding."

"Both of us can read it, Uncle, and we're both Human and it says Humans can't break the warding."

"Who else can read Trollen?"

"Trolls."

"Then a Troll must break the warding!"

Baladar smiled at his mentor. He felt better about the old man than he had ever felt about his own mother.

•• 22nd day of 4th Month ••

Accosta had been exhausted after the creation of her magical guardians, but she needed one more safeguard. If the Palace was breached—if the cube was found—if the shield was passed—if the ice was touched—then what? She tied a spell to the touch of an outside hand or tool to the ice.

"*Charlanta-asta-eleph-charlanta.*"

The sound of the air being sucked out of the room as it whirled around made Accosta cover her ears. Then the whooshing air streamed into the floor under the huge ice cube containing the Queen. Accosta was content but if she thought of something else—she would make that happen too!

•• 22nd day of 4th Month ••

Miraden and Baladar stood in the King's room, in front of the High Throne of Urk—the Troll King. They explained their predicament, but Urk was reluctant. He was still upset over the death of the Hero of the Trolls—the boy, Boncaster.

Baladar did a daring thing—he 'popped' to a sitting position on the Troll King's knee—high over his own head, if he were to be still standing on the floor.

"King Urk, one of the evil ones who killed Boncaster will be defeated if you help us," Trollen words sounding oddly on the boy's lips.

The giant face of the Troll bent closely to the tiny boy on his knee.

"Besides, Great King, today is my tenth birthday. And this would be a wonderful present to me and also to the memory of the great and noble Boncaster!"

The giant face in front of the boy nodded and began to laugh.

"I like this new boy, Miraden. He is a smart one."

"Indeed he is." Miraden remarked, dumbfounded at the wisdom and audacity of the child and surprised and pleased that it was his birthday. The boy had told no one.

"Who will you send, Noble King?"

"I will send no one!"

"But...?"

"I will go myself!"

All in the room were dumbstruck. Had the boy bewitched their King? Or had the King merely been as charmed by the lad as they all had been? Does it matter? It worked!

The Troll King was going to help!

•• 22nd day of 4th Month ••

As the Dwarf, the MerPrince and the Son-of-the-Circle strode on into the night of the Northern Reach, where the Archer's Arrow had pointed them northeast, Miraden and a boy and a mountain of flesh stood in front of them, blocking their journey. It had been a long walk for all.

After introductions and explanations, and the reversal of an interrupted trek had been made, Miraden and Baladar 'popped' home leaving the group of four to begin the journey again at the border between Caladon and the Great Northwestern Reaches.

To cover the ground more quickly a harness that suspended three pouches was hung across the giant's broad chest. Sean and Kwuktw hopped into their traveling compartments. Gladenwreath, still preferring the power of his own legs, reluctantly climbed into his. The Dwarf was soon content and amazed as they sped along to their goal—where the right angle of the Archer bisected the line from the Polestar. The Troll had made up any loss of time in less than an hour. The Dwarf sighted and Urk strode on to the Northeast, heading for a distant mountain range and eating away the leagues with his stride. Finally, Gladenwreath admitted that it was faster. Not better! But faster.

•• 18th day of 4th Month ••

The swamp had been hot and humid. All but Holder had stripped to their waist. Evermon smiled. He was becoming more sure each day.

There had been no traps, no dangerous creatures in this

swamp. It was like an incomplete imitation of the real thing—a shadow. It had been unpleasant but not dangerous. As they stood there in the muck and the mire, what appeared as a great hedge at the edge of the bayou opened. Two clear and sparkling pathways were displayed before them. Evermon, for the third time on the journey, chose the Right Path and they dripped from the water to the dry dirt of the path that led to a giant clearing.

As they entered the clearing they were beset and besieged by swarms of insects. Stinging. Biting. Buzzing. Huge, hairy swarms descended on them. They ran about swatting and screaming. The bugs filled their mouths, ears, noses and eyes and dug their way under their clothing, biting them in places bugs don't normally reach. They ran back to the path—Alan dragging them farther back into its perceived safety. The buzzing around them stopped. After a few more twitches and itches and many well-placed slaps, the bugs ceased their buzzing and the air cleared. Evermon, Alan and Nathan ripped off their clothes and in their loin-wraps shook them out, beat them against trees, trying to get them bug-free. Holder was riffling his hair and he noticed that the boys were busy, so he slipped into the woods behind a tree and shook out his clothes and reappeared as the others were getting dressed.

"Where'd you go?"

"I had to take care of business. I know we're brothers and all—but we don't have to share everything!"

The three males laughed, leaving Holder to join them. After debugging, they sat and ate some bread and cheese. They could hear the insects waiting for them down the path—mandibles and probosci flexing in anticipation. Then Nathan stood.

"Personal wardings!"

"That's fine for you and Alan but Holder and I have no magical powers."

"Not necessary. I can enward both Holder and Evermon. Alan can take care of himself."

Within five minutes four people with purple patinas paraded past the parasite-infested clearing.

•• 22nd day of 4th Month ••

The deep blue of the night was a comfort to the Troll and the Dwarf. Night was home. The beauty of the stars in the skies was a solace to all four travelers. Urk stormed on toward the northeast—straight as an arrow—never seeming to tire—until they came to the mountains separating the Northern Reaches from the Northeastern Reaches.

The river was behind them, Urk having crossed it without getting his shirt wet. The mountains rose up sharply in front of them. Urk and his fellow travelers threaded through the passes and valleys of the tall peaks of the eastern north. As the sun came up they settled down on the north slope of a peak and slept.

•• 19th day of 4th Month ••

Nathan, Evermon, Holder and Alan had passed the bugs but they were in another quandary. They remembered eating when they were hungry but no one remembered sleeping—or even the sun going down and giving them darkness. Time seemed immaterial in this forest and that thought brought them to a halt. They decided to take a nap before moving on to the next set of paths—just in case they really needed one!

When they awoke they could not know how long they had slept. They felt rested. That's all they knew. They didn't know how much of this path was left but they marched on. Again, the path ended and the shrubbery surrounded them. As Nathan stepped forward, this time the left path was dark. As they turned to look down the brightly lit right hand path a very large paw, with razor sharp claws, raked the air in front of them. They all jumped back and the portal closed in front of them. Panic. Had they just destroyed their progress? Was this fourth path necessary to get to the fifth? How could they know?

With saddened and troubled hearts they stepped forward again, behind Nathan, and the bushes reopened. No darkness on the left and no paw on the right. The left path led into a lake and the right path led into a cave. It was different from the dark claw but there was still a cave in front of them and the memory of a clawed paw in the air before them. They stepped forward tentatively into the darkness because they had to. They could not let another choice pass away.

Total. Absolute. Black.

"Light!" was spoken by Nathan.

Darkness reigned. Alan reached to the floor and searched for a rock—he found several boots attached to people he knew before his hand found a rock. He lifted it up, holding it tightly and it squished flat in his hand.

"Ahhhh!" He dropped it. "Bear dung!"

He heard laughter coming at him from out of the darkness. He used a charm and brushed his hands clean. He even got the smell to come off. Evermon reached into the satchel that was tied to his waist and extracted a coin.

"Nathan—here!"

They groped for each other in the darkness. Hands were guided to other hands in their blindness.

"Who touched me?"

"Sorry!"

"Watch your hands!"

"How can I watch what I can't see?!"

"Got it! Light!"

The little coin shone a bright golden glow around them and revealed trees. Evermon plucked three other coins and they were magicked and passed to the other members of the party. Their surroundings only got stranger.

It was a forest, all right. They were in a cave—truth! It was dark except for just around them and their coins. They peered through tat darkness to see that the trees just beyond the edges of the light were silver. Alan strode up to one and knocked on the trunk. It resounded—metallic and hollow. The path was clear, so, Nathan took his turn and led them through the eerie silver forest, walking on a path of shimmery quicksilver, leaves tinkling like tiny pots and pans, in a cave darker than night with a ghostly golden glow casting frightening, bronze shadows all around them.

•• 23rd day of 4th Month ••

They had slept the day away. After a quick meal from the packs of the little people, Gladenwreath, Kwuktw and Sean were ready to start again. Of course they were! Urk was doing all the walking. As Urk awakened he wandered off into the forest around the base of a nearby mountain. He came back munching on a 'deer-sickle', crunching contentedly through bones and all. The three little people were somewhat sickened but they didn't want to offend their new friend (or their mode of transportation) so they suppressed their queasiness. When Sean stepped into his pouch and his boots were surrounded by blood, he lost it and threw up his breakfast all over the front of Urk's tunic. The King laughed.

"Sorry, young Human. I always was a messy eater."

They all laughed as Sean grinned gamely and showed them a leg bone from the deer and threw up again as it dropped out of his hand.

The pouch was cleaned and the four were set to be on their way just as the Bear rose out of the horizon in the east.

"'Under the belly of the bear' is straight ahead. Good job, Urk!"

The Troll King smiled his stumpy-toothed, Troll-like smile and lurched off following the Belly of the Bear.

It was safer going on the tundraed plains of the north than in many other regions of the Realms. Broad—flat—empty. It seemed like they had been traveling for just a few hours before Urk stopped in the darkness and stood in front of the sea on a point of land familiar to Nathan. Troll Island and Pine Island were shimmering darknesses just across the moonlit sea. He settled to the ground. They must wait for midnight.

•• 23rd day of 4th Month ••

The Circle had revisited Pine Island. The warding there was gone. The underground lair—still flooded. The Portal was in ashes. No one had returned. All was good on Pine Island.

Others of the Circle were at Norstok. A cold and forbidding darkness crept over each member as they witnessed the overwhelming gloom of the Castle on its hill above the small port, once inhabited by Dajinn. Twenty Circle members walked through the streets. They were glared at—gawked at—hated, feared, distrusted. It all radiated from the eyes of the locals. Gloom seemed to pervade the hearts, minds and lives of the people here. Blad and Dajinn's legacy had left an infusion of darkness and oppression over everything. Also, a distrust—a hatred of magic and those who possessed it.

They reached the castle. It had a magnificent presence; but sorrow surrounded it, also; enveloped it—invaded it and infused it. The Circle agreed it had to come down.

They surrounded the empty structure. No one had dared even to enter since Dajinn had left. They began with the towers— toppling them inward to the central courtyard; then the battlements—pushing them over into the bailey. The people of the town gathered around them, keeping their distance, but watching in rapt, horrified attention. As the outer defenses crumbled, the Keep and its towers were revealed. The destruction commenced. Minarets, parapets, walls, windows, all tore themselves apart and sought to bury themselves in the earth for the shame of the place.

As the dust settled and the eyes of the populace rested on total emptiness—not a rock left just dust in great piles—a loud cheer ascended from the long-deadened hearts and the unused throats of the townespeople. It was harsh but exhilarating for the shouter and the listener. The Circle, as a unit, nodded to each other and disappeared, stopping the shout at the very apex of its sound and leaving total, sudden silence.

The people were grateful, releasing pent-up emotions and frustrations, shouting, clapping, cheering, hugging each other carefully; unused to the display of affection, wondering if it was real or just a dream; fearing they would only wake up to more terror. In the silence of their emerging joy they began to sense the reality of their situation and they celebrated.

Now—they had a story to tell—a Circle story of their own—a story each of them had witnessed for themselves. A story that could and would be retold: all about the magic strangers who had come and provided salvation and freedom for each of them; even if it was only freedom from their own thoughts and fears, which are powerful things.

•• 23rd day of 4th Month ••

Accosta felt a shockwave run across her, through her, almost pinning her to the bed. She ran, donning her robe, to her lab. She grabbed a handful of silver powder and strew it across a basin of darkened liquid.

"Show me Norstok!"

Somehow she knew. Even as the image floated to the surface of the water, she knew. Her home looked different; something missing. She stepped back from the basin. The Castle was gone! Completely! Vanished! She felt weak and reached for a chair. The loss of Norstok was not a fatal blow to her power base, but it was a considerable blow to her emotional base; something that was none to steady at the best of times.

Most of what she had needed she had already transported from there. What she had left behind would not be missed. The fortress was gone! You will never know how important something is until you no longer have it.

The Circle must be active again. She ran back to her room and dressed. Then she 'popped."

The Castle of the North was still there! Thank, Dal! She ran quickly up its steps and bounced off the front door and fell to the ground at the base of the steps. She got up and crept up to touch the castle wall and was shocked as her hand could not go any further forward—she could not touch the stone of her home!

She tried to 'pop' inside. As she disappeared, she again was bounced off the warding, reappearing and hitting the ground. She screamed and 'popped' home to the Ice Palace. The ice would come in handy. She had seriously bruised her backside!

•• 23rd day of 4th Month ••

Baladar smiled as, through the image of the tree growing in front of him, he saw Aral's eyes grow wide as he stood beyond the tree. Baladar shaped and twisted the beautiful tree until its green branches formed a near perfect sphere on the edge of the lake called Salah Mal.

"Uncle Miraden, I don't know of a better birthday present! I feel—good! Aral, thank you." The boy bowed to the Hegemon

145

"You are the most apt pupil I have had since Daniel and Boncaster." He patted the boy on the head and sent him away. As Baladar skipped stones, occasionally looking back over his shoulder at his tree, Aral talked to Miraden.

"Such power—so young—I hope it is not his undoing."

"I hope so as well."

•• 20th day of 4th Month ••

The silver trees were behind them. The dark rock of the cave wall stood in front of them. Spectres still seemed to loom over their shoulders. The golden glow of the coins refracted and reflected off of everything in leaf shaped apparitions. Evermon stepped forward. The fifth pair of paths presented themselves— cold, dark, uninviting—the pair of them. Again he stepped back. The three companions verbally challenged him. He placated them with a hand gesture.

He stepped forward again and the wall of rock peeled away from in front of the travelers. To the left was a path that looked suspiciously like the outer edge of the Shifting Forest—the beginning, while the path to the right revealed a long, narrow clearing with trees on the right side and tall, strong cliffs on the left side. About a league away—jutting out of a cleft in the cliffs—was a gleaming white structure surmounted only by the large flight of steps in front of it. Evermon looked around at his companions, took their hands, and they all stepped forward into the brightness of what he believed to be the Valley of the Path Once Found. Now found again!

•• 24th day of 4th Month ••

The sun arose in the east, molten, dripping fire into the sea, and the party of the Dwarf found, as they moved forward to the edge of the precipice, a shadow of light emerged from the surface of The Rock to block out a portion of the rising sun. It was the shadow of the glorious, many-towered Ice Palace! As they stepped away to the side, to the left as the right would have taken them over the edge of the precipice, they lost the image of the castle but found the shape of a pile of very large stones.

They scoured the stones, recognizing them as the cairn Miraden had spoken of. Urk called to them from around the other side of the cairn.

"There's writing here."

"They all scrambled to where Urk was pointing.

"What language is that?" asked Kwuktw.

"It's Old Speak."

"How do you know, Son of Elias?" asked Gladenwreath.

"Miraden taught me, Noble Dwarf."

"What does it say?"

"Speak of my...love and I will...take you...across it."

"A riddle. Just what we were told."

"Speak of my love and I will take you across it."

"What can you take across your love?"

"Not 'your' love—'its' love."

"What can you take across what it loves?"

They rolled the phrase around in their individual and collective minds for several minutes. Broaching a solution, then rejecting it as silly or implausible. The sun rose far away from the horizon and The Rock was no longer silhouetted when the solution came from the least expected source.

Urk was chuckling to himself.

He laughed louder and shouted, "The Sea!"

The rock with the writing on it hinged open like the lid of an old trunk. The precipice split at the front of the cairn and opened like the blades of a pair of scissors. Out of the maw of the rock sailed the largest ship that anyone but Urk had ever seen. It was a Trollen merchant ship. Urk's eyes widened to the size of wagon wheels and he clapped his hands in childish glee as the square-sailed, single-masted barque floated free of its moorings.

The four scrambled down to the beach. Kwuktw then slid out of his chiton and handed it to Sean and dove off the cliff for the water. Feet changed to fluke and he glided though the cold wet of the northern sea. He swam to the side of the massive vessel, re-emerged from the water as a Human, and climbed into the safety rigging hanging over the side. As he reached the sprawling deck Urk was reaching over the stern, to the shore, and hauling Sean and

Gladenwreath aboard.

They settled themselves in the prow of the ship, up on boxes, nestled against the rail and just barely able to see over it. Urk corrected the course of the ship a single point to port and the bow nosed directly at The Rock as the sun lifted itself further overhead.

ൡ

CHAPTER ELEVEN—
QUESTS AND COUNTERQUESTS

•• 24th day of 4th Month ••

The prow pointed eastward. The sun was now to starboard. The Rock stood barren in front of them. Urk suddenly turned the wheel, point after point, to starboard and came up on the island's windward side. He tied off the wheel and lowered the sail while Sean, Kwuktw and Gladenwreath chopped at the Troll-sized anchor release rope with sword, axe and halberd. Once free the capstan spun and the anchor dragged its rope until it hit bottom and the ship was caught in the shallow bay. They were just a few dozen spans away from the jetty thanks to the piloting of the King Of Trolls, but the tide had not been high enough to get near enough to tie up. Urk lowered a longboat and they clambered in and were off. As they tied that smaller boat up at the jetty they looked up at the cliff. It loomed hundreds of arms overhead. The steps were Troll-sized and the little ones had to climb back into the harness. As Urk began the ascent the waves crashed mercilessly upon the jetty and rocked the longboat, endangering its safety. What could they have done if the ship had been tied up there? There would be no more jetty!

•• 22nd day of 4th Month ••

As they stepped through the Right Door and entered the Valley of the Path Once Found their walk was lighter, happier. It was not the weary plodding of travelers in the middle of their journey—(Are we there yet?) or maybe still in the middle of a cave—(eeew!)—but it was the spring of the adventurer in sight of their goal.

As they emerged into the clearing beyond the Shifting Forest they heard a scrabbling on the rocks.

"Is this just another part of the test?" asked Alan. "Can't we banish them with magic?!" he hoped as he watched the skeletal creatures approach them.

Nathan put up a protective warding around the four of the travelers awaiting the arrival of the strange creatures. Not true skeletons—more like cadavers with flesh oozing and dripping. Nathan and the others observed as the bags of bones leaped toward them. Then the warding was hit as the creatures battered it with their long swords.

"Is this part of the path?"

"I don't think so—but it could be."

"Did we go right or left as we came out of the forest?"

"I have the funny feeling that we bore to the left."

"That's exactly what we did!"

"Then we're on the wrong path."

"What do we do?"

The four inside the warding had also drawn their swords. The four cadavers timed their next blow to all hit at the same moment. Their bodies may be rotten but their brains weren't. The warding shattered. The cadavers advanced. Nathan, Alan, Evermon and Holder met them blade to blade. Each, try as he might to stay at each other's backs, was drawn into a separate skirmish away from the protection of the others.

Alan was fierce and relentless. He threw out his hand and the cadaver magically lost its head. No brain no gain! The body kept on fighting. He tried another spell and the legs blew off the torso with a sickly scrunch, but the body remained suspended in the air, not moving from its place but turning to meet each of Alan's blows. Alan feinted to his left and then swerved around to his right and thrust his sword through the ribs of the thing's hanging body. Its movements stopped and it clunked to the earth. Alan reached over and pulled out its sword and the body revived and was up and swinging again. He stuck it once more and it lay still and silent. He then took the thing's own sword and stuck it also into the body on the ground, jamming it in to the hilt, and then pulling out his sword. The body stayed down this time—pinned to the earth.

He looked around. Holder needed help. He had also seen his father who was currently dismembering his opponent's corpse and was not in need of help. Evermon was also slashing fiercely. As Alan arrived at Holder's side he thrust into the body of Holder's attacker. The body fell quickly to the ground. Alan again dispatched it with its own sword and withdrew his.

"Thanks.

"You're welcome!"

They ran off to attack the creature fighting Nathan but he had taken care of it with its own sword before they got there. Like son—like father. Then they saw Evermon backed up against a tree, defending mightily. They ran for him. The cadaver thrust and sliced and batted Evermon's sword out of the way and thrust his own repeatedly to the Prince's center. Evermon dodged right and left and the dead thing's sword stuck into the bole of the tree. The Prince, with a clean and perfect swipe, removed the creature's head, arms and legs. Then he pulled its sword from the tree while the arm attached to the sword flailed around and hit him in the face as its former shoulder joint sprayed a sickly brownish blood all over the Prince. He thrust the sword (with arm attached) through the torso on the ground. Its arm went slack and Evermon wiped his sleeve across his sweat and blood-ridden forehead.

Alan arrived and checked him over.

"Not a scratch! You and Holder—not a mark on you!"

"Just lucky, I guess," was said with a deprecating smile.

After regaining their breath, taking a drink from their water skins, and pronouncing what had happened 'really strange', they turned and faced the forest again to retrace their steps to the point from which they had entered the clearing. Once there, they turned around once more and, facing the cliffs, bore to the right this time and re-entered the clearing which was now empty—well, at least the cadavers were gone!

They covered the intervening league before they knew it and found themselves in front of the sheer cliff that rose for hundreds of spans and extended both to their left and to their right for leagues and leagues until the walls of rock were lost from their view by the bend of the valley around the trees of the Shifting Forest.

"The Temple!"

Indeed, the face of the rock was different in front of them. The capitals, columns and steps of the Temple protruded into the valley from a small cleft in the rock wall, while the Temple filled it completely, like the cork in a bottle's mouth. Evermon reached the steps first and sank to his knees at the bottom, panting and wheezing. Holder arrived just ahead of Alan and Nathan. Holder was hardly breathing. Nathan bent over with his hands on his knees, gasping. Alan smiled at him. Holder smiled at them all.

"Don't pour salt into the wound, Holder. The air is much too thin up here. I am used to living at sea level. Mirador is the same altitude as it is here, after all," Evermon protested.

A glance from Holder at Evermon was all the Prince needed.

Holder recovered quickly. "I knew you'd come up with some poor excuse."

After they had regained their ability to take in sufficient air for their lungs, Evermon rose, took another swig from his water skin, passed it around, and walked up the steps to the towering doors in the Temple wall. Made of brass and wood, they had, engraven into their surfaces, scenes of the creations of various animals. Evermon recognized it at once. The others noticed Evermon's attention to the carvings and they trooped up the steps to join him.

"Look! There's Miraden creating... Dragons!"

"And the Unicorns."

"This is a history of our Realms!"

"Well, almost. It is at least a history of the creation of the magical beasts."

"I thought that was all a myth."

"Then you've been mythinformed!"

"Correct." That drew a stare from Alan. "If they are a myth how do you explain Istramere?"

"Then the legends are true?"

"Yes, Alan—every word."

"It would have been an honor to live back then; see all the magnificent beasts." He was trying so hard to sound older than fifteen—and attempting to make up for the gap in his lack of knowledge.

The others didn't mock him but only nodded silently in agreement. They looked up. Across the lintel, above the door, were the words "TEMPLE OF THE ANCIENTS' in the large block letters of New Speak. Odd. Shouldn't it have been Old Speak? After the sharp edge of their awe faded a bit, Evermon pressed his hands against the right panel of the massive door—The Right Panel—might as well stick with the pattern!

•• 24th day of 4th Month ••

The Troll King's giant stride was very compatible with his boundless energy. He never seemed to tire. The staircase up the cliff had been solid and the ascent was over. Urk untied his pouch and lowered it to the ground. Gladenwreath rolled out and stood mighty but diminutive in front of the monumental Troll. Sean and Kwuktw dusted themselves off and arose searching for the location of the Palace.

The horizon was blank. What they had seen from afar was indeed invisible from their now closer vantage point on the island.

"It stood in the center, didn't it?" asked Sean.

"As near as I could reckon, yes, Son-of-Elias."

"Urk can you see the center of the island?"

"Yes. We will still follow the point of the rising sun. Am I not right Noble Dwarf?"

"Right as rain—King Urk!"

"How come it is so cold here?" Kwuktw was shivering as he donned his chiton and adjusted his body temperature.

"A warding of cold keeps the place frozen," offered a laughing Dwarf. "The Trollen ship was the only way through the warding."

Sean started off and the others followed. Urk remained just a little bit behind his smaller companions in order to have the better perspective and keep them going on course—direction was everything. Sean was fast and strong and young, with an average stride and an easy gait. Kwuktw, although tall and strong, was not as easy on the land as he was in the water and had to struggle a little to keep up with Sean. Gladenwreath, poor Dwarf, although used to keeping up with Humans and their longer legs, trotted along just behind Kwuktw.

Then there was Urk. Sean would cruise along for ten steps, fifteen for the Dwarf, Urk would laugh and take one step and pass his smaller friends. The giant turned it into a jolly game and had all enjoying the stroll across The Rock.

Then Sean stopped, stock-still. They were leagues away from the 'center' of the island.

"Do we have to walk all the way? Or did we just have to walk to the cairn in order to fulfill the requirements of the spell?"

"I understood that we had to travel together and follow the stars. There are no more stars here to follow. Why do you ask?"

"I can 'pop' us closer and closer. At least I think I can. Gladenwreath, you can help!"

The Dwarf smiled and nodded his head. He climbed up onto the toe of Urk's boot.

"Ready, King?"

As the small figure of Gladenwreath looked up at Urk, he sensed a little fear in the giant's eyes. "I am ready, Dwarf."

"Give me your hands Gladenwreath, Kwuktw—we'll 'pop' to that ridge! Right by the small bush? Do you have the picture in your mind, Gladenwreath?"

"Aye—firmly—to the right!"

Pop!

Gladenwreath arrived on the turf next to the bush right on target, and next to him were only Sean and Kwuktw. All were still holding hands, but Urk bad been left behind. Urk loped up to the three beside the bush, laughing and shaking.

Sean spoke quickly, before Urk's arrival. "Maybe Trolls can't 'pop.'"

"Maybe we just needed to hold his hand."

"Right. And how do we do that?"

•• 22nd day of 4th Month ••

The door did not budge. Evermon hammered once. The echo

rang through the interior of the Temple and they listened to it reverberate through its corridors. They sat, stood or stared at the door. Alan moved closer and began to study the panels. He ran his fingers over the bas-reliefs themselves and then his fingers found their frames; the decorative borders that surrounded the friezes were ornate in their own right. There were strange little markings, dots and lines, crossing and joining.

"What are these strange markings?"

The other travelers crowded around and began examining the borders. They were puzzled and they took time to muse over the strange shapes. Holder lingered longer, reverently caressing the dots, dashes and lines.

"These are musical notes."

"What?"

"It's how they write songs down so that others can learn them."

"You mean that you don't have to memorize them all?"

"That helps, but it isn't crucial."

"Can you sing it?"

"It's not in a useable form. They're just scattered around haphazard random like decoration."

She stood back and examined each frieze. They began to make sense. They had an order.

"This door is not just a representation of separate tales. Put them all together, in order from top to bottom and they tell the story of the "Calling of the Beasts of Magic."

"Do you know the story?"

"Better. I know the song!"

"Well, sing it!"

"I think we can go no further until I do. It is the key to open the doors."

"Miraden didn't mention that."

"Maybe he didn't need to," added Evermon. "Because he knew 'Holder' would be with us."

Holder reacted to the strange emphasis of his name but got out his harp and plucked the strings.

"In the Age of Magic when the world was new;

Before men, before Dwarves, when Enchanters grew;
The Creators charged them with an awesome task:
Magic Creatures are needed. It is what we ask.
A pair of Dragons for every Realm;
To build, to teach, to guard;
To own the skies and the mountains, too;
To live, to grow, to ward.
Then the Unicorns to roam the meadows and leas.
Dryads and Nymphs to care for rivers and trees.
Sprites and Pixies to help shrubs and grains.
Gnomes for the hills, Trills for the rains.
But each will bow to the greatest of all
The mighty Phoenix will rise and fall.
Miraden blessed each magic life
And his creatures kept the world from strife.
The Creators blessed us long ago
When the Calling of the Beasts was a magic show."

There was a whirring as of the workings of a clock in its tower. Then a clanking as if a massive bolt or beam was being shuttled back and forth within the walls. Then a silence as the doors pulled open.

The room seemed cavernous. There were tall, slender, fluted pillars all along each of the four walls of the room which held the lintels that supported the enormous tiled roof. It was also devoid of any color but the natural, striated highlights of the rock. The walls behind the pillars were marked with a stripe of books. Hundreds of them, tying the walls together. There was nothing else in the room except for a door at the exact opposite end and a block of stone located dead center at the rear.

"The altar."

Nathan and Holder noticed Evermon's eyes following something. It was a beam of light that seemed to move across the opposite wall in no particular pattern at all. As they crossed the room and passed the altar, they noticed a small, circular cut-out-rounded-out shape in the exact center of the slab of stone.

"What fits in that depression?"

Evermon was silent, thoughtful and observant for a few seconds more.

"What was the first answer?" They looked at him in puzzlement. "Miraden's answers!"

"The opal," called Holder. "Where is it?"

Evermon pointed straight up. The strange light that was darting around the far end of the room, above their heads, emanated through a jewel near the ceiling.

"How do we get it?" Alan queried.

"We have to hear the riddle first. There must be a trigger somewhere. We must answer the voice after it asks us a question—I think."

Evermon rounded the head of the altar, by the other doors, and noticed a different colored tile laid in the white floor. He motioned his friends over and raised his eyebrows at them. They nodded.

He stepped on the tile. They heard the sound of rushing wind, the kind of sound that air makes as it passes through something narrow or confining; almost like a deep sigh. Then:

"Welcome. You may not pass until I have an answer to my riddle and you perform the task the riddle implies. If you are wrong you will not be able to pass."

The voice was booming and more than a little frightening.

"Are you ready?"

"Yes," was their weak, concerted reply.

"I will begin. Remember this: death awaits you if you fail. Leave now and no harm can come to you. Once the riddle is spoken it must be answered."

"We are ready."

"What glitters that is not gold?
Sparkles but is not light?
Twinkles that is not a star?
And waits to fit its mold?"

"The Opal in the Temple of the Ancients," Alan blurted out.

The voice seemed to pause, as if looping to another disk, or tape, or crystal. "That is correct."

The voice sounded almost disappointed.

"Place it and pass through the inner doors."

"Is there a time limit?"

Alan thought, *'good question!'*

"How long do we have to get it?"

"As long as it takes to do it right! You may only do it once!" and the voice fell silent. The wind seemed to stop its rushing. The Temple was as still as a tomb at the MidWinter Festival.

Evermon looked up at the source of the wandering beam. He moved over against the inner door. The beam passed over his arm. It burned! He ran away from the wall and back to the safety of his friends. Alan came over to him and healed the slight burn. They all looked around the empty Temple. There was nothing. No more pressure plates on the floor. No levers, no buttons...Wait!

"What is that square, flat area on the center pillar of that wall?" Holder said, pointing to it.

Nathan moved over to the pillar. He pressed his palm against the flat surface and another trembling noise started to shake the building. Soon, they couldn't believe what they saw—the altar started to lift out of the floor as a column of solid stone. Evermon jumped atop the altar as it rose.

"Be careful!"

"I'll try!"

The altar continued to rise unhampered by the weight of the Prince. Evermon looked down. He was at least thirty feet from the floor and still twenty feet from the Opal in the ceiling of the Temple. He continued to be thrust upward. Soon the Opal was within his grasp. He reached up and his hands were burned slightly by the Opal and its light.

"I can't touch it. It's too hot!"

The altar continued its upward movement. Evermon was squatting—then kneeling—now laying out flat!

"It's going to smash you!"

"How can I get the Opal?!"

"I don't know!"

"Off—hang from the sides, my boy! Quickly!"

Following Nathan's advice, Evermon slid over the edge and hung from his fingers. The altar closed up the space between it and the ceiling and then stopped, just short of crushing Evermon's fingers, although they were being held tightly. As the altar stopped the noise of the machinery that was lifting it up ceased also. Then they heard a sigh, like an exhalation of breath, and the altar started to descend. Evermon's fingers almost lost their grip at the sudden release.

"Hold on! It's coming down!"

As it did Evermon's fingers began to slip little by little from the first knuckle—to the second to the third—until be was hanging by his fingertips, forty feet from the floor. Thirty. Twenty. It's a good thing that the altar descended faster than it went up.

"Let go!"

"What?" Evermon panicked.

"Let go! It's safe."

Evermon stopped holding onto the top edge of the column of rock and his feet dropped through the air and contacted the floor where he fell backwards onto his rear. Holder and Nathan helped him to his feet. Nathan checked his hands. Nothing that needed healing. The altar was still disappearing into the floor, however. As the top of it came into view, they noticed that the depression in the center of the altar was filled with the Opal. He hadn't even needed to ascend with it to retrieve the stone at all! As the altar settled to its original position, a small crystal remaining in the ceiling's opening sparkled and sent a shaft of light directly down to the top of the Opal. As it hit the jewel, the light diffused through the gem and then shot out as a flat plane of light to all of the walls in a simultaneous blanket of a beam along the top surface of the altar, and the bottom rail of the surrounding bookshelf. The group saw it coming and ducked under the beam before it reached them and cut them in half. (If it could have cut them in half. No sense in risking what didn't need to be risked.) This seemed to have caused the door at the inner end of the Temple to pop open as the light raced along the rail, met, and flashed. The four crawled forward and pushed the door to its full-open position. They went outside into the brighter sun where they could stand upright. The blanket of light blinked out but the door remained open.

As they turned to continue, the path was again blocked.

•• 24th day of 4th Month ••

As they wrapped their hands around Urk's down-thrust fingers, Sean 'popped' with Gladenwreath's assistance. They had spied a rise in The Rock about a league away. They headed for its center, where they found themselves rebounded to the ground, again without the Troll, at the outside edge of the large circular rise. Urk soon caught up to them and they knew they had reached the warding. They had bumped into nothing and that nothing had shimmered as the impact occurred.

As they gained their feet, dusting themselves off, they spread out along the warding; this warding that Urk was supposed to defeat. As they touched it the warding did not feel like a warding. There was no elasticity no give and take—just a hard shell separating the space they were standing in from the invisible space beyond in which they wanted to be standing.

They had received no instruction as to how to dismantle the wardings of the Ice Palace. No clues, no keys, no spells. All they knew was that Urk had to do it. Urk began to walk around the warding—testing, examining. He was not pushed away. He was not shocked; but he was not welcomed, either. The other three roamed around in the other direction getting shocked and repulsed by the warding.

As they passed each other on the opposite side of the huge empty circle, Urk was very intent, as opposed to the others, who seemed like they were out for a stroll. Once back to their starting positions, Urk walked away a few spans and returned with a large boulder he had ripped from the surface of The Rock. The stone's size would have smothered the Humans completely, or caused the Dwarf to disappear beneath it.

He raised the boulder over his head, drew it back slightly and smashed it into the warding—once, twice—three times! Gladenwreath, along with Kwuktw and Sean, heard a tinkling like crystal, a cracking and then saw a silver shimmer come into their sight and then disintegrate.

Accosta, inside her sanctuary, felt her Palace shudder at the impact. She enwarded herself in the blackest of wardings and 'popped."

•• 23rd day of 4th Month ••

Were they now trapped? The Temple behind them—a tipping rock in front of them. Yes, they could go back—the door was open—but could they really? Or must they move only forward? Alan crawled back up the steps and in through the Temple's door. He touched the sill of the doorway and the blanket of light shot out again. They would indeed have to move forward.

Looking ahead they found sheer cliffs on both sides of the very narrow canyon. No way up—no way over—no way around. The walls of the canyon looked like rock but felt like glass. Then ahead, their way was blocked by the biggest boulder any of them had ever seen. It was shaped like a giant version of the Opal, except that it was flat on the bottom, with sides curving gently upward to an evenly rounded, almost pointy top. Where the Opal of the altar fit its bottom into the cupped space on the altar, the opal-rock was balancing on a point of stone that supported it; first the right side and then the left side, as it rocked back and forth daring anyone to avoid being smashed when passing underneath it. The rock rose well over thirty feet in height above its fulcrum. There appeared to be two declivities placed in the lower right and lower left corners of the opal-rock, as it faced them. These declivities were fairly large and empty. At least large enough so that one of them could curl up inside it. As to their true purpose, that was a mystery.

The four scoured the rock, the walls, the ground, for another trigger as the giant Opal continued to crash back and forth. How could they tap into the voice for their next task? There was nothing to pull or push, step on, kick at, slide...

"What's this?" Holder was pointing to a small lever, like a toggle switch, slightly bigger, that was on the left hand side wall of the door through which they had just used to exit the Temple. They looked at the rock, tipping back and forth, waiting to crush them—inviting them to be crushed. Evermon looked over at Holder who looked at Nathan who set his eyes on Evermon who nodded. Holder flipped the switch! The sound of air rushing came again, like a vast bellows for a primitive pipe-organ starting up.

"Congratulations on your first task," the voice wheezed. "You did not fail. Now, for your question—and the answer will be in the doing, not in the speaking."

"What bars your way on left and right?

How do you pass? With just your might?"

"I await your trial."

"The answer is 'the rock.'" Evermon whispered to Alan.

"That rock rocks," Alan whispered back.

"No, that's not it."

"If we could keep one side down we could slip through under the other side."

"Which side?"

"The rhyme—'might... right' points to the right. Throughout the entire forest the answer was 'right.'"

"Those holes in the rock. Use one side to stop the rock from tilting?"

Evermon grabbed onto the right-hand pocket and hauled himself up into the declivity. The rock continued to tilt.

"Nathan! Help me!"

Nathan grabbed on as the rock tipped into his reach. As he hung there, Evermon holding onto his hands, the rock became almost but not quite stationary.

"Hurry through!"

"But how will you get through?" shouted Holder.

"This isn't the answer, is it?" he confided to Nathan, just below him.

"I don't see how. The riddle doubted that 'our might' would even help us."

Nathan let go and on the next down-tilt Evermon jumped from the declivity to the ground.

"Fill in that hole with rocks!" cried Alan.

As the rock tilted down again and the four of them piled stones large and small into the space provided. The tilting of the rock slowed again. More rocks and the rock stopped; right side down and left side up. Evermon scrambled through, followed by Nathan, Alan and then Holder.

"Number two—we beat you!"

Silence.

•• 24th day of 4th Month ••

As the black lightning from the black warding of the black-hearted Accosta hit the Troll, she cackled in-glee. Then Urk turned to face her—his power undiminished.

Sean threw up a warding of two purple and one red bubble that included Gladenwreath, Kwuktw and himself. Urk reached for the itchy place on his back where the lightning had hit him. He ran over to Accosta's warding and she threw more lightning at him. If it doesn't work the first time—try, try again; that must've been Accosta's mantra!

Urk dodged the bolts with an agility way beyond his size. As he was within range he backhanded the bubble of black and Accosta was tossed and rolled across the landscape. Urk ran after the bubble and began to beat on it and bat at it. Accosta screamed and scrambled unsteadily to her feet and 'popped,' leaving an empty, rolling, black bubble that soon popped on its own as Accosta had employed her second mantra: 'Save yourself first—at all costs!'

Urk ran back to the warding surrounding the Ice Palace, now that his toy had vanished. (He was just beginning to have some fun!) He rammed his shoulder into it at full speed. A shimmery blackness cracked into view and shattered to the ground with a crash and a large splash of dust.

Accosta watched from the inside of the castle and was astounded by the Troll—both as to his size and his alliance with the Realmers. She was completely unaware that her wardings had taken on all of the properties of Estrella's original wardings. Estrella had meant them all as a game for her friends, the Trolls. The Palace was to be theirs. Then Accosta had shown up with Orthon, both completely ignorant of all of Estrella's plans and setups. (Well, mostly ignorant!) They killed Estrella, stole the palace and placed secondary wardings. The Sorceress knew nothing of the Trollen ability to defeat, or demonstrate an immunity to, magic. She was woefully, egotistically uneducated. But so then are all people who take power unto themselves, rather than wait for it to be bestowed upon them.

Accosta had her Wraiths, her Demons, her guards, her magic and Aradon's Queen! The Dwarf, The Prince of the Sea and the

Circle-boy would pay for their effrontery!

The Palace shook and shadows of blue fell to the ground. The Wraiths began to whirl around the inside of the spires, waiting for their victims. The Demons shook inside the bars of their restraint.

Her guards eyes were wide with fear. She placed herself in front of the room of pearlescent-pink leading downward. Her new black warding, swollen, was discharging its own bolts of energy—automatically—saving the ones from her hands for when she would need them.

•• 24th day of 4th Month ••

Baladar and Miraden sat on the shores of Troll Island facing The Rock to their south. They were anxious, nervous, expectant—helpless. They could not aid or advise in any further way. They had not filled the quest; had not walked the path across the Reaches. It was not their mission. So, they sat, waiting, watching for the sign of battle. Hoping for the appearance of Miraden's sister's palace of ice; (which could signal the defeat or destruction of Accosta.) Baladar stood and pointed—a silver shadow glimmered and disappeared.

"Uncle—look!"

It would now only be a matter of time.

•• 24th day of 4th Month ••

Accosta summoned her brush, not only out of nervousness but also out of necessity. She had to be her youngest self possible. The brush screamed through her hair, infusing her with youth, beauty and power. Another item stolen from the magical Estrella. In addition to the age reversal, each stroke served to calm and complete her self-assuredness.

Once again, they were shaken—both the palace and her self-assurance. She trembled as the original golden warding of the Palace shimmered, like a video picture does when it is faulty. The golden warding did not shatter—with attack after attack, all around the perimeter of the palace, the warding sloughed off as giant sheets in some places. In other places it melted off and dripped to the ground like a dish too-full of ice cream sundae. As it completely disappeared the sunlight streamed in through the spires of ice topping the palace.

Bolts of lightning and roars of rage made the ebony doors of the palace tremble and quake as they were repeatedly forced inward. As the doors flew open, smashing against the interior of the fluted walls, four silhouettes were outlined in the huge frame. A dwarf, a boy and a MerPrince stood on the threshold, enwarded in personal wardings of purple or red—or both. A giant Troll filled the space behind them nearly blotting out the orb of the sun which was starting its journey to the horizon beyond their silhouettes.

•• 23rd day of 4th Month ••

The organ-like air bellowed and rushed at them and in the dimness of the secluded canyon past the tottering Opal, another bright shimmer appeared, this time, on the rock face to their right as the breath of the Creators tumbled them to the dust. Laughter preceded the announcement of "Well done! You have passed the first half of the four tests awaiting you."

"Four? But we were told of only three!" protested Alan, always quick to point out inequities.

"Four there are and four you will solve—or die."

Alan stammered.

Nathan interrupted—"Oh, Ancient One, give us the new riddle. We shall solve it. We shall not disappoint you." He hoped he had said it correctly since this could be one of the Creators and he had never addressed a god before.

"I hope not. Are you ready?"

"Yes."

I am open to all, but closed to you.
I am free to all, but if you fail, you will pay.
I hold each in his sphere, but I am not a sphere myself.
I can be still and placid—or full of motion and fury.
Send me to the well and you will move on;
What am I?"

"What's to keep us from walking over to the well right now?"

The figure on the rock face motioned, placatingly, toward the well with his hands as if saying, 'go ahead.' Alan took off running but soon was enmeshed in a giant, invisible warding that, at once, enveloped him and then propelled him backward toward the tottering Opal.

"The barrier is your separation. Hope that it does not become your desolation."

The white figure on the wall vanished like a vision from an Orb. Holder, Evermon and Nathan admonished Alan with a look and then approached the barrier—touching gently—feeling, sensing. They began together, to pick apart the riddle.

•• 24th day of 4th Month ••

As the four stepped across the ebony threshold the bars holding the Demons released and they surged forward. Sean had his sword. Gladenwreath had his halberd. Kwuktw, in a triple purple felt the warding sparkle as Sean added an outer red and the MerPrince began to roll.

Black lightning came at them but their carefully built wardings enclosed and protected them. Demon after Demon was sliced at with Human and Dwarven weapons—but none fell. The Demons only sizzled as Kwuktw ran over them, incinerating not only the Demon but the animal inside. The six remaining guards fell quickly to the lightning of Sean and Gladenwreath. Had Accosta underestimated the Circle—again?

Then the Wraiths descended. They swarmed around Urk. He batted them away with his giant hands and arms. Then he grabbed hold of a door and ripped it off its hinges. He swung it through the air connecting with Wraith after Wraith (and their swords.) The Palace was absolutely full of them and the battle raged on with Accosta sending lightning at the three enwarded attackers only to have it bounce off the warding and obliterate a Demon standing too close. She couldn't break through their magic shields but her force was strong enough to move them around in their wardings as Urk had done to her outside.

Just as a dozen Demons, clawing and raking toward the MerPrince in his bubble, were near enough to try to do some damage, a bolt of black hit Kwuktw's bubble and sent him backwards into those Demons, flattening and sizzling them like bacon on a griddle as the lightning also bounced off the bubble and tore through their flesh releasing the animal inside.

Urk felt the small piercings of the Wraiths and their long, thin blades. He just kept swinging the door, collecting their swords in its surface like a pin-cushion, and scattering their ethereal bodies with the solidity of the door itself. The Wraiths who evaded the door were the ones that he would shake off in his fury while exterminating the persistent, stinging insects.

Accosta panicked. (No surprise there.) It was different being in the battle from what it had been just supporting and sending the troops as she had done with the Arikkans. Her black warding rolled as the Dwarf and the Human hit it with coordinated bolts of energy. As she righted herself she saw black—nothing but solid, door-shaped black. She rolled again as her warding rang with the sound of the impact of Urk's door. He battered her around, as if he were a professional Field Hockey player, with an occasional swing at the Wraiths, until she was at the very edge of the pearlescent spiral. She was tumbled and confused and couldn't think clearly of anything that she could do except 'pop.' After her warding was empty Urk hit it with the door and it careened over the edge. Luckily, it winked out of existence before it had a chance to hit the block of ice suspended at the bottom of the well.

•• 24th day of 4th Month ••

Baladar was pacing and Miraden grew worried as he watched the boy stress over things the boy could do nothing about. His agitation was peculiar. Was he worried over the outcome? Was he just impatient? Was he concerned that his mother would be destroyed?

"Take my hand, Nephew."

"Where are we going?"

"You'll enjoy it."

"But what about... ?"

"We can do nothing here until their task is finished; maybe not even after that."

Baladar reluctantly placed his hand in Miraden's.

Pop!

They were at a lake which Baladar had not seen before. The boy watched as the Enchanter waved his arms and muttered some magic words he couldn't hear quite clearly. He was too confused and agitated to listen. Miraden finished with the incantation and pulled the boy back gently as rock after rock began to pile itself one upon another. Baladar's look of confusion was erased by an over-imaginable sense of excitement and curiosity.

Miraden led the boy into the tunnel that was revealed by the absence of rocks. It arched high above their heads and seemed to go directly out under the lake. Torches flamed into being on the walls. Baladar marveled. Miraden had done it without a word or a gesture. He had just thought it!

The aroma of...something he could not place...assailed his nose. A moistness seeped through his clothes and attached itself to his body. At the end of the main corridor they turned right into the last room. There was another doorway across from them. As they entered the room beyond, the floor tilted down, ramp-like, and curved deep into the earth. The smell hit Baladar again—stronger—he stopped. Miraden urged him on.

As they wound deeper into the earth Baladar saw a strange, orange glow up ahead. As magically mature and as keen as Baladar's perceptions were, he was letting his childhood imagination overtake him. He looked up, fearfully, at his mentor, who merely nodded and continued to guide him forward.

The tunnel-ramp opened up to an enormous cavern at its bottom. With all of the orange clay, the orange torchlight flickering everywhere, Baladar almost missed the huge pile of orange rock at the center of the cave. Then it moved.

So did Baladar—to right behind Miraden. The Enchanter smiled as he realized that the boy's imaginings had gotten the better of him. Good! He was still Human.

The mound of rock grew and almost reached the ceiling. Baladar recognized legs—with claws! He shut his eyes. Why would Miraden lead them here to be torn apart? He opened his eyes when the claws didn't rake his flesh, and saw a tail—or something like it—unfurl from the orange mass, its delta shaped tip relaxing onto the floor of the cave. Then at the other end of the—body—yes, it was a body—a long sinuous neck curled around and soon two golden eyes were staring at Baladar's brown ones. Baladar shut his eyes tight again. This was all too much, too fast! He wouldn't be torn apart. He would be eaten!

In the darkness of his tightly shut eyes he heard laughter, both Human and something else—deeper—hungrier, he thought—was Miraden only the pawn of an evil beast that controlled all the Realms through him? Was he, Baladar—just a small boy—to be the sacrifice to this unreasonable god? Had his mother told the truth about the Realms after all?

"Baladar, you must meet Istramere—my friend," the old man's words were kind—calming.

"Please no! Please—no! Please, no! Don't eat me!" was whimpered through nearly silent, petrified lips.

Then he felt something inside him. It was like a presence but it was nothing he could hold—only something felt—but yet tangible—and it didn't seem angry or hungry.

"I am Istramere," it said. "I have been waiting for you, Baladar."

"Oh no, please don't eat me!" was shouted into the darkness by the terrified boy.

More laughter! How could Miraden laugh, when he, an innocent boy, a prodigy, a friend, an apprentice, was about to be eaten in front of him? Then he felt Miraden's hand on his back, comforting him—small circles, easy pressure—as his mother had, sometimes, in that time before. He felt something wet and rough snake along his face and neck.

"What i-i-i-is an I-I-Istramere?" asked the boy.

"A friend. Open your eyes. I was Boncaster's friend. Maybe I can be your friend, too. You can certainly be mine."

"What are you?"

"Open your eyes."

Baladar shook his head 'NO' with all his might. Then he felt that presence again, deep inside. Baladar relented, opened his eyes and Istramere pulled his massive head back so that the boy could get a really, good look at him. Baladar couldn't speak for a few moments as the enormous reality of the creature in front of him pressed its way to the surface of his consciousness. Of course! He was seeing a Dragon. It all made sense!

No, it didn't!

Dragons did not exist! His mother had told him so! It was in front of him! His mother had never been very truthful anyway.

Baladar reached out a hand. Istramere lowered his head again until he rested it on the floor of the cave directly in front of the boy. Baladar's hand came in contact with the hardened scales and skull first, then the soft warm neck. The Dragon tipped his head and Baladar laughed and scratched under the Dragon's bearded chin.

•• 24th day of 4th Month ••

The Demons still danced over the intruders and the Wraiths writhed around the Troll. Sean summoned a second sword and magicked it into Kwuktw's hands. Sean then collapsed the Prince's warding until it fit him like a second skin. Sean stepped forward finally remembering the stories of Demons that his father, Elias and Uncle Daniel had told him. He stabbed forward into a Demon's abdomen and ripped the skin open up to the neck. The skin fell away and a harmless little forest creature emerged to scamper off toward the door. The three enwarded rescuers began slicing. The Demon skins fell away.

Urk, holding the pincusion-like-door saw very little room on it for more swords; so he turned the door over and swung the empty side at the last of the waves of Wraiths. Their swords were impaled in the ebony and their spectral forms were dissolved by the attack of the massive door. Urk stood there, bleeding from thousands of tiny sword pricks—as if giant mosquitoes had attacked him without finishing their job. He was tired and his orange skin stung but he was smiling from ear to ear. He picked up Demon after Demon and with a sword, the size of a toothpick to him, taken from the door, he carefully incised the skins and set the animals inside free.

The hall was soon empty except for the thousands of red skins. It was silent—except for the heavy breathing of the heroes. That is what they were, now. The task at hand demanded that the heroes become saviors, rescuers, before they could be released from their task. They searched through the vacant palace.

Room after room glistened with the emptiness of Accosta. The little group came upon a chamber that was curtained off from the others. As they drew back the draperies, red, white and gold lights sparkled across their faces and bodies, and their fascination at the source of their illumination drew them into the room.

The lights looked like they were trying to fuse together, but were unable to join for some reason, to form a single beam. As they approached, Sean recognized the Frosted Flask, The Blood Rose and the Golden Sceptre, beautifully and carefully mounted and displayed; but were they works of art or siguls of power? Whatever you considered them, they were pretty! Startlingly so.

"We'll pick them up on the way out!"

"I think we ought to 'pop' them to Miraden now!" said Sean.

Kwuktw and Gladenwreath nodded their heads. Kwuktw then had a second thought.

"But will it interrupt the magic of our quest?"

"It might."

"Best wait, then, Son-of-Elias."

"Maybe you're right."

There was an archway covered with the same material leading off to their right. In the next room they found a bed.

"Accosta's chambers."

There was another room off of that one that was full of glassware, vials, ampules, trunks crates, shelving stacked high and piled deep with the detritus of Accosta. Kwuktw found a large black crate and picked it up from underneath the table. It looked like it might be important. He opened it and the plush, black, satiny material shone in the refracted light of the room. There were three familiar but empty shapes in the box.

"A box for the Talismans?"

Sean nodded. "Looks like it. Maybe we'd better at least pack them up."

"We also need to come back for all of this equipment. Miraden could use it."

They left the room and headed back to the chamber with the

dancing lights. They carefully removed the Talismans from their receptacles and placed them in their respective homes inside the black box. They shut the box and the light in the room winked out. They left by the door into the main hallway. As they crossed the hall, a pearlescent pink drew them to its archway and into another chamber. They found the spiral ramp and ran down it to its base. There, the ice towered above them, and in it they saw the form of the Queen—imbedded. Gladenwreath wept tears of sorrow at the Queen's predicament mingled with tears of joy at her discovery. The four paused to share a moment with their leader.

They stepped forward and a wall of water shot up in front of them. They raced around the cube trying to find a way through it, but the water completely surrounded it, cascading upward from a ring-like pool that was fifty arms across. They could not get near the Queen.

•• 23rd day of 4th Month ••

"Open to all—free to all—not a sphere—still and placid—full of motion and fury." The words reverberated in their heads.

"It's what stands in our way!"

"What?"

"The barrier! What is it made of? All wardings are made of it."

"What?"

"Air!"

Holder had solved the riddle! How did he know so much about magic? Must be his/her father and mother, hmmm? Evermon was grateful, but even more puzzled about the enigma that was Holder.

"So, what do we do, now?"

"Send me to the well and you will move on."

"I'd like to but how do we get through the barrier?"

"No—not me-me. The air-me!"

"And?"

"We have to push the warding back with our own magic air!"

There was a moment of stupid silence—that kind where you realize that the answer was staring you in the face all the time but you were too preoccupied to see it.

Nathan and Alan created a ward of air and sent it, in a

continuous flow, towards the warding that restrained them. They felt it move and they slowly walked forward until a loud crash was heard in front of them.

"Stop!" cried Evermon.

They stopped walking and the magic air dissipated. Evermon walked forward. There was no warding there.

"I am impressed." The Voice wheezed. "You brought intelligence with you that was beyond your understanding, but you have also the wisdom within yourselves. The Well of the Waters is your final barrier. Inside you will find what you seek."

There was silence after the wall of light had vanished with the being's image and voice.

•• 24th day of 4th Month ••

Baladar had run his now ten year old hands over all of the Dragon that he could reach. He kept looking from the body of Istramere to Miraden, to Istramere's eyes, to Miraden—just to make sure that it was really happening and not some sort of illusion.

Istramere placed his snout behind the boy who was atop his scaly back. Miraden 'popped' out of the way at a mental nudge from the Dragon.

Istramere began to run. Out the doorway, up the ramp. The boy yelled as he dodged the stalactites flying passed him and he clung tightly to the scales and ridges of the Dragon's back as he also flattened himself to it, nearly missing each depending piece of rock.

The entrance was sighted and Istramere poured on the speed and the clay walls rushed by the boy's blurry vision. When they hit the light Baladar couldn't believe his eyes. They were airborne—immediately. He was flying on the back of a Dragon!

•• 24th day of 4th Month ••

The four stood in front of the wall of water. Kwuktw removed his chiton.

"I know now why Miraden summoned me to be with you on this quest," and he dove into the wall of water. Sean, fascinated, began to heal the tiny wounds on the Troll's body, all the time watching the body of the MerPrince fly through the currents of the water as they tossed him in their eddies and whorls.

•• 24th day of 4th Month ••

Evermon looked up - and saw the other building more clearly than before and it hushed their celebration as they beheld a building that appeared to be a cube with a large door in the front similar to the Temple. It was difficult to look at because it was shining like it was the personal residence of one of the Creators.

All over the building there were luminescent scenes of water: lakes, rivers, streams, waterfall—all carved, painted, etched around the outside of the structure. The colors were vivid and the scenes that they depicted were many and varied.

The door this time, seemed to be made of gold, not brass, and more scenes of water action were carved into its surface—except for one bright oval-shaped spot: the outline of an opal with a rounded bottom and the sides curving gently upward to an evenly rounded, almost pointy top. It was placed in the dead center of the door. The words, "The Well of the Waters" were inscribed above this single-panel door. There was a bell pull of spun gold hanging by the side of the door. Holder pulled it. The wheezing, rasping sound of the wind began again.

"You have succeeded again. Further congratulations. Now for your final test:

"What door, without a keyhole
Can be opened by a key without a shaft, teeth or handle?
Can this design be filled?"

Well, 'key' was the third answer."

"But we have no key."

"The key has no shaft or teeth so it may not look like a key."

"No handle either."

"The door has no keyhole."

"Come here and look closely." Evermon was at the door staring at the oval shape.

"There's a depression in the center of the white oval. It has both rounded and straight edges and another oval depression within its design."

"But..."

Evermon reached over and pulled the chain out of Holder's shirt. Holder jumped a little at first. Evermon noticed that Holder clasped the neckline of his chemise closely to him.

"Sorry!"

Evermon carefully took the amulet off the chain and turned it around in his hands trying to match it to the outline of the design within the oval shape. He found the correct rotation for the amulet and pressed the special 'key' into the door with the jewel fitting perfectly into the center of the depression.

The straight edges lined up and the rounded edges matched! He then applied a little more pressure and the entire white panel moved into the door. There was a gasp by all, until it shot back out at them, raising itself above the flat surface of the door—then there was a scream. With one hand still on the oval shape, holding the amulet in place, Evermon's other hand rotated the entire contraption to the left.

There was no give. It wouldn't turn. *To the right—always to the right!"* he thought. He turned the white piston to the right and the door slid backwards into the cube and then shifted over to the right side. Air and dust were expelled and Holder's amulet disappeared behind the wall with the door.

"My amulet!"

"How did you know, Evermon?"

"I've seen it peeking and hanging out of your shirt many times. It must be why you are here."

"But I've had it since I was young. Mother says that it was Miraden's once."

Evermon looked long and hard at Holder—knowing something more, but not understanding it all, yet.

"It was our destiny to meet in the forest, Harper."

What followed was an eerie silence. Then a tiny sound emerged out of the darkness. A drip-drip-drip-drip.

Cautiously, Evermon, Holder, Alan and Nathan crept into the 'Well of the Waters.

Inside the cube they found a deep, oval pool in the center of the building. A small, clay pipe dripped constantly from the back wall into the calm, blue water. The water was so clear that the bottom of the pool, which looked a few inches deep, was actually over thirty arms deep. The room was lit by the same kind of opalescent reflection of the sun as the Temple had been. Nathan took out an empty bottle from his rucksack and dipped it into the cool waters. He then stoppered it and placed the treasure in a special area of the pack where it wouldn't leak or spill.

He hadn't, as of yet, noticed, but the room was becoming brighter as he dipped, then replaced the bottle. Soon a white figure appeared, standing in the room.

"Well, done! Well, done!"

Evermon stood, disbelieving the vision in front of him. It was, well, at least it looked like...

"Boncaster?"

"Yes, cousin."

Caelith's eyes lit up also but she soon hid her recognition of the figure in front of them.

Evermon ran forward and threw his arms around the vision. A vision isn't supposed to be solid. This one was. Holder/Caelith could not help it. She stared often at her former playmate—the boy she had grown up with. For he was just as she had remembered him—only white now, like her father. He winked at her and she kept her silence, but he attracted her eyes back to him with a gesture of his hand. Out of the neck of the gloriously white tunic he pulled a chain. On that chain was an amulet. Caelith/Holder gasped slightly. It looked identical to her amulet! The one that was now lost behind the door. Boncaster formed the word "Miraden" silently and dropped the bauble back between his tunic and extra white skin.

"I have missed you, Boncaster."

"And I you, Cousin, but I was sent to congratulate you, not reminisce."

"You haven't changed!"

"I know. You have. I have been impressed by what you did with the limited information Miraden gave you. The Right Path, forgive me for this, but I have to tell you; the Right Path could have brought you here sooner!"

"I knew it!" Alan broke in. "If we had chosen the seventh pair first it would have been the Right Path to the Right Path."

"Correct! But you did figure it out, Evermon. And remember this:

The Right Path will not kill you.
The Right Path will challenge you.
The Right Path will reward you.
Here and in the future!"

Evermon, Alan and Holder were finished filling their vials and stood to face Boncaster.

"Will this really cure my father?"

"And much more. Remember this also—it is the quest for, not the possession of a thing, that is important; that makes it worth the finding. Go now. Aradon needs you. You must first exit through the Temple. Then you can 'pop' home."

The foursome turned around and left the well, leaving Boncaster alone. Evermon couldn't stand it. (Caelith was also having a hard time.) Evermon hugged his brother/cousin. Holder/Caelith smiled and waved, a tear in his/her eyes. Boncaster waved back and vanished. The door began to move outward as soon as the last of the four was standing out on the steps of the Well house. The door pressed itself into its original position. Evermon took the amulet out of its place in the door and returned it to a grateful Holder.

"Let's move!"

As they ran across the clearing they felt a wall of air rise up behind them. They pressed themselves through the passage under the tilting Opal. As Alan, at the rear, stood again between the Rock and the Temple, the stones fell, or were pushed, out of the declivity, and the Rock started its motion from left to right again. As they went through the inner door of the Temple, the altar inside was already moving upward, the blanket of light rising along the wall with it. A door closed. They rushed to the front door of the Temple in time to have the beam of light start its wandering passage around the Temple chamber. The doors closed behind them as they found themselves standing on the front steps of the

Temple with the dust settling at their feet.

"Well, right back where we started."

"Speaking of where we started—we had better get there."

They stood up and walked down the steps of the Temple. The sun was high overhead and they were trudging away from the object of their Quest—that object having been successfully obtained. Then with a look back at the Temple, just to make sure it had all really happened, they stepped into the coolness of the forest road (that wasn't there before) and the Temple disappeared from their view. Then they remembered, and joined hands.

Pop!

•• 24th day of 4th Month ••

Kwuktw flailed his fluke and pulled himself through the waters with his strong arms. The others ran around the circular well of waters encouraging him, marveling at his strength and ability. Kwuktw's head popped out of the water on the inside of the circle after several minutes of struggling against the magic currents within and he fell to the floor. The waters immediately ceased their movement and disappeared back into the pool that had surged them upwards. He landed on the tile of the island under the ice cube. Fire roared out of the center of the floor, from directly under the ice cube and out across the entire island like a back-draft. A back splash of the waters, arrested in their descent, momentarily covered him and protected him from the flames but as they blasted out laterally across the floor, and the waters receded, Kwuktw was singed before he could scramble back into the protection of the pool.

Flames leaped toward the ice cube and it started to melt.

"This could be a good thing—couldn't it?"

"The Queen will boil!"

Sean and Gladenwreath began magicking the waters of the pool towards the center of the flames. Little spurts did not seem to be working. They joined their efforts and pushed a wall of water across the island towards the fire. As it rolled under the cube the wave extinguished the flames. As the maelstrom ceased, drips were the only sound to break the silence, until:

"Where's Kwuktw?"

They searched and saw the MerPrince floating at the outer edge of the pool, half in and half out of the water. They hauled him all the way out of the water and saw the horrific burns to his feet and lower legs that were the part of him out of the water.

Sean, with a little help from the Dwarf, began the healing process and Kwuktw's pinkish-blue skin began to re-knit itself. The charring of the flesh gradually disappeared and was returning to its normal Skwatwael coloring. Kwuktw's chest rose and fell in a more even rhythm, now. He would be all right. Urk stood in the pool—up to his knees—and lifted Sean, Kwuktw and the Dwarf over to the island of marble tiles under the gigantic cube of ice.

"That fire could have melted this ice."

"But it would have roasted the Queen."

"True enough."

"What is supporting that block?"

"Only magic—no ropes or chains—no invisible pedestal."

"How do we get her out of it?"

"Urk—can you lift it?"

Urk wrapped his three-span-long arms around two edges of the cube. He lifted, shifted, pushed and pulled—as the others stood behind him. As he strained, the cube came loose from whatever had held it in place high above their heads. Urk set it down on the island with a deep, dull, resounding thud. This was a Trollen castle after all. Most of the magic could be or should be able to be defeated by a Troll.

Gladenwreath began to chip away with his axe as the boy Enchanter melted portions of the ice with the flames generated from his hands. Kwuktw hacked at it with his sword. The ice either dripped or was chipped away until the danger of the fire or blade grew too close to the Queen. Gladenwreath worked carefully onward. His blade coming expertly within a hair's breadth of touching the frozen monarch.

Then she was free! The Dwarf had done it! They placed her still frozen but breathing body in the palm of Urk's hand and followed him as he carried her across the pool and up to the top of the spiral walkway. Urk then slogged through the Demon skins, kicking them out of his way and stood at the front door, waiting.

Sean wanted to leave a beautiful castle—an intact palace. After all it was intended as a present to the Trolls. He began to quickly incinerate the skins with Gladenwreath's help. Soon the floor was clean, almost as it would have been back in the days of Estrella. The thousands of swords were removed from the door and it was replaced, by magic, back into its frame. The black box containing the Talismans was taken in Sean's hand. They heard a large crack. Dust spilled out of the room where the Talisman's had been displayed.

Once outside, the door closed and they started walking. Gladenwreath realized that he must get the Queen back quickly. They had no time to walk all the way home. They turned around and gazed at the absolute beauty and perfection of the Ice Palace—Estrella's creation, not Accosta's—as the wardings no longer hid it from view. It would truly be a tale for the Harpers and Bards. Alan had always wanted to be part of a story for the Bards to tell.

This part of the tale was now over for one member of their company. He could not transport with them back to Aradon. So, Gladenwreath, Kwuktw and Sean bade farewell to their new friend, Urk—King of the Trolls. Urk ran off towards the ship which they had moored at the western end of The Rock. It would be a short trip back home for him to Troll Island in a new ship created for the Trolls by Estrella—one of their greatest friends. He quickly disappeared from view and they, holding the still stiffened body of Rose, and the case of the Talismans, 'popped' to the White DragonMount to see Miraden.

•• 24th day of 4th Month ••

Accosta was frantic as she paced her cave in the Blue Mountains of Aradon. She had found it one day when she had left Baladar alone at the Purple Lake. The mountains had called to her and led her to this remote pass in the heart of the Blues. She always had a back-up plan—and it was a good thing that she planned ahead that way—because she always needed the plan she thought she wouldn't need—whether she was working alone in her own incompetence, or with others of a similar mindset and ability. In yet another new place, she summoned everything that she could think of from her laboratory in the Ice Palace. (So much for Miraden getting the equipment.) Her cave filled up with all of her most important items. Except for the Talismans! She was not a terribly happy camper but she set out to start over—again and alone.

She looked into her mirror. It always helped her think when she brushed her hair. A hundred strokes at a time—no more, no less. The brush ran through her long, though now black locks. She saw another face staring back at her from that mirror—a sort of shadow face that appeared superimposed over her own: that of Queen Rose. She reached out to touch the mirror as the brush continued to thread through her hair. She also sent a trailing of thought back to the Ice Palace and she didn't feel her loss. The Queen must still be encased in the cube. The rescue had failed and those simple fools had been burned alive by her surprise from out of the floor. (Well, she could dream!)

The thought comforted her. A Troll, a Dwarf, a MerPrince and the Son-Of Elias of the Circle. Not a bad tally of dead enemies. Maybe she would be returning to the Ice Palace someday. She smiled. Rose's smile gleamed out of her mirror at her. Accosta began mixing potions.

ML

C. MICHAEL PERRY

CHAPTER TWELVE—
QUEEN AGAIN!

•• 24th day of 4th Month ••

Alfrond and Elayda were seated on the thrones of Aradon
dispensing judgment and assistance to their citizens. Alfrond was
unsure. Elayda was uncomfortable. Each case brought before them
was unique and wisdom was not just something you could turn on
or give out as a pill or a balm or a salve. Alfrond realized that he
was inadequate to the task; which is the first quality of any great
leader. Because of his inborn sense of honor and the integrity that
had been fostered into him by his parents and older brother, he
managed to send his petitioners away satisfied; content that there
was fair judgment again in Aradon.

A red-robed and hooded petitioner stood in front of the
newly-royalled couple. There was a silence in the room as the
acting King and Queen waited and watched. The guards tensed.
They didn't like the feeling of this one. The room held its collective
breath. A voice pierced the air with power and clarity.

"I have a petition of thanks to offer to King Alfrond and
Queen Elayda. The wisdom of Aradon has returned. Your subjects
are happy. I can make them even more happy."

The crowd gasped at this being's effrontery. You could hear
metal scrape against metal as swords started to leave their
scabbards. Then the red robe was unfastened and was dramatically
dropped to the floor. A startlingly beautiful woman stood in front
of the Royals. As recognition dawned, astonishment filled the
room. Alfrond stood and approached the woman.

"Sister!"

Rose smiled and welcomed her brother-in-law to her arms. She and Elayda greeted each other with kisses as the audience buzzed with excitement. Applause started in the assembly and swords were re-sheathed. A cacophony of sounds rose to a fever pitch as Alfrond and Elayda led Queen Rose to her throne. As she seated herself the applause died out to an expectant silence.

Rose's body seemed to shudder with pleasure as she took her place on the throne, ran her hands along its arms and thrilled once more to the feeling of power inherent in the chair.

She wrapped her hand around the silver sceptre and caressed the rampant Dragon at its top; the only Dragon she had ever liked. She struck the ball-like lower end of the Sceptre against the pad in the arm of the chair. Alfrond and Elayda took their places at her side. Then the question they all dreaded came from her lips.

"Where are my husband and sons? On a mission somewhere?"

The sad stories were told: of Emeron's illness, the disappearances of the older brothers, and of Evermon's treachery. The Queen slumped, sagged and gave into her sorrow. Malika, the Circle representative in her husband's absence, and Elayda comforted the heavy-laden Queen. The Chamberlain called off the audience for the morning—to be taken up again tomorrow.

The Queen was led to her husband's chambers where she touched his cheek and cried a little. It was also explained to her that a search for the cure was on, led by Nathan of the Circle. If successful the King would be restored; or so Miraden had said.

"Miraden!... is not the answer to everything!"

"Whatever you say, My Lady."

"Leave me."

And the room emptied. Rose's shoulders sank over the prostrate body of her husband and began to heave.

•• 24th day of 4th Month ••

Two dark-robed figures huddled in the shadows of the city waiting for word from Miraden. When they received it they would have to move swiftly. Evermon had not returned. Gladenwreath had not returned. Many days had passed without word. Suddenly

Mara, Nathan and Malika's oldest daughter, burst into the darkness of the stables.

"Queen Rose has returned and has taken back the throne! Mother sent me to get you. She has gone to Miraden."

The two Seers looked at each other and followed Mara out into the streets and toward the castle.

•• 24th day of 4th Month ••

As Malika arrived in the cave of the Magician it was crowded and busy. She saw Miraden and Sean and Kwuktw and Gladenwreath along with Daniel and Tilly. She had interrupted something. But then she saw what she was not prepared for: the face of Queen Rose.

"Your Majesty! How did you get here so quickly?"

The group laughed.

Holding out her hands to her old friend the Queen said, "Dear Malika, years have passed since I have seen you."

"But I just left you—in Aradon."

The proverbial pin would have crashed to the floor after that comment sunk in. Concern immediately overcame the faces in the chamber and Malika rehearsed the story of the Queen's magical appearance in the Purple Palace.

"I am Rose. This other is an impostor."

The company nodded in agreement.

"She always has been an impostor. Accosta—no doubt—or Alindra—whichever?"

Then Malika noticed the boy in the corner.

"Baladar!" she ran to him and hugged him. "I thought we'd lost you!"

He was unaccustomed to this type of a display of affection. It had been a sparse thing in his young life, but he permitted it; even enjoyed it, for he was smiling broadly. How could he not? Malika was pretty.

"I'm so glad you are safe."

Rose then patted her knee and the boy reluctantly left Malika and came over to sit with the Queen.

"So, the son of my enemy is now the enemy of my enemy.

Does that make him my friend?" and she peered into the boy's face, searching for the answer.

Baladar thought a moment. "I am Evermon's brother!"

"Then you are more than friend to me, Young Prince of the North."

"Why do you say that? Prince of the North?"

"Your bloodline. Your heritage."

Baladar hung his head in shame. "I have learned that it is bad blood."

"It is not the blood that turned bad, Baladar, but the hearts that pumped it. It was the people who were consumed by lusts they could not or would not control. Your blood is what you are born with. Your life is what you choose to make of it."

"I'm a real Prince? Just like Evermon?"

"As real as Evermon—wouldn't you say so, Miraden?"

"I would agree completely. Your noble blood comes from Accosta herself, daughter of a Prince and heir, no matter what we think of them. Your magic—it comes from both your mother and your father."

Baladar was silent again. A fear, recurrent and persistent, scrabbled up the back of his mind and forced him to speak it. "What if my magic is more my father's than anyone else's?"

"Your father had great powers—like your mother does—but they chose to serve Darkness. You are not condemned to that choice or fate. Your choice is your own to make."

Miraden was kneeling, now, in front of the boy. Baladar chose to wrap his arms around the surprised old man.

"Then I choose your magic and your way."

Those assembled smiled in hope, and in relief, and in joy. Another battle won, for the moment. So many battles that could be lost were in the future.

Just then—a vial 'popped' onto Miraden's work table. "It's time!"

•• 25th day of 4th Month ••

Another day. Another council session. Another day closer to normalcy.

Rose was in her place on the throne. Malika was back and standing by her side. Alfrond and Elayda sat close by. The Chamberlain rapped his staff on the stone floor of the courtroom. Hooded figures dotted the room's edges. Evermon and Nathan entered, robed and cowled, side by side. Holder and Alan went to stand among the other robed figures by the wall.

Evermon's eyes, and hopes, grew as he saw who was on the throne. "Mother!!"

The Queen arose, horrified, staring at the youth who was fast approaching her. How could he? Unless he had... ?"

"Guards! Seize the boy!"

They intercepted the confused youth by surrounding him, reluctantly, with pikes and spears. The entire crowd was thrown off balance. They had expected a joyous reunion! The hoods began to move about the room—coming closer to the front.

"Mother?"

"Silence!"

"But I have the Waters of Life!"

The Queen, a vision in red, seemed to swell in stature. "Merely a ruse to finish the poisoning of the King—your father." Then she spoke to the room. "The plot against myself and my husband is far reaching. My sons have been infected by it and behind it all is the truest evil in all the Realms—the Magician, Miraden—now unmasked in his own masquerade."

The hall was stunned.

"The King was poisoned once already. I was abducted and my sons were duped into the schemes of an old Sorceror who has managed to kill off all of his enemies and now reigns supreme and unchallenged as the only Enchanter, but is really only the Darkest of Sorcerors. Our Talisman is missing. Seek Miraden and ask him what he has done with the Gentle Jewels."

"The Talisman is here, Noble Queen." Two dark-robed men stepped forward withdrawing the Jewels from their robes. The Gentle Jewels sparkled and their light played about the room.

Rose spoke. "Your prophecies have no more powers here, failed Seers. I do not recognize you or know you.

"But you lie again, oh, Queen!" Their staves dropped to the

floor and they removed their robes. Raileon and Galderon stood in front of the throne holding the Gentle Jewels. Evermon's jaw dropped to the floor along with their robes. "Dearest Mother," spoken in derision, "our youngest brother did not commit the atrocities attributed to him. You know that in your mother's heart. Unless you are not our mother."

'Mother' was confused. Things were happening too fast and not at all as she had planned them! "Why have my sons stolen the Gentle Jewels?"

"They were 'placed' in our care."

"By whom?"

"By myself—your Majesty--" and Miraden stepped forward and loosed his cowled robe to the floor.

Those present in the room reeled again. What was going on here?

"I gave you no permission to do anything!"

"You are not the one with whom permission rests. Permission is mine to give and is also vested in the true King and Queen of Aradon."

"I am the Queen of Aradon! Does this form before you lie?",

Another robed figure stepped forward, dropping her robe to the floor revealing the identical twin to the Queen on the dais. A weaker member of the court swooned to the floor—among the discarded robes.

"Yes—it does Alindra." spoke the real Rose.

Soon, revealed before her, robes dropping everywhere, were Gladenwreath, Alan, Nathan, Sean and Kwuktw—among others. Then a small figure stepped forward and dropped his robe. He held his hands in the air and a hand-mirror and brush magically appeared in them—summoned by the boy from wherever they had been. With tears in his eyes he dashed his mother's precious mirror to the floor and broke the handle off the brush. Placing the bristled end on the floor he took the axe from the Dwarf, next to him, and cut the bristles to pieces.

The Queen upon the dais, now standing in shock, shrieked as her hands went to her face. The eyes of the audience watched as her image shuttered and the blush of a Rose diminished to be replaced by the fear of Accosta. It was the face of Alindra, but with darker hair.

"Mother?!" cried the boy.

She continued to writhe. Miraden and Gladenwreath held Baladar back as Alindra was seized by the changes overwhelming her body. Her hair turned grey; her hands and face aged—not terribly as she was still younger than Miraden—but her youth disappeared from her flesh and left her just—older. Her false immortality had been stripped away from her. She rushed forward and grabbed the vial out of Evermon's hands, pulling the stopper and tipping it into her mouth. She laughed as she wiped her mouth and licked her lips and fingers to get all the potion possible. She ran back to the throne and as soon as she had, black lightning erupted from her fingers, shooting out across the room, deflected from their targets as she clutched her stomach in pain. The fire spread throughout her weakened body. She collapsed to the throne, leaning heavily on its arm.

"Mother!"

She turned—pain and rage mixed in the miasma of her face. For a second—a single glance—Baladar saw the mother who had loved him, taught him, protected him, trained him—but then she was replaced by rage and hatred as she staggered forward and tumbled down the steps to her son's feet. The boy kneeled down and took her hand in his. Her rage was now a thing of the past.

"I only ever wanted you to love me, Mother."

Every mother's and father's heart in the room cracked a little at the simplicity of that haunted statement.

"Why, Miraden?" she croaked through drying lips. "How?"

"There is an old magic that none of you of the second generation, or even the third, knew anything about. You were all too impatient for power. You wanted it now. You weren't willing to work for it—to learn, to grow. It is a sad fact but the old magic will always supercede any other. When the Creators anointed the Waters of Life, they were sealed then with this promise:

Those, who ill, that drink this wealth
Will cure themselves of all that ails.
Those, who well, drink their own health,

Will find that only death prevails."

Accosta sank weakly back to the floor, so quickly were the Waters of Life overcoming her. She groaned and whispered to her son.

"I did..."

"What, Mother?" was said through brimful eyes.

"I did love you," and the battle that had raged within Accosta for over two millennia was finally quieted.

Rose—the rightful Rose—knelt down and pulled a sobbing Baladar into her arms. There was no celebration—no victory at the death of this hated foe. How could there be? She had been a mother. Her child was loved by all who came in contact with him. There was no victory in this death—only the relief at the elimination of a great threat. The boy quieted, and Rose gave him over to Miraden and approached her own flesh and blood sons— Evermon, then Galderon and finally, Raileon—only to smother them in the Queen's motherly embrace. As the family stood at last in each other's arms the room began to quietly, respectfully applaud. It wasn't a thundering ovation but a simple pean to their reunited and beloved leaders.

As the Royal Family filed out, Evermon motioned to Baladar, who was staring again at his mother's lifeless body, to accompany them. Baladar stooped to try to pick up his mother. Evermon rushed to his side and lifted the once-upon-a-time-mother into his arms, and carried her out of the public view with his new little brother at his left and his own mother and brothers on his right.

•• 25th day of 4th Month ••

Rose and her sons, along with Miraden, Nathan, Alan, Sean, Kwuktw, Gladenwreath and Holder had assembled at the bedside of King Emeron. Evermon stepped forward and asked for a vial of the Waters. Three vials appeared—one each from Holder, Nathan and Sean. Evermon chose the one from Holder and placed a little of the precious liquid on his father's dry lips. As those lips fell open he poured the remainder of the vial slowly into his father's mouth—drop by drop. The greyish pallor that had haunted the King for many years gave way to a pinkish, healthier color. The eyes of the monarch, not yet old, fluttered, opened, and beheld his love—his wife—his Queen. He did not move. He was too weak. As his Queen placed a gentle kiss on her husband's lips, three sons took their father's two hands in theirs and the throne of Aradon was whole again.

ML

CHAPTER THIRTEEN—
ANOTHER BEGINNING

It was a cold day as the clouds glowered out of the west and the winds blew from the north across the little party that stood in front of the tomb of Orthon. Once he found out about the tomb, from the stories told and exchanged over the days following Queen Rose's return, he insisted that his mother be buried with her ancestors. No one could begrudge him this request. Then he asked that the tomb be sealed forever. He owed her that much and no more.

Daniel and Tilly, Miraden and Lily, the Brothers of Aradon and their parents stood with their newly adopted son/brother as the final wardings were placed on the tomb by Miraden and Daniel. They quietly transported back to the panoply of the celebration in the Purple Palace of Aradon. The somber duties were done and it was time to honor the living—the heroes—the rescuers—and all the success that Accosta had fought so hard against.

Baladar was not entirely up to the festivities yet, so Evermon left him alone for the afternoon until, finally, near evening, the Prince of Aradon corralled the Prince of the North. With his arms across the shoulders of his young brother, the two of them walked into the celebration, Baladar's eyes beaming and his heart—filling—not full—but getting there.

Gladenwreath, Kwuktw, Sean and the absent Urk were proclaimed heroes for returning the Queen. A celebration on Troll Island would be held later to also induct Urk into the newly formed "Order of the Orb"—for service performed to the Realms.

Evermon, his unearned shame forgotten by all, along with

Nathan, Alan and Holder were proclaimed heroes for the cure of the King. (Order of the Orb, for sure.)

Gladenwreath was awarded a special status as "Protector of the King" and the Gentle Jewels were re-ensconced in the reconstructed Room of the Talisman, entrusted again to be guarded by the Clan of Wreath, Gladen's Dwarven Bretheren. Gladenwreath was also named 'Court Astrologer'—there to understand the stars and their movements—to predict, to reassure and to console when needed.

Caladon, Mirador and Panador had received the return of their Talismans on the previous day.

Kwuktw and Raileon celebrated their reunion. They had missed each other at Evermon's last birthday. For several years they had not seen each other as the brothers were on Miraden's quest of protection for the Talisman. They cemented their friendship and brotherhood and pledged the mutual cooperation of their two Kingdoms.

Raileon was then anointed to become King of Aradon—as the eldest it was his inheritance. He hemmed and hawed in his acceptance of his title and finally got around to utter the words that were in his heart. It was a long and convoluted speech, but he eventually revealed his love for Lindara; and his wish for her to become his wife and the future Queen of Aradon. Lindara rose and accepted his public proposal. She wrapped her arms around the Crown Prince and kissed him soundly. Evermon, happy at this turn of events, looked over at Baladar—whose face wrinkled up in prune-like fashion. Evermon laughed. He couldn't help it. He remembered that it wasn't so long ago that he felt the same way.

Galderon then stood and requested, from King Mistral, the long-awaited hand of his daughter, Orinda—Princess of Caladon. The King gave his permission and a second happy couple joined the ranks of the to-be-wed. Miraden then proposed that since Panador was left without an heir, the House of Valor, represented by Queen Snow, would be succeeded by Galderon and Orinda as their new King and Queen when the present monarch stepped down.

"Hear! Hears!" filled the hall and right then and there Miraden and Daniel stepped forward and anointed Galderon and Orinda as heirs to Panador, with Queen Bianca smiling in approval.

Well, the time seemed right—the air was ripe with proposal so Capostral found his way to his feet and officially announced what everyone already knew—that he and Raelle would marry and stand in line for the throne of Caladon. Their marriage would be in just a few weeks, in Mirador, and that maybe the other couples in the room would like to join them and have a really big ceremony!

Cheers and shouts were sent around the hall. Then Evermon stood and called for attention. He was young—just barely a man at fifteen. He then proclaimed his love for the Princess of Mirador. Capostral strongly objected. Raelle was to wed him! It had been arranged for a decade!

"No—not Raelle, although Capostral is a lucky man! The other Princess of Mirador!"

No one really understood his statement. He explained that over the last few weeks he had fallen hopelessly in love with her. All present were in a quandary as that particular Princess was still missing from the celebration; the one dark spot in their joy.

"How can this be?"

"You have both been missing for the same amount of time. She was not on the quest with you!"

Miraden smiled and pushed a reluctant Holder forward. Holder was smiling and winked at her great-grandfather. The court was somewhat confused until he removed his hat and floor length cloak to reveal the beautifully gowned, but short-haired Caelith—the runaway from Mirador. Shock spread across the room as joy overcame Daniel and Tilly who embraced her, almost smothering her to death. As the room quieted, they faced Evermon.

"She is our first—and now our last. She is yours."

Evermon smiled and held out his hand and Caelith ran into his arms.

"When did you know?"

"Almost from the first. When you couldn't stop looking at me I knew that you were not Holder—or at least there was more to you than Holder explained. In a few days I knew who you really were. I saw the girl I had admired from afar—the one I secretly hoped for, but thought I could never have."

"I, too, have loved you since we were children—but I didn't realize it until we were thrown together in our Quest. Then, when I knew it, I couldn't let you know. It was so frustrating!"

Laughter filled the hall.

"Why didn't you unmask me, Evermon?"

"You had your reasons for your disguise. Besides, your Great-grandfather told me to take care of you. It wasn't until I knew who you were that I really understood him."

Now, Daniel was flustered. "Grandpa—you knew all the time where she was and didn't tell us?"

Miraden shrugged his shoulders. "I couldn't risk it."

"One thing I must know, Grandfather; Evermon could have died or have been killed at anytime during the Quest. He has no magic. How has his life been sustained?"

"You were threatened also, Caelith, but your amulet protected you. Evermon also had the protection of the Creators, completely unknown to me until recently. They arranged for him to find his protection."

"How, Miraden?"

"You were led to it amid the rubble of the Fortress of Fear."

Evermon's hand went to his waist and he withdrew the dagger and its sheath from the bandolier beneath his robe. He held it up in both hands. Miraden was nodding.

"Anandoral's Dagger has been missing since before the Great War. We had thought that Orthon had stolen it—he probably did—but we never knew where he had put it. He must have given it to his father for safekeeping."

"There was a lone closet left standing, undamaged, in the rubble of the Fortress of Fear. It must have been the protection of the dagger itself that kept the closet intact until I found it. I have wondered why it was the only thing not destroyed."

Miraden spoke in hushed tones. Everyone strained to listen. "My brother's dagger is a very potent Talisman. If the possessor never draws it in anger, and as long as he keeps it on his person and wears it in honor—he can never be harmed. If you were to draw it in anger it would lose its potency for you. Or if you leave it off your body, as Anandoral did once, when he was killed by Tophet's son, Orthon, you will also be able to be killed."

"Orthon? My grandfather?"

"Yes, Baladar."

"I do not like my family."

"You do not have to. Besides, you have a new family now, in Aradon," Rose spoke reassuringly to the boy.

He drew close to her. She held him lightly, protectively.

"Here, Miraden."

"No, No, Evermon, that dagger and your life are now entwined. The one who will rule Mirador must have protection for Mirador rules them all—it is the Central Throne..."

"The prophecy!" shouted Baladar.

"Yes, Baladar. The Prophecy. This does not concern Daniel— now there is another prophecy for Mirador and the Realms."

Baladar ran to Evermon and hugged him tightly. "You are the Prophecy now, Evermon. It came true."

"But shouldn't it have been Daniel's?"

"I think not, Evermon," spoke Daniel. "Our destinies are not the same, although they head in a similar direction."

Evermon clutched the dagger and Baladar slipped his hand into his brother's and squeezed it. Then, as Baladar dropped his hand, Evermon held it out to Caelith who took it and let herself be drawn to his virgin lips. They kissed as the room sighed. (Well, all but the boy at his brother's side.) The action of love was imitated by every couple in the room, newly betrothed or not! Those left without a second and clinging pair of lips looked around and smiled in guilty pleasure or in frank embarrassment.

The Realms of the Crystal Orb were safe again. This time it was due to many hands other than just Daniel's.

"And Baladar," spoke Miraden, "you, too, are a Prince and you will also have a Kingdom. The Northeast Reaches are yours by right of birth, and also by the right of your honor and behavior."

The boy beamed.

A brightness came into the room, it stationed itself between the Royal Family and Baladar, near the throne. Queen Bianca and Princess Lindara, last of the House of Valor of Panador, wept happy tears as they saw their son/brother—Boncaster—blessing the Realms; especially Aradon and most particularly, Baladar.

This is truly how it was supposed to be!

The ongoing work done in the Northeastern Reaches by the members of the Circle had been extensive. Out of the less than a thousand inhabitants they had formed a Circle for the new Realm. They had all been inducted and instructed. Now the new Circle of Anandor—named by Baladar in honor of Anandoral—stood behind the leaders of the Circles of the Realms as they all stood in front of the ruins of Mountain Hold.

Daniel and Tilly, Elias and Nancy, Aloshtu and Leah, Serrantu and Shanla. Kalaal and Dalarra, Nathan and Malika, Timothy and Reahtu and Arik and Jessica were shoulder to shoulder with the newly crowned boy-King, Baladar. (Well, waist to shoulder, anyway.)

Weeks of planning and redesign had gone into this moment. All understood their duties. Baladar raised his hands and the portcullis stood on its pointy end as the Barbican of the vast fortress began to rise around it, out of the dust and detritus, and reassemble itself. No one else moved yet. They were all too astonished at the power of the ten year old King of Anandor. Soon, they also were raising their arms and raising the rocks and stones of the ruins to form the towers, walls, parapets, battlements and keep. In the morning sun that crept into the valley from the east the stunning bastion of Baladar's family renewed itself.

After the difficult work of a late Spring morning, the Walls and towers of Mountain Hold stood before him and the others. Miraden and Lily were there to give it a coat of glistening sparkle—something to overlay the darkness of the volcanic rock of the region that had made up the original fortress.

Baladar suddenly 'popped' away. He had to check on something.

"Light!"

The torches flared up as he ran down the hallway toward his father's study and former laboratory deep within the mountain itself. He heard whining and whimpering. Then, as he stood at the door, he heard several growls. He quickly enwarded himself in a purple personal and advanced into the room. Once again he was on his back beneath a growling wolf as the growl soon turned to a whine and a lick as recognition dawned in the eyes of his wolves. He was surrounded by the eager, licking cubs and their parents and he vanished his warding. He then reached out and pulled the wolves closer to him.

Just as the assemblage in front of the castle was beginning to worry about the absence of the Prince, now King, Baladar 'popped' back. (Wolfless.)

"We are full of surprises, are we not, little brother?" chided Evermon. "I didn't know you could do... what you have just done!"

"Well, I can—sorry."

Kalaal leaned into the conversation, "Are they all right?"

Baladar smiled up at his friend and rescuer, "Yes, they're fine!"

Aloshtu, Kalaal and Serrantu all smiled.

"Who?" asked Evermon.

"The wolves who saved me," whispered Baladar.

"I think, little brother, I need to hear a story—sometime soon."

"I'll tell you tonight after the weddings!"

"But I will be busy with—I'll be with Caelith tonight."

Baladar blushed. "I forgot. I finally get a brother and lose him to a girl!"

"You're not losing a brother—you're gaining a sister!" protested Caelith.

Baladar harumphed. "So, when shall I tell you? After you finish, um... tomorrow morni... no—he blushed again. "When?"

"Tomorrow night you will tell us all in front of the fire in your own Great Hall."

Baladar looked up and smiled out of his embarrassment at Evermon—the soon to be married man. Man?! He was only five years older than his younger brother! Would he, Baladar, also be expected soon to... ? Gross! Yuk! Baladar 'popped.'

He stood on the battlement of the barbican, above the open portcullis of the Fortress. He had to do something to get his mind off that stuff! It was time anyway.

"I have learned of a new name for this fortress. I found it while I lived here during my banishment."

The crowd rustled uncomfortably for a moment that such a thing had had to happen to a boy, or anyone at all.

"Mountain Hold was also called by another name by some of those in this Circle. As King of Anandor I name this fortress 'Twelve Towers.'"

Miraden appeared by the boy's side.

"Our new King has spoken and spoken well. It is a tribute to all, spoken from the lips that are connected to a heart that will never fail him or us or the Realms. This Twelve Towers will be Baladar's home. A city will grow here in the valley and thrive. Baladar, as a ward of Aradon, shall rule here. But he has other things to do as well to further prepare him to rule. I have officially accepted him as my apprentice. As you have seen he has talents and abilities well beyond his years. He will learn and grow under our careful tutelage and Twelve Towers and Anandor will soon take their full and rightful place in the Realms of the Crystal Orb."

Daniel 'popped' up to Baladar's other side—"And now— friends and family—to Mirador for the weddings of my daughter and Evermon; and that of Raileon, Lindara. Galderon, Orinda, and Raelle, my other daughter and Capostral. Mirador, Aradon, Panador and Caladon united for all time under the powers of the Creators.

There was thunderous applause. Baladar tugged on Daniel's sleeve—he asked, maybe a little too loudly and in that always deafening silence that comes amid great applause, "Can we hurry up with the mushy stuff? I have magic to learn!"

Mixed laughter and applause were renewed as a chorus of howls joined the celebrants who soon 'popped' away for the festivities in Mirador, leaving Baladar and Evermon alone for a moment, with Caelith, patient in the background. They stood there on the battlement and the air was punctuated by the occasional muted howl of one of Baladar's friends.

"It isn't as bad as you think, Baladar!"

"Uh-uh! No way! No how! No girls! No mushy stuff!"

Caelith barged in and placed a big kiss on Baladar's lips. He stood there wiping it off, sputtering.

"We'll see, little brother," said Evermon, laughing, "we'll see!"

THE END

THE EXILE OF ARADON
CHARACTER LIST

BOOK FOUR—Same time period as Book 5 (Flaming Sword)
YEAR: 2726

KING EMERON—King of Aradon, lies ill b.2682
QUEEN ROSE—Queen of Aradon, missing b.2684
PRINCE RAILEON—Prince of Aradon, 'lost' b. 2704 (can transform to Mer-person)
PRINCE GALDERON—Prince of Aradon, 'lost' b. 2706
PRINCE EVERMON—Prince of Aradon, the exile b. 2708
QUEEN ALINDRA—New Queen of Aradon, appears in her early 20's
BALADAR—Alindra's son, Immortal, Sorceror's Apprentice b. 2713
PRINCE ALFROND—Emeron's brother, Ambassador to Caladon b. 2685
PRINCESS ELAYDA—of Caladon, Alfrond's wife b 2786
TESTRA—daughter of Alfrond and Elayda b 2708
PALANCA—daughter of Alfrond and Elayda b. 2710
TWO SOOTHSAYERS—men in dark robes bringing news from Colabos
MIRADEN—Master Magician, born before Time was
DANIEL GREGORYSON—King of Mirador, The 'Miracle', The 'Prophecy', b. 2689
TILLY—Queen of Mirador, b. 2689
ELIAS MATTHEWSON—Leader of the Circle of Light in Mirador, b. 2691
NANCY—Wife of Elias, b. 2691
NATHAN JAMESON—Circle Leader of Aradon, b. 2689
MALIKA—Wife of Nathan, b. 2689
ISTRAMERE—The Orange Dragon, b. 2702
PRINCESS LINDARA—Princess of Panador, b. 2705
PRINCESS CAELITH—Princess of Mirador, Daniel & Tilly's daughter b. 2705
PRINCESS RAELLE—Princess of Mirador, Daniel & Tilly's daughter b. 2707